A sudden, bi[...] the left. Shar[...] and swirled a[...]

"Get your cloaks over your faces," Petia yelled. "The ice will slice our flesh to bloody ribbons." She grabbed the edge of the blanket and flung her arms up to protect herself.

"At least someone has blood left. More than I can say for myself," grumbled Keja.

Squinting, Giles tried to find the wind's source, for a moment he saw nothing but the eddying ice. As it fell toward the floor, four creatures stepped out of the tunnel mouth.

Taller than humans and more massive, the creatures stood on icy legs planted firmly. They ranged themselves across the cavern. Their frozen torsos presented an excellent target. The monstrous creatures stood gazing at them from sockets without eyes, and it was obvious the demons knew exactly where the humans stood.

"Ice demons!" Keja shouted, as Giles drew his sword . . .

KEY OF ICE AND STEEL

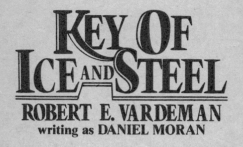

KEY OF ICE AND STEEL

ROBERT E. VARDEMAN
writing as DANIEL MORAN

A TOM DOHERTY ASSOCIATES BOOK

KEY OF ICE AND STEEL

Copyright © 1988 by Daniel Moran

First printing: May 1988

A TOR book

Published by Tom Doherty Associates, Inc.
49 West 24th Street
New York, NY 10010

ISBN: 0-812-54606-7
Can. No.:0-812-54607-5

Printed in the United States of America

0 9 8 7 6 5 4 3 2 1

For those printing fools from Stayton, Oregon

Dale and Ginny Goble

Mike and Susie Horvat

Chapter One

Rain pattered against the sodden leaves arching like green umbrellas above the four riders. Fat drops fell into the puddles dotting the forest trail even as distant thunder rumbled with the promise of a more vigorous storm. Although the trees protected the riders from a direct onslaught, they sat astride their horses soggy and miserable.

Keja Tchurak raised his hand and wiped drops from the end of his straight, aristocratic nose. "Can't we stop and set up camp soon?" he whined.

Giles Grimsmate turned in his saddle and stared with flinty gray eyes until Keja became uncomfortable. He averted his gaze, feeling that he again slowed them, that he kept them from their fabulous quest because he disliked being cold and wet and uncomfortable.

"You do well to look away, Keja. Look around you, man." Giles swept his heavily muscled arm in an arc encompassing both sides of the trail. The low ground ran with water, gathered into pools, then burst through dams of leaves and twigs to run away in rivulets to even lower ground. "If you want to build camp in this swamp, you're welcome. I'm as eager as you are to climb down

1

and find shelter, but not so stupid to want to spend the night up to my arse in water. When I find some high ground, we'll stop."

Giles stretched his arthritic, tired limbs and studied the others slumped in their saddles, soaked blankets over their heads lending little protection. Petia Darya and Anji, the two Trans who made up half of the company, said nothing. Miserable, hissing like the part feline that she was, Petia barely guided her horse. Young Anji let his mount plod behind. Both seemed content to let the more experienced Giles make such decisions.

Giles stared into the dripping forest and muttered a small prayer that they would find high ground soon. He wanted out of the wet as much as anyone. He hoped that the foul weather was not an omen of things to come on this, their last adventure.

They traveled two miles before the track began to rise. Giles sat erect in his saddle and peered into the rain, finding a knoll worthy of a campsite. He called back to the others.

"That ought to do." He swung down from his horse, tying it loosely to a nearby tree.

Keja slid from his mount, also. His foot landed in a puddle of water, and he slipped on the leaf mold beneath it. He sprawled, cursing all the gods supposedly protecting thieves from such ignominy. Petia foresaw Anji's laugh and motioned quickly with her hand, cutting him off before he began. The trail had been long, and tempers frayed. Anji's mirth would only provoke an angry outburst from Keja.

She dismounted, grabbed Keja's arm and assisted him to his feet. Then she turned quickly to Giles before Keja could mutter that he didn't need any help from a woman.

"We'll need to build shelter," Giles said. "Branches from those conifers will shed the rain. I'll cut some small limbs for the framework."

They worked silently, their mood so depressed by the weather that they didn't dare talk to each other. Giles' long years as a sergeant during the Trans War enabled him to build a shelter quickly. The others simply cut and carried and let him work. The sooner the shelter was built, the sooner they had a chance of finding a modicum of comfort.

By the time Anji had found the first dry wood, a lean-to shelter offered protection from the storm. Anji arranged the stacks carefully, making sure that there would be enough wood to last through the night. Assured of adequate—and dry—fuel, he went to bring the horses into the woods and find the best shelter possible for them. The animals were Anji's special love. Giles paused in his work and watched the boy. At times he wondered if the Trans could speak with the horses. He shook his head, sending droplets flying from his thinning gray hair, and returned to his work.

Keja warmed with the activity and his mood improved. He silently helped Anji unsaddle and remove packs and wipe the water from the animals as best they could. When they returned to the shelter, a small fire blazed into life, Petia carefully encouraging it.

"Make you wish you were back in the desert, Keja?" Giles grinned at the small thief.

"The next quest we go on, let me choose the place," Keja said. His tone came lighter and joking. "Somewhere moderate, balmy days, cloudless nights, and no snakes, please. And women. Lots of willing, wanton women eager for a passionate night with one such as myself."

"Impossible," scoffed Petia. "Not even passing through the Gate of Paradise will give you all that."

She ducked when Keja tossed a pine cone at her.

"What do you think lies behind the Gate?" he asked. "*I* think it is riches and leisure."

"At the moment, all I want is dry and warm," muttered Petia.

As the fire burned higher, the companions spread their blankets and cloaks to dry, and Giles and Petia tended the kettle of stew.

3

The sound of rain and the occasional stamping of the animals disturbed their meal. Each kept to his and her own thoughts. Only when Giles stuffed and lit his pipe did they stir from wild dreams of what finding the fifth and final key to the Gate of Paradise would grant each of them.

"I told you we should have waited until spring," Keja said. "We could be sitting around a warm fire in the inn at Sanustell. And keeping an eye on those people at Callant Hanse. I don't trust them."

Giles chuckled. "The keys were still there, weren't they? You insisted on seeing the other three when we deposited the fourth. They brought the box out and we all had to sign before they opened it, just as we agreed. What makes you think that they'd risk a two-hundred-year-old reputation to steal our keys? Especially when those four keys to the Gate are worthless without the fifth?"

"Yes, but these are keys to the Gate of Paradise. They're not just your everyday keys, you might say," Keja said. "I sweated rivers in the Bandanarra desert and faced a snake as big as a room and hungrier than a beggar to get that last key. And I say that the closer we are to having all five keys, the bigger the risk leaving them there."

"You have no faith, Keja," Petia said. "Giles is right. A mercantile house like the Callant Hanse isn't going to throw over a reputation it took centuries to build, even for keys to the Gate of Paradise. Only fools like us do such things."

Giles laughed and tamped more tobacco into his pipe. "They don't even know what those keys open," he pointed out. "If I hadn't thought the keys were safe, I'd have never left them, now would I? We've suffered too much to lose them casually."

Anji pulled his blanket closer about his shoulders. "I'd rather be back in Bandanarra than in this miserable dripping forest," he said.

Giles gazed at the boy, kindness in his eyes. "Desert

heat *is* normal to you. We were all born here in the north and are used to cooler weather. But even I could do with a little less of this autumn rain." He peered out from beneath the edge of the lean-to. Clouds obscured the stars and he saw no moon. "I don't think it's going to stop."

"Does it ever quit?" The boy looked plaintively at Petia.

She reached out and tousled his wet hair. "You've forgotten already how beautiful it was on Bericlere when we first arrived. We have seasons here. Autumn begins with the summer heat still in it and slowly gives way to the cold of winter. You'll become accustomed to the diversity it lends to our lives. It's not like the desert where each day is like every other, the entire year round."

"That's not true!" The boy pulled his head back angrily from beneath Petia's hand. "It rains in the desert," he said. "Just because you never saw it . . ." He lowered his head and sulked, trying to feel more sorry for himself than he actually was.

Petia stared at the two men and shook her head. They understood and fell silent. Anji had been through much —more than any of them. Petia had rescued him from slavers. She knew, in part, the prejudices the boy had endured because of his Trans heritage, but she came from Trois Havres where most were Trans. Petia stroked the hair on Anji's head until the boy's tenseness faded.

Keja poked at the fire with a stick, then rose to fetch a piece of rope from his pack. He settled again and worked at binding the frayed ends.

The boy's voice broke the silence again. "We were followed today."

Keja's fingers grew still. Giles leaned forward, his eyes searching the boy's face. Petia drew a breath.

"By whom?" Giles asked.

"I don't know," Anji said. "Maybe the man in black we heard about in Bandanarra. The desert people knew nothing of him, but I think he was there to watch us."

5

Petia nodded. "I felt the mind of a catamount today. It was upset, but I thought that we had intruded on its territory. I didn't give it a second thought, except to make sure that it kept its distance. But there might well have been someone else."

Giles shook his head and reached for a fire brand. Between puffs he said, "It's a reminder that we need to be on guard." He turned to Anji. "How do you know we were followed?"

Anji looked at Petia. "She's been teaching me to use my Trans senses. Nobody ever did that before. When my mother sold me into slavery I was a dumb fetch-and-carry servant. So I've been practicing hard. I heard the catamount, too." Now he avoided Petia's eyes. "But I tried to go beyond the big cat. There were several horses and I caught the barest sense of men. They were quite a ways behind us, I'm sure."

"I'll backtrack in the morning," Giles said, venting a huge sigh. The old soldier wondered if he would spend the rest of his life looking over his shoulder, waiting for the knife to descend. "Thank you, Anji. I had hoped we wouldn't need to do this so soon. Let's set the watches."

Even when the others stood watch, Giles lay awake, listening hard and worrying. He knew they had been lucky thus far—in spite of their travails, they had been lucky. With the man in black actively following, even if it was the mysterious stranger in the desert, danger mounted for all four of them.

When the wet, gray morning came, Giles ached in every joint. He ordered the others on ahead, then went tracking.

The following evening they sat in the common room of a rustic mountain inn nestled in the foothills of the Adversaries, a mountain range stretching several hundred miles toward the even colder northlands. Giles, bone-tired, wanted to retire early. Petia pressed him for what he had learned.

With some trepidation over worrying them needlessly,

Giles said, "I found hoofprints all right. But they turned east, forded a stream, and continued into the forest.

"So they don't appear to be following us. It goes to show, however, we must keep a sharp eye out for the unusual. Keep your senses alert, Anji." The boy grinned. "You, too, Petia. We're too near success to be beaten now."

"What success can that be, I ask you?" a man spoke up from across the room. "There's naught to be done in this foresaken wasteland."

Giles sucked on his pipe and nodded to the man who had interrupted. He offered him his tobacco pouch when the man's pipe sputtered and went out. "Do you know this area well?" Giles asked.

The man puffed solemnly for a moment, tamping his pipe to make certain that it burned evenly. "You might say so." He nodded in emphasis. "I'm a peddler by trade. Been traveling these parts for a good many years."

Giles motioned for Petia, Anji and Keja to be silent, then pulled a map from his tunic. "Maybe you can tell what we have ahead of us. We're traveling through these parts for the first time."

The peddler hunched forward over the map, one grubby finger tracing familiar routes until he had found the inn. "Which way do you go from here?" he asked.

"North," Giles answered.

The peddler's eyes widened. "Argh, it's a bad time of the year you've chosen," he said. "Snow coming any time now. Even in the best of times it's not a pleasant place you're heading into. Mountains and secluded valleys and the people most inhospitable. They tolerate me for my goods, but not much more. I wouldn't care to be snowed in there for the winter. I'm heading for the coast, where it's warmer and the ale isn't so bitter."

"Tell us about the snow," Giles said.

"I can only tell you what I've heard from others," the peddler replied, puffing blue clouds of smoke that veiled his weathered face. "I don't take any chances. I make certain that I've finished my rounds and am well away before the winter comes hard. The people tell stories of immense storms, of being snowed in for weeks. They may be exaggerating, but they make it sound as if you shouldn't be caught out in the open."

Petia leaned forward. "I don't like this, Giles. We can take the wet, but snow is different."

"It's cold *and* wet," grumbled Keja, used to city amenities.

Giles leaned back, puffing thoughtfully on his pipe.

The peddler bowed toward Petia. "Good evening, miss. We don't see many Trans in these parts, not since they came runnin' in this direction during the War, beggin' your pardon. Understand, I don't have any problems with your people. I've traded in the Trois Havres and have always been treated honestly."

Petia sat back, steeling herself to hear how he wasn't prejudiced against the Trans. She watched the peddler as he swallowed half a tankard of ale before returning to the pipe fueled by Giles' tobacco.

"You and the boy had best be careful, though. These mountain people are strange. They don't like outsiders of any persuasion much, and I'm not sure how they'll react to a pair of Trans. Some of them are all right, I guess. They're honest folk, but they have some funny ideas. I'd keep a sharp eye out."

Petia tensed. Giles rested a hand on hers, cautioning her to silence. He didn't need her emotion-sensing talents to realize that the peddler was wondering how he could use information about the four to his own advantage.

Giles rose from the table, yawning and stretching. He picked up his pipe and tobacco pouch. "We've had a long day on the road. I hope you'll excuse us if we retire."

The others followed him after curt "good nights" to the peddler. At the top of the stairs, Giles paused and whispered, "We'll discuss it in the morning. Let's sleep late and take our time in the morning." He grinned wryly. "It might be the last time we sleep warm and dry for a while."

In the morning they ate a leisurely breakfast, much to Keja's delight. Not only did the food please him, he couldn't keep his eyes off the serving maid. When the maid had cleared their bowls, Giles said, "I think we ought to stay here another day and talk this out. The peddler's news last night wasn't particularly encouraging. We should consider whether to continue or leave this venture until spring."

"I agree, Giles. You're right. Very right." Keja smiled broadly and winked at the maid, who seemed equally inclined toward the small man.

"No! I, for one . . ." Petia was stilled by Giles' huge hand.

"Let's enjoy the morning. With no pressure, we can think more clearly about continuing or waiting. Another day isn't going to hurt our plans, one way or the other."

He rose from the table and went to the window, peering out. "It's clear at the moment. I'm going for a walk. Fresh air helps my thinking." He slung his cloak around him and left the inn, closing the door carefully behind him.

Keja stared after him, as if unable to believe his good fortune. "I guess he means it. I'll be damned." He stood, straightened his tunic and announced, "I do my best thinking in bed." He disappeared up the stairway.

Anji looked questioningly at Petia, who glumly nodded. "The maid went upstairs after she took our dishes. I think Keja will be well occupied for the rest of the day. Are you up for a game of Threes and Fours?"

"What's that?" the boy asked. Petia got a leather cup filled with dice from the innkeeper and spent the day showing Anji how to play.

At dinner, Petia was nearly ready to burst. The inactivity had worn on her, as much as she enjoyed the time with Anji. Giles was not to be hurried, however, and only when his pipe was lit did he begin the conversation concerning their immediate future.

Keja, sated after a day with the winsome maid, felt magnanimous and allowed Petia to speak first. He leaned back, hiked booted feet to the table and laced his nimble fingers behind his head.

"Spending the winter in one of the cities of Trois Havre would make me crazy," she said. "I can't stand inactivity. I want to push on. I have Anji to think about and the sooner we get the final key and pick up the treasure behind the Gate, the sooner Anji and I can get on with our lives."

Her speech came out in a rush and was the closest she had ever come to saying how much the boy she had purchased at the slave market meant to her. The boy from Bandanarra had become a part of her life—a significant part.

Keja smiled to himself. The boy was changing Petia, and not in subtle ways. He imagined her as a middle-aged homebody, having supper ready when Anji returned from schooling. The thought amused him. In five or six years the boy would be old enough to go out on his own. What then for Petia? He wondered if she had thought of that.

What then for Keja Tchurak? The thief scowled now as he realized how much Petia meant to him. He tried to shrug off the feelings. It'd never do for him to be tied down like that. A home? Petia and Anji? Keja snorted and shook his head at the insane idea.

"So you're for going on?" Giles nodded. "Let's hear what Keja has to say, and then Anji."

Keja brought his feet to the floor and leaned forward. "I'm still wanted, so to speak. I saw some old handbills while we were in Sanustell. They were faded, of course, but the reward is real. I imagine the man responsible is the father of my one-time paramour from whom I stole the first key. And back on Bericlere there was a trivial matter of the theft of that overly endowed woman's jewels. What was her name, anyway? I'm good at figures, but I never was good with names." He grinned. "I could find somplace to hide out over the winter, I'm sure, but you know me. I'd just get into more trouble." He put his feet up again, finished.

"Anji, you may be the youngest, but you're part of our pleasant little band. What do you say?"

The boy looked at Petia, but she simply nodded as if to say, "Go ahead, say what you think."

"I don't like the rain, and I don't think I'll like snow, although I've never seen any. Petia says it can get bitterly cold. I don't see how I can get any colder than I already am, but I trust Petia." The boy paused, gathering his thoughts. "She wants to go on and get it over. When she bought me in the slave market, I promised I'd follow her anywhere. She wanted to set me free, and I guess I am, but I'm going to stay with her. If she goes on, I'll go, even if it means freezing to death."

"That leaves you, Giles," Petia prodded. "Your turn."

"Yes, my turn. Anji is the only one who has spoken of the hardship from the cold and snow. I'm an old man . . ." He held up his hand to stop the protests forming. "You know how many years I spent fighting in the Trans War. Twenty years took a lot out of me. I'd be a lot more comfortable holed up in some inn for the winter, toasting my bones in front of the fire. But I'm a bit like Keja. No posters out for my head, but I'm not well liked among the Flame Sorceress' worshipers in Sanustell. Not after I killed her to get the Flame Key. So none of the Trois Havres towns for me, either.

"But let's get down to cases. Do we have enough warm clothing to make it? The horses are in good shape, well fed, capable of getting through the winter, I'd say." He saw Anji nod vigorously, eyes shining. "The people we can ignore. Nothing can be more hostile than the Bandanarra desert, and we survived that. We should be able to cope with these hill folk, even if they prove surly."

Petia spoke up. "We packed woolen cloaks. If it's as harsh as the peddler said, we need skins and furs. But I think we'll make out all right. We won't freeze, Anji."

The boy smiled at her, adoration in his eyes. He would follow her anywhere, even if he had no clear understanding of her need to find this fifth key to what the boy believed to be only a legend.

"No strong arguments for going back, then," Giles said. "We'll continue in the morning."

"I'll see to our gear," said Keja. "The serving wench hinted that she might have a special waterproofing for our cloaks."

"I'm sure," Petia said sourly.

Keja eyed her curiously, wondering what was bothering her. Whistling, he set off to find the maid and attend to their cloaks.

"Anji, go see to the horses. We want them ready for a long ride tomorrow," said Giles. "And, Petia, I want you to memorize this map. I've opened and closed it so many times, the paper wears thin. I'd not like to be the only one knowing the terrain."

She nodded, knowing what was on the man's mind. If anything happened to him, Giles wanted the others to be able to return. Giles and Petia bent over his map, looking up only when Anji rushed back in.

The boy burst into the inn's common room, shouting. "Giles, Petia, someone's cut open the saddles and the bags."

Giles shot to his feet and nearly ran Anji down getting out the door. Petia ran a pace behind him.

They found the riding equipment exactly as Anji had said. Their gear had been scattered about the stables, each piece tossed aside after close scrutiny. Someone had made a thorough job of it. The seams of the saddle skirts were split, as was the joint between cantle and skirts. The cloth linings had been ripped free and now hung in tatters. Saddlebags had been emptied, and spare clothing and blankets thrown aside to drape over the bales of straw in one corner.

"Somebody's searched thoroughly," Giles said, collapsing onto a pile of loose hay. "It looks as if they hunted for something very small—and we know what that means. Someone knows we have the keys." He picked up a saddlebag, turning it over to see what damage had been done.

Anji checked the horses carefully, crooning to them. He lifted each leg, checking their hooves to see that no injury had been done to them. He saw Giles' questioning look, and said, "In Bandanarra the desert raiders often damage the hooves of their enemies' horses. I have to make sure we will not ride out, only to become stranded in a day or two."

Giles sighed. He rose and began to gather the pieces. "Help me sort this out, Petia. We no longer have a quiet evening before us. Everything needs repair. Anji, when you've finished with the horses, fetch Keja. He can repair a saddle as easily as I can. A catastrophe here, danger behind, and . . . what ahead?"

Giles shook his head. "It looks as if we're in for more trouble."

He hoped that the final key to Paradise would be worth the effort.

Chapter Two

At breakfast, Giles glowered as the others took their places at the table, muttering a barely sociable "good morning." Keja started to tell him that their position wasn't too bad, but Petia nudged him in the ribs and silenced him. The small thief subsided, seeing she had more accurately gauged Giles' mood. And talk now would turn bitter.

They had dragged the saddles into the inn after supper and worked late into the night repairing them. The longer they had worked the more angry Giles had become, and it was apparent that the night's sleep had not brought any change.

Finished with breakfast, Giles growled, "Someone is after us, that's certain. I thought everything would be safe at an inn. We should have set watches. And from now on we will. These saddles are almost worthless. Maybe we should turn back."

"Not on your life!" Petia exclaimed. "We made the decision to go on, and we're going to. We'll ride on saddle blankets if we have to. You just didn't get enough sleep last night. You're acting like an old grump."

Keja turned away and stared at the fire, hiding his

grin. Petia could get away with that; he couldn't. If he had said anything like that to Giles, he would have had a fight on his hands.

"I didn't want to go on this crazy treasure hunt in the first place," Giles muttered. "Even before I met up with you two, I got hit on the head and accused of murdering a priest in a temple. Then I nearly drowned saving you two in the Flame Sorceress' cave. Then some mysterious stranger followed us all the way to Bandanarra, as if we didn't have our hands full with the Skeleton Lord and his snakes."

He headed toward the door. "Why can't we just this once retrieve the key without somebody harrying us all the way? I'm fed up to here with this." He gestured against his throat with the side of his hand and went out, slamming the door.

"Let's give him a few minutes to simmer down," Petia said. "Anji, check our room to see that we didn't leave anything."

The boy, whose eyes had widened at Giles' outburst, nodded. "I've never heard Giles like that before," he said. "I didn't know he had such a temper."

"He doesn't, usually," Petia said. "He'll come out of it, once we're on our way. It's always the start of a journey that's the hardest. Now, get on with you. Check that room."

When they reached the stable, Giles was still muttering, but he had two horses saddled. The saddles were no longer things of beauty, but the repairs looked as if they would hold. Anji went to each of the horses, greeting them in a soft voice. Keja and Petia saw to the packs and saddlebags, while Giles completed the saddling.

When he had pulled tight the last cinch, he moved away from his horse, craning his neck to scan the sky. "Looks like the day won't be too bad," he said, and stepped up into his stirrup. The others hastily mounted and trailed behind him as Giles rode from the stableyard.

For an hour the track remained level. Wispy, rainless

clouds came and went, turning the day gray, but as long as the weather became no worse than this, it would be pleasant enough. By mid-morning the road began to turn upward into the Adversaries. Giles pulled the map from inside his tunic and halted to study it.

"The road rises to Honiton Pass," he said. "The map seems accurate. I was afraid that it might not be."

"It's the map we found in Shahal, isn't it?" Keja asked. "The one in the giant skeleton's hands?"

"It's a copy I made," Giles answered. "There was some information on the original that I've left out, just in case it falls into other hands. Some XXXs nobody else needs to know about, if you take my meaning."

"You think it will take us to the last key?"

Giles clucked up his horse. "If it continues to be as accurate as it has been up to now," he said.

They rested at noon and ate a sparse lunch, taking the opportunity to water and feed their horses. The companions had not resumed their journey for long before Keja remarked on the number of tree branches scattered along the road. "There must have been a big storm through here recently," the thief said. "Those weren't cut; they were blown off the trees."

It wasn't long before they found the road completely blocked by a fallen tree. They rounded a bend and found an ironhorn laying aslant in the road. To their right gaped a hole in the earth, and the massive root system jutted up, exposed. The trunk, several times the thickness of Giles' waist, was crushed into the ground. There was no room to lead the horses through.

They dismounted and surveyed the tree. "There's a giant for you," Giles commented. "And we had been making such good time, too."

He strode to the left side of the road, following the length of the tree into the forest. "It must be over a hundred feet tall," he said. "The underbrush is thick on both sides of the road, but the shortest way around is past the roots." He gestured to the right, and began to tug his sword free from its scabbard. "Tie the horses,

Anji, and we'll start hacking a path through the under-
growth. Time to work up a sweat, my friends."

Anji tended the horses while Keja and Petia pulled
their swords and began helping Giles hack through the
thick foliage. Anji tethered the horses and watched as the
three cleared ferns and the sturdier *salal* and *tamra*
grape. He tested the reins, took a deep breath and then
slipped into the forest.

The Trans boy moved through the underbrush swiftly
and silently. He did not return to the road until he came
to the other side of the bend. When he emerged, he
stayed close to the verge, looking behind him. The road
stretched empty and uninviting. Anji broke into a trot,
watching carefully as far as he could see up the road. He
had sensed something when they had stopped for their
midday meal. He hadn't heard it, just sensed it. He was
sure that someone—or something—followed. Giles may
have found tracks leading off another direction, but the
travelers were still being followed, Anji was certain.
He'd prove his worth to them by discovering the identity
of that persistent tracker.

Petia paused to wipe a drop of perspiration from the
tip of her pert, upturned nose. She picked up a clump of
brush and threw it behind her. "Anji!" she called.
"Come and clear the cut brush." She moved forward
and hacked at the bottom of a particularly rugged *salal*
bush that blocked their progress.

Keja straightened to stretch cramped muscles. "Dam-
nable stuff, isn't it?" He massaged the small of his back
and together they bent again, his eyes on Petia. Although
she ignored him, he felt her nearness and thrilled to it.
His attraction for her had grown from simple physical
desire to something more complicated, unlike anything
he'd experienced before.

He snorted and redoubled his efforts, forcing such
thoughts from his mind. So what if he found himself
actually admiring her tenacity and courage? She had
rebuffed his advances over and over. And weren't there

enough serving wenches and maids such as the one at the inn for him?

The next time Petia paused for a breath, she looked back to see what progress they had made. The clump which she had asked Anji to clear away still blocked the trail. She raised her voice. "Anji." No answer. "Where did he go?" she muttered, planting her sword in the soil.

Petia made her way back to the road. The tethered horses grazed contentedly, but of Anji she saw no trace.

"Anji!" she shouted, but the sound became muffled by the massive trunks of the ironhorn. She ran back along the road, rounded the bend and saw—nothing. She called again but received no reply.

Petia hurried up the track. "Giles, Keja! Anji's gone."

Giles emerged from the brush, wiping his forehead. "What?" Keja stumbled after him, and sat on a stump to catch his breath.

Her heart pounding, Petia arrived breathless. Between gasps she managed to get out, "Anji . . . he's gone . . . I called . . . he's not here."

"Easy, now, lass," Giles said. "Catch your breath and then start over." He guided Petia to a place where she could sit. "Now what's this all about?"

She gestured weakly. "Anji. He's gone. I asked him to clear some of the brush we'd cut. He didn't come. I went to look and he's gone. He tied the horses up neat as you please and then slipped off. He must have. There's no sign of anyone else."

Giles gestured at Keja to go look, then returned his attention to Petia. "Maybe he's just gone off to play and didn't hear you. He's still a boy, remember."

Petia gazed at him, despair in her eyes. "He's a boy with experiences that turn young men gray. In eleven years he's lived forty." She took a deep, calming breath. "He's not playing, Giles. He's gone. He said that someone was trailing us the other day. He's gone back to find out. I know it! You backtracked the other day and said that everything was fine. Then our saddles and packs were ripped open. Anji must still think someone's behind us. He knew I wouldn't let him go if he asked, so he's slipped away when our backs were turned. He's got courage, but I'll tan his hide when I catch him."

"You're not going to catch him," Giles said. "You're going to wait right here until he comes back." He looked up at Keja's return.

"No sign of him," Keja said. "But Petia's right. No sign of a struggle with anyone, either."

"I'm going after him," Petia said. "There's no telling what might happen to him." She started to get up, but Giles pushed her back.

"Wait a moment, before you go running off. Never mount a campaign without planning. And sustenance in the belly. Keja, fetch some water from the packs."

When they finished drinking, Giles settled crosslegged on the ground. "Keja says there was no struggle. You say the boy has gone off to find out if we're being followed. Could well be. Both you and he have senses that Keja and I don't. It seems like this would be a good time to use yours."

Petia stared at Giles for a moment. "I'm sorry, Giles. Worry wins out over common sense every time, I guess. Be still while I concentrate."

She composed herself, closed her eyes and began to drift mentally. She sensed animals scurrying through forest and open country; Petia had known of the roving catamount for days. She allowed her mind to relax even more, then reached out along the track they had traveled, exploring both sides of the road, attempting to soak up any trace of animal or human.

"Getting anything?" Keja asked, but Giles silenced him with a wave of his hand.

Impressions came to Petia of tiny animals, shrews and voles, and once a stoat. In a moment, as she stretched her mind even further, a deer and fawn made their way cautiously to a secret watering place. But no indication of the boy came, not the slightest clue to show where he had gone.

Petia raised quivering fingertips to her temples and rocked back and forth, attempting to intensify her empathy with Anji. Nothing. At last she opened her eyes

19

and looked at Giles in quiet desperation. "I can't find him. I don't *feel* him anywhere."

Giles touched her shoulder reassuringly. "That doesn't mean he's not there, Petia. You've been training the boy, teaching him how to use his Trans senses. Perhaps you've taught too well. The boy may have more natural talent than you know. He may have found a way to conceal his presence from your mind."

Fear seized Petia. "Why would he do that?"

Giles laughed. "Didn't you ever do anything you didn't want your mother to know about? He knows you'll be angry with him and will come after him if you find out where he is. It's just self-preservation."

"I've got to find him and bring him back. He may be in danger."

"You'd be the one in danger," Keja observed. "If you can't reach him—*feel* him—you'll never find him. You'll walk right on past him and be the one stumbling into something. If Anji is right and we're being tracked, he'll return to tell us." Keja shrugged. "For that matter, he'll come back anyway."

"Keja's right," Giles said. "Anji will come back, I have no doubt. You told me, Petia, that he's crammed forty years into his eleven-year life. He knows how to be wary. I don't like the idea of his going off alone, but we're not dividing forces further to search for him. Meanwhile, we still have to get around this fallen tree. The best thing we can do is keep working and be ready to continue when Anji returns."

Petia saw the wisdom in what Giles and Keja said. Anji was no ordinary boy. He had lived by his wits and knew better than to tangle with whomever followed. But she was still angry with Anji, and he'd know it when she got him alone. The two men had convinced her that it was foolish to go looking for him, but she still worried, and would until he returned. Petia took out her frustration by hacking away at the brush.

They worked steadily for more than a half hour before taking another break. They barely sat down to rest when Petia jerked upright and twisted, looking back toward the road. "Anji!" she called.

The boy stumbled toward them, out of breath. Giles passed him the waterskin. When Anji had recovered, he grinned at the three adults.

"I told you someone trailed us." He saw the anger on Petia's face. "I had to go. I heard something earlier when we stopped to eat. Didn't you hear or sense it, Petia? It wasn't really a sound, I don't think, but I was sure something was back there."

"Well?" Giles asked, impatient.

"I didn't go far enough to see them, just far enough to use my senses, like you've been teaching me, Petia." He looked to her for approval. She signaled for him to continue.

"Somebody *is* following us. I got the impression of five men, mounted on horseback, and a pack of dogs, about ten of them, I think."

"What sort of men?" Giles lightly fingered his sword. That many men—and dogs—boded ill for them.

"I don't know, exactly. I wanted to get close enough for a good look, and I would have, too, if it wasn't for the dogs. They would have caught my scent. The men wouldn't have ever known I was there. I could have hid from them easy. But I was afraid of the dogs."

"Describe the men," Giles ordered.

"One of them was huge, and fat, and sweaty. I could tell that," Anji answered. Keja and Giles exchanged glances. "Another gave off a feeling of power, but I couldn't tell anything else. The others were just servants, obeying orders and hating it."

"What about the dogs? What kind?"

"Big, hunting types. In Bandanarra we call them *felji*."

Petia's eyes grew large. "Segrinn! He's found me again!"

"Don't worry," Giles said. "If it is, we'll deal with him. People like him need to be taken care of. Permanently."

Anji stared at Petia. Fear haunted her eyes, something he had never seen before. Petia was strong; Petia had bought him in a slave market and set him free; Petia wasn't afraid of anything. He knelt by her knee, his eyes searching hers, looking for reassurance. "Who is this Segrinn?" he asked.

She smoothed Anji's hair. Her anger at him for running off had drained from her the moment she realized whom Anji described. "He's a bad man," she told him. "My mother indentured me to Lord Ambrose, his father, something like your mother selling you into slavery. Segrinn wanted me to sleep with him, I ran away, and he's never forgiven me. He caught me once before, but I escaped. It looks like he's never going to give up."

"We'll stop him this time," Keja said with bravado.

"If it is Segrinn, we had better finish cutting this trail through and be on our way." Giles picked up his sword and walked away.

Keja laid a hand on Petia's shoulder. "It will be all right. Come on. Neither Giles nor I will let anything happen to you or Anji."

She eyed him strangely, then nodded. They returned to their task, hacking away with renewed energy, uneasy about enemies at their backs. They finished the job quickly, not caring that it was untidily done. Anji fetched the horses, and they mounted and were on their way.

The road continued to rise steadily toward the haze-hidden pass. Ahead the sky gradually turned gray, the clouds lowering until by mid-afternoon the light shone more like dusk.

Giles shook his head. "It's going to snow," he said. "I can feel it in the air. Maybe we can get through the pass before it gets too bad." He pulled his cloak closer about his shoulders.

Giles' prediction came true. Small flakes began to fall, growing larger the farther they went. Anji stared at the white, fluttering crystals in fascination, not knowing whether to rejoice in seeing his first snow or to worry. By good fortune they found a shelter as the snow began to drift knee-high along the trail.

To the right of the road, they found a tiny log hut with a sturdy roof and thick door. Keja pulled the door open onto a sparse interior. Four ledges along the wall provided sleeping space, and a small firepit had been dug in the center of the earthen floor. A small protected vent hole in the roof allowed the smoke to escape.

They made a meager supper and ate with no real appetite, their minds on Segrinn. The companions settled down to sleep soon after with little conversation. None slept easily.

In the morning they awoke to the baleful whine of wind blowing dry snow against the shelter. They didn't bother with a fire, eating the cold remains of last night's supper.

"Enough of this place," Giles said. "I want to make the pass before midday." He stuffed his bowl into his pack and went to open the hut's only door. It wouldn't budge. He put his shoulder against it. "Snow's piled up against the outside," he said. "C'mon, Keja, lend me your body."

They pushed the door open enough to allow Anji to slip out. He cleared away enough snow for the door to swing open, then stood, his hands clasped between his legs, as the adults sidled out through the opening. "Is snow always this cold?" he asked, and didn't think it funny when the others laughed.

Giles gazed toward the obscured road. It was covered with drifted snow, which provided beautiful scenery but a barely distinguishable track. "We've got to get through the pass." He stared up at the sky. "It could snow again at any time. See where the snow falls away at the side of the road? Keep several feel away from that and we should be all right. I don't want anyone going over the side. Do you understand, Anji?"

"Yes, Giles," the boy said as he swung up onto his horse. "Just don't forget who rescued us from our temporary prison." His eyes twinkled.

Giles snorted and watched the silvery plumes hover in front of his face. He mounted and led the way.

They found the way slippery and the road indistinct. At times one of them would dismount and feel their way along the road, picking a safe path for the others to follow. Fog cloaked their progress until the road began to descend, with only an occasional rise in the ground. They had passed the summit. Elated but tired, they guided their horses through snow deeper than their horses' fetlocks. Light snow began to fall again.

"We'd best find shelter," Giles said. "I don't want to be on the trail in a blizzard."

"You feel such a storm coming, Giles? What does it *feel* like?" Anji wanted to know. Even though the boy's nose had turned to a cherry-red button, he still stared in wide-eyed awe at the snow.

"Can't tell you," Giles said. "Might just be my joints stiffening on me." Anji looked disappointed and, not for the first time, Giles envied the Trans for their powers. But he knew others found nothing to envy in unknown power—they hated what they didn't understand. The Trans War had been fueled by such prejudices.

"Giles, there," shouted Keja, shivering with the cold. "Through the snow to the left. A light. Fire! A farmhouse!"

Giles motioned for Petia and Anji to follow. Keja surged on ahead, eager for the warmth promised by the farm.

The reception they received reminded them of their conversation with the peddler. The stout woman who came out to confront them in the barnyard wiped her hands on a greasy apron. She squinted at them and asked in a gravelly voice, "What do you want?" Not waiting for an answer, she called her husband from the barn. Silently the pair faced the travelers.

Giles pulled the hood back from his face and tried to smile. His lips cracked from the cold. Wincing at the small pain, he said, "We're looking for a place to stay the night. We've just come over the pass, and we've spent the last two days battling the snow. We thought you might have a place for us to spend the night. A place to sleep. And maybe a meal."

"This ain't no inn," the wife said.

Keja took a step forward, but Giles gestured him back. "We knew this wasn't an inn, madam," he said smoothly. "If there were an inn, we would have continued on to it. We'll pay for accommodations. We understand that it will make extra work for you."

The farmer's eyes glinted. "Mother, they could sleep in the barn. And we might find some bread and cheese for their supper, eh?"

Giles suppressed his smile at the greed written upon the dirty face. "Bread and cheese and fresh straw will do us just fine," he said, dismounting. "If you'll just show us the way, please."

There were no stalls for the horses, but they were inside and protected from the snow. The travelers had tasted better than the moldy bread and bitter cheese, but at least they didn't go hungry.

"We know now," Keja said, as they wrapped themselves in their cloaks. "Strangers are not welcome here, just as the peddler said."

Chapter Three

IN THE MORNING, THE FARMER, WITH A VICIOUS, SNAPPING barnyard dog at his heels, came to the gate and leaned on it, watching them go. The dog barked at the horses, making them skittish, but the farmer silenced it with several strokes of a gnarled stick.

"What an awful place," Petia said when they were out of earshot along the snow-packed road. "And despicable people. I don't think they've ever learned to smile. Last night the woman acted as if she were giving away the last morsel of food for their winter, even when they were well paid for it. The man had only money on his mind. And making us sleep in the barn." Petia snorted derisively.

"Didn't you sleep well?" Giles asked. He remembered all too well the times he'd slept in freezing mud and was glad for even that. "Believe me, you slept better than if we'd been in the house. Unless you like bedbug bites. I think the man was jealous of us, too."

"Jealous?" Petia said, eyes widening in disbelief. "He hated us!"

"See the way he stared when we rode off? He'd love the freedom we have. There was real envy in his eyes."

Petia shuddered. "Shall we try for an inn tonight? I'd

26

like to wash the straw out of my hair."

"The map shows a village called Malor still a good day's travel ahead," Giles said. "Any good-sized village ought to have an inn, but I make no promises on that score. The map doesn't show such detail."

The day turned clear and crisp, with the snap of real winter in it. The snow on the road had crusted from an overnight freeze. The horses' hooves broke through, making the going difficult until the sun softened the surface and turned the road to a muddy slush. Even so, Giles and Anji dismounted periodically to examine the horses' feet and fetlocks for ice cuts.

When the road widened, Giles beckoned Anji forward to ride beside him. He questioned him closely about what he had sensed when he backtracked at the fallen ironhorn tree.

"How far did you go?" he asked.

"I don't know, Giles," the boy answered. "I can't tell distances with all these tall trees. If we were in my desert, I could have told you."

Giles stared at the sharp azure sky, trying to remember how long the youngster had been gone, and doing sums of the distance in his head. "You couldn't have traveled more than a couple of miles in the time you were gone," he said. "Do you have any sense of them still following?"

"No," Anji answered. "I've been staying alert. They seem to have disappeared, or at least are beyond my range."

Giles called back to Petia. She shook her bridle and trotted up to ride on his other side.

"Can anyone block you from sensing them?" he asked.

"I don't know. Another Trans might. If you're thinking about those who were following us, Anji is certain they weren't Trans."

"Have you been listening?" Giles asked. "Sensing?"

Petia nodded, her expression grim. "My mind seeks constantly now. If it is Segrinn back there, I'll know it."

"Sing out the instant you know anything," Giles said.

In late afternoon, they rode into Malor, which proved to be a larger village than Giles had expected, but certainly not a town. Winter had shut down any industry that might have flourished during warmer months, but Giles doubted Malor prospered even then. The entire village had a curious, dead feeling about it.

"You, good sir," he called to a man who was standing in the road and motionlessly watching them. "Is there an inn nearby?"

The answer was nothing more than a vague wave of the hand. The man turned and walked off in sullen silence.

"What wonderful hospitality," grumbled Keja, who had complained of the cold all day. "We'll find this inn and discover it closed. Wait and see." He shivered and wrapped his arms around himself for the scant added warmth this provided.

Giles shook his head in wonder. Anji ought to be the one suffering. The boy seemed to enjoy the novelty of the cold. But Keja? Giles pushed all thoughts of the small thief from his mind. If Keja wasn't griping about something, *then* Giles would worry.

The sign hanging over the inn door needed repainting, but the members of the quartet made out the name: THE BREAD AND WATER. A plain loaf of bread, no butter, and a tin cup only half full of water portrayed the words.

"If this is someone's idea of a joke," Keja said, "we might be better off in their gaol."

No ostler ran out to help with the horses, and Anji and Keja were left to hold the reins while Giles and Petia went to see about rooms. They were aware of surly glances from heavily dressed men standing nearby, but amused themselves by whistling an old folk song in two-part harmony. "That ought to cheer the old place up," Keja said. "It certainly looks as if it needs it."

The onlookers silently left, as if Keja and Anji's tune offended them.

When Giles and Petia returned, Giles said, "The color of our money seems good. We have rooms and a meal, but not much else. I've never seen anything like this." He took his horse's reins from Anji's hand. "The stable is around in back, and we take care of our own horses." Giles looked around the glum village, then added, "We set watches tonight" The others nodded, remembering all too well their problems at the last inn.

The meal had been edible, but not much more could be said for it except that it proved better than the moldy bread and bitter cheese of the prior night. Giles and Keja ordered mulled wine after dinner. The wine was poor but tolerable because of the spice stick overpowering the taste.

Just as they settled down comfortably by the large fireplace, the inn door swung open and a guard officer entered. He ordered an ale from the innkeeper, then turned to survey the room. Keja watched his eyes light up as he saw them. "Here it comes," he whispered to the others. He loosened his dagger in its sheath, waiting for the inevitable to come.

"Let me tell our story," Giles whispered back.

The officer seemed content to leave them alone, but Giles had served in the military long enough to know the type. While Giles was fighting in the Trans War, this overdressed upstart of an officer was probably hiding beneath a haystack, only coming out to boast of his noble exploits.

The companions sat quietly, chatting, and ignored the officer. When he swaggered over to their table, Keja finished telling the story he had begun and paid no attention to the man. Everyone chuckled at the end of the story, and Giles poured more wine into Keja's cup. At last, settled again, he looked up as if he was noticing the man for the first time.

"Good evening, sir. Would you care for a cup of our mulled wine?"

The officer leaned back against the neighboring table, knowing full well that he had been purposely ignored. "Strangers here, aren't you?"

Keja snorted in disgust at such an obvious question. Petia restrained him before he made a flip reply.

"Just passing through," Giles answered mildly. "On our way north."

"North?" The officer's voice was tinged with sarcasm. "At this time of year? What would you be going north for?"

Keja leaned forward, but Giles spoke before a single sarcastic word left the younger man's mouth.

"We've heard, on good authority, that a great deal of mineral wealth in the north country offers itself to the bold. We're going exploring." He leaned back and took a sip of his wine. "Sure you won't have some?" he asked. The story was a poor one, but the officer might not care. He might be content with running them out of town in the morning, claiming to have done his duty. What worried Giles the most was that the officer was entirely right when he had mentioned that, with winter coming on, it was the worst time of the year for prospecting.

Keja spoke up now, and Giles assumed that his friend would follow his lead.

"Actually," Keja said, voice dropping low, "we're looking for gold. A source we can't name, a noted explorer from Bericlere, told us where we might find it in the northlands."

Giles marveled at Keja's skill. He made the tall tale sound almost plausible. Giles had to admit that Keja performed his chosen profession well.

The officer turned his head inquiringly. "Where might that be?"

Keja leaned back and chuckled. "Now, you don't really think we'd tell you, do you? We may look stupid, but we aren't going to give away that kind of secret."

The officer gestured at Petia and Anji. "Your wife and son?"

"No," Keja said. "Although . . ."

Giles broke in. "Partners in our venture. We've traveled a good bit together. This isn't the first time that we've joined up."

"Trans, aren't they?" The man said it as if his mouth were filled with muck. "Why'd you pick up with Trans?"

Petia flushed. Her anger made the veins along her temple jump. She opened her mouth to answer, but Giles touched her knee under the table, signaling for her silence.

"These two are good at prospecting. They have the knack of finding all that's worth finding." He touched Petia with his knee again, pleading silently with her to hold her temper and let him and Keja do the talking. Giles decided to see if he could elicit some pity. "Petia's husband was killed during the War."

"Your choice," the officer said, not bothering to hide his contempt. "We don't like Trans much here. Don't like strangers, either. I'm going to have to report your arrival to my superiors. Meanwhile, stay close to the inn. No telling what might happen if you get to wandering around the village."

"That's no problem," Keja said. "We're only staying the night. We'll be on our way in the morning."

"You'll need a pass to continue," he said, painfully drawing his chop on the bottom of a tattered sheet of paper. "Here's a temporary authorization to be in Malor. Don't go anywhere until you see me again—and don't leave Malor." He laid the authorization on the table. "See that you keep this with you and show it whenever you are asked by any of the uniformed soldiers."

He swaggered to the door, making an obviously rude remark about the quartet to the men sitting nearby. He raised a loud guffaw for his efforts, winked at the innkeeper and left.

"Nice people," Keja commented. "We haven't even done anything and they hate us."

"Unusual, indeed," Giles murmured. "I wonder how they feel about each other. Are they ever happy? Well, drink up." He poured into Keja's cup again. "Petia, would you like a small glass? It will make you sleep better."

Giles frowned when he saw that she had turned somber, melancholy written all over her face. He reached out and touched her hand. "Petia, what's the matter? Don't worry about that guardsman. They're all alike, all wanting to make their power known."

She raised her head, twin tears running down her face. "What you said to him was true. I *did* have a husband, and he *was* killed in the War. I never told you before. I thought I was over it. I . . . I'm not."

"I'm sorry. I would never have said that if I had the slightest notion it might be true. I was simply making up a story to satisfy that oaf. I truly am sorry."

Petia dabbed at her eyes. "It's all right, Giles. It seems like such a long time ago. Being indentured by my mother, escaping from Segrinn, being married, the War. Do things ever settle down? Is there ever any peace in life? When this is all over, I don't think I want to see either of you ever again."

Giles and Keja were stunned by her words. Unsure what to do or say, both turned back to their mulled wine. The silence between them became oppressive.

"You can come up for air now," she said after staring into the dancing flames in the fireplace. "I apologize. I shouldn't take out my feelings on you. It must be this place. I'm starting to be as inhospitable as the villagers."

Keja stretched. "It's not the friendliest place I've ever visited." He picked up the pass. "What a regimented country. I wonder if the locals are allowed to move around without a pass. Maybe they don't want to. Can you imagine being stuck in one place all your life? Not me."

"The only reason," Giles said, "you've moved around so much is because someone is always after your thieving hide. You'd probably love to settle down in one place, but you won't admit it."

"Not true, Giles. I could have stayed with l'Karm's daughter. I thought about it."

"Except you thought about the gold key more," Giles

32

said, "and ended up stealing it. Her father's men are still after you for that. Face it, Keja, you'll never settle down."

Keja tried to work up a scowl, but his face broke into a crooked smile. "If I did, I wouldn't pick Malor. Unfriendly people, tin soldiers marching around, snide remarks about visitors, terrible ale, ugly women. I wonder what other problems we'll have."

"Giles, I would like a small glass of your wine, after all."

Giles gestured to the innkeeper. "A glass for the lady, please." He heard a snicker from the nearby table, but when he turned a cold eye in that direction, the men fell silent. They read danger—and death—in that unwavering look.

The innkeeper brought more wine and the extra glass. Giles gestured for him to sit and share a cup with them. The man nodded and fetched his own mug. When he had poured the wine, Petia said, "Having to carry a pass is absurd."

The innkeeper's voice rang out deep and robust. "Everyone needs a pass here, even the people who live here." He pulled a brass sliver from his apron pocket and waved it.

"What sort of place is this?" Keja asked. "Not even the citizens are trusted."

"It's getting so we don't even trust each other, much less strangers. It wasn't always like this." The man drained his mug and set it down with a loud, empty click.

Giles moved forward and refilled the innkeeper's cup. "Tell us about it," he said.

"We're a good people, but lately there's been a big change." Even this obvious statement caused the innkeeper to drain another mug. Giles obliged, refilling silently. "Simple folk, living here in the foothills of the mountains. We used to help each other out. Then the soldiers came. Said we couldn't go anywhere without a damned pass. Threw people in gaol if they didn't have one. Scared us good, they did."

"Aren't they your own soldiers?"

The innkeeper paused and thought on this. "Guess we had soldiers of our own, once," he said. "But we never saw them, except once in a while when a troop would march through. We might have to billet them for a night. Never came back after the War, not a one of them. But now we've got a contingent of *them* here all the time, struttin' around, askin' to see our passes."

"Who's your ruler?" Keja asked.

"Lord Onyx," the innkeeper said. "We've never seen him. He wasn't the ruler before the Trans War, but now he is, it seems. Nobody knows how that happened, but we've got new laws. And the soldiers." He sighed. "Ain't much we can do about it, but it grates on you after a while, the way people have shut up and become so secretive all the time. People just ain't the same as they used to be."

"We're going north," Keja said. "Can we expect the same treatment all the way?"

"I'd think it likely. We ain't allowed to travel much, as you probably can tell. People is keepin' things close to themselves. They's bein' especially careful around strangers. No, you ain't got much welcome to look forward to. Not from the people or the land. You're goin' deep into the Adversaries, and in the winter time they ain't very forgivin'."

"I thought we were already into the mountains," Giles said.

The innkeeper leaned forward and looked at him as if to see if he was making a joke. "You're only in the foothills. If the weather would clear a little you could stand in the middle of the street and see the mountains up ahead of you. I wouldn't care to be heading that way, not at this time of year."

"The weather?"

"Oh, that, too, I reckon. I was thinkin' about the ice

34

demons and the snow demons. We don't see them much. They've only attacked a couple of times in the last five years. But that's because Malor is so far away from their lairs. The closer you get to them mountains, the more likely you are to be attacked. The ice demons live in ice caves, so don't go takin' no shelter in them. The snow demons, well I guess they build caves, too."

"You believe in spirits?" Keja asked. He licked suddenly dry lips at the idea of meeting such beings.

"Oh, yes. You'd better, too. I could take you down to the end of the road near here and show you a log cabin with the sides ripped right out. You'd believe me then. Tell you what, son. You go on up to them mountains and keep them demons busy. Then they'll leave *us* alone this winter." The innkeeper sighed and swallowed the last of his wine. "Don't want to tell me what you're going after, I don't suppose?"

Giles stuck to the story he had told the guard officer. "Doing a little prospecting, looking for gold, mostly, but anything else we might find: silver, lead, iron."

"Bad time of year for doin' that." The innkeeper gazed vaguely at a ceiling beam. "I don't believe you for a minute, but you stick with your story." He winked at Petia and put his hand on Anji's shoulder. "Back to work. Thank you for the wine and the talk." He wandered off to take care of the other guests.

The companions sat quietly, pondering what the innkeeper had said. Giles drew circles with the drops of wine that had spilled onto the table. Petia studied her fingers.

At last Keja broke the silence. "It doesn't sound good, Giles. Ice and snow demons and the winter coming on."

"No." Giles' statement was more of a long sigh than a response. "Maybe we ought to sleep on this." He rose and walked away, deep in thought over how far they had come, how close they were to success. The fifth and final key that opened the Gate of Paradise lay ahead. Could an old man with sparse years remaining pass up such a tasty morsel as Paradise?

The gods insisted that it wasn't going to be an easy decision.

The innkeeper served them a big breakfast. Giles deciphered the man's expression as a nostalgic remembrance of older times when people had been friendlier to strangers—and one another. A loaf of fresh brown bread, a platter of scrambled eggs and salted fish, and mugs of tea brewed from the leaves of a native bush were set before the four. Anji's eyes sparkled as he dug in. The others ate stolidly, knowing that a decision must be reached whether to go on or to return to warmer climes. If they ventured deeper into the mountains, there'd be no turning back.

When they were finished, Keja moved the platters aside and folded his hands on the table. "Well, Giles?"

Before Giles could respond, the door opened and the guard officer of the previous evening stalked into the room, accompanied by two soldiers. Petia saw others outside. "Trouble," she whispered.

The officer strutted over to their table. "I see that you didn't sneak off in the middle of the night," he said.

"Why should we do that?" Giles asked. "We're simply traveling through."

"Your pass." He thrust out his hand for the scrap of paper. A frown came over his face as he stared at it. "This won't do."

"I don't understand. Are you revoking our pass through this country? What's the reason?"

"Place them under arrest!" Those with the guardsman moved to obey. The officer smirked.

Giles and Keja shot to their feet. "Why? What's the reason?"

The two soldiers stopped, tugging at their swords. The officer held them back with a wave of his hand.

"Be careful, you two. There are more soldiers in the street outside—if needed." He sneered openly.

"We haven't done anything!" protested Keja.

"This pass is invalid."

"But *you* gave it to us!" cried Petia, outraged.

"I'm only following orders," he said, with obvious enthusiasm. "All with revoked or out-of-date passes are to be arrested."

"We don't understand," Giles said patiently. "You've got to give us an explanation."

"I don't have to give you anything," the officer snarled. "I have my orders and I carry them out. That is all you need to know. Now get your belongings."

"I'm sure there's some mistake," Giles said. "I'd like to see your superior. Then we can straighten this out."

The gleam in the man's eye told Giles that he'd get no more satisfaction from the higher ranks than he got from this lowly officer.

It took only a few minutes to gather their packs and reassemble downstairs. The innkeeper stood silently. He gave a minute shrug that told the four he was sorry for them. The officer gestured grandly and followed them into the bright sun.

"Run for it?" Keja whispered.

Giles shook his head. "No good. We need the horses, and they'll have someone posted at the stables." He glanced at the troop standing at ease in the street.

The officer slammed the inn door behind him and commanded the party to step down from the plank porch. Four soldiers led their horses from around the corner of the building. They were saddled, but their bridles were tied loosely to the back of the saddles.

"We'll bring your horses, but you'll walk. Since my men don't have horses, I see no reason that you should be allowed to ride."

Anji went to the horses and spoke softly to them, rubbing each of them on the nose. A soldier jerked him away and shoved him back toward the others.

Townspeople lined the street, gathered to see what had caused the commotion. The officer pushed the four into

37

the road, and soldiers formed around them. He gave the orders to march. Cheers followed them, punctuated with jeers at the strangers. "Stay out of Malor. We don't want strangers here. Get out, dirty Trans. Kill them all!"

Giles squeezed Petia's shoulder. "It's all right."

She nodded, but her face showed that it wasn't.

Chapter Four

"WHERE ARE YOU TAKING US?" GILES GRIMSMATE ASKED.

The soldiers surrounded the party and stood awaiting orders from their officer. Giles received no answer, nor had he expected one. He took the opportunity to examine the troop. An old soldier's habits die hard. Giles had commanded his own men for far too many years not to deduce a great deal about the men who hemmed them in—and about their officer.

He found them to be a slovenly bunch. If they had been in his company, he would have given them extra duty until they turned as old and gray as Giles himself was. With snow on the ground, he could understand their boots being dirty, but the snow did not reach to their belts or to the brass buttons on the front of their coats. Leather belts hung in untended tatters, the buckles hadn't been polished in months, and tarnish had accumulated so thick on the buttons that Giles began to wonder if they were brass.

Giles turned in disgust from these so-called military men and took a step toward the officer. Several soldiers tensed at the movement and prepared to seize him. A single cold stare froze them in their tracks.

He again demanded, "Where are you taking us?"

"He won't answer," Petia said. The cat-Trans hissed in disgust. "He's having too much fun lording it over us and playing to the crowd. One such as he wouldn't know, anyway. He has to wait. He has to be told. He's only someone else's lackey." She put her arm around Anji and observed him to see how he was taking their arrest. The boy looked up and winked. He wasn't afraid and seemed to be enjoying himself.

Giles wished the boy showed more sense in this. These men might not be good soldiers, but they *were* soldiers.

Keja stayed aloof, not deigning to acknowledge the soldiers. He looked past them to the jeering crowd standing along the road. The small thief elevated his nose and tried to appear as haughty as possible. Giles gave him a quick nod. Only by maintaining their aloofness and superiority over these country yokels would they escape. Keep the enemy off balance and wondering what he'd done wrong. And never show fear. Never.

Giles turned to Petia and tapped his forehead with his finger. She frowned, but the silent instruction became clear when he nodded slightly toward the officer.

She paused, collecting her mind, and sent it searching for the slightest clue in the man's mind. The officer's thoughts swirled in confusing eddies devoid of real content. He worried about promotion, his wife, something about blackness. The Trans scowled, angry at her inability to figure out what tore so at the officer's emotions. She couldn't read minds but her skills in empathic communication allowed her to discern more than what was carried by simple words. Usually. This wasn't one of those times, however, and she shook her head at Giles and shrugged.

The officer argued, gesturing wildly, but the innkeeper remained adamant. About what? Giles tried to edge closer to hear more distinctly, but one guard drove a hard elbow into his side. Giles avoided the worst of the blow and glowered at the soldier, who turned pale and stepped away.

"You *will* pay, by all that's holy," the innkeeper said, loud enough for all along the street to hear. "You take them before they pay, fine. That's your business, Brellon. But I will get my money for their board and room."

"This is none of your concern," the officer said, licking his lips nervously at the crowd forming around them. It became increasingly obvious this arrest wouldn't be done quietly.

"Then let me collect from them. They've retrieved their belongings. They have the coin." The innkeeper tried to shove past the officer, only to be knocked to the ground.

"Stay away from them. They're prisoners."

Giles saw a chance for sowing even more discord in their captors' ranks. "You won't even allow your poor citizenry to receive their rightful pay? This country is worse than I had imagined!" He took a large coin from his pouch and flung it toward the innkeeper, aiming in such a way that the man missed it by an arm's length.

A scramble of children pouncing for the coin ensued. They ended in a pile, arms and legs going every direction until one boy came up with the coin. He took it to the innkeeper, and Giles saw the man pull a smaller coin from his pocket and present it to the boy. Perhaps a little good and truth and justice lived in the town, but it was very little.

In spite of the moment's inattention, none of the companions had a chance to slip away from their guards. Giles' action effectively ended the argument, but the officer realized that the jeering crowd had become restless.

"Get moving," Brellon ordered. "Now!" He kicked several of his soldiers to make them obey. Giles heaved a sigh and shook his head.

Just give me these churls for a month, no, two weeks, and I'd turn them into real soldiers, he thought. Still, their slovenliness afforded a chance for escape at some time in the future. All Giles and the others had to do was wait, no matter how difficult that proved.

41

They moved off, boots scuffing through the snow. The jeers faded as the people realized that the entertainment was over and their feet were cold. The town fell away behind them and, when they rounded a corner in the road, vanished completely.

"We're well away from there," the pudgy officer said. "March easy, men."

Their display for the townspeople, such as it had been, was finished.

The ranks opened and stragglers slowed their pace. Some of the men pulled pipes and tobacco from their pockets. The officer fell back from his position at the front of his squad and walked beside the four prisoners.

"A beautiful day," he said, squinting in the reflected sun. "Not bad for marching, since it's marching we must do."

"Now will you tell us where you're taking us?" Giles asked in exasperation.

"Can't do that. I have my orders," Brellon said. "But there's no need for us to be uncouth about it. I haven't had anyone new to talk to for a long time. These louts"—he waved a pudgy hand at his squadron —"can't talk about anything but drinking, gambling, and women. I hope we can pass the time with more interesting talk than that, don't you?"

"What else is there but—" began Keja, but he subsided when he saw that the officer continued his little talk without waiting for an answer.

Keja raised his eyebrows, with a suggestion of resignation. The man was garrulous, no doubt about it. Maybe Brellon would stumble upon an interesting topic, but for the moment the officer seemed intent on bragging about his importance.

Giles silenced the others and allowed the officer to ramble on while they settled into a steady pace. The officer didn't seem to notice that they were not taking part in the dreary monologue of his tedious life, his tepid loves, his insignificant travels, the places he had been, the dull people he had met.

42

Brellon still flowed over with the verbal diarrhea at mid-morning, when he realized that he had not given his men a rest. He halted the troop, split it into groups to relieve themselves, and allowed the prisoners the same privilege, but under close supervision.

"You will *not* assign a man to watch me at my toilet!" the Trans snapped. She hissed and raked at the air in front of his nose.

The officer stepped away, wide-eyed. "But you're my prisoner, and I'm responsible for your well-being," he said, befuddled. A smile slowly crossed Brellon's face as the dilemma worked itself out. "You can go alone, if you promise not to attempt escape."

"I give you my word," Petia said with ill grace.

Giles almost wished she would vanish over the low rise and keep going, but he knew she wouldn't. She'd given her word—and Anji had stayed behind. The officer apparently missed the closeness between the two Trans. For that Giles heaved a sigh of relief. Until they discovered more about their destination—and the one ordering them arrested—he wanted only physical impediments to their escape. If the officer discovered he could use the boy as leverage, he might do something they'd all regret.

Giles had seen Petia angry. Her cat nature rose to the surface and turned her more animal than human. Even the bovine officer didn't deserve such a fate.

"Come on, you slugs," the officer shouted at his squad. "There's ale for you at the day's end and billeting in the inn, but not if we don't arrive there. You'll be sleeping under a sword tree tonight if you don't crook a leg."

"We travel for more than one day, then?" Keja asked.

"That's more than I care to tell," the officer said slyly. "Might that not be your destination? The end of your road, so to speak?"

"We," cut in Giles, "are simple prospectors, nothing more. We stay at inns for the time being, looking for the right place to sally forth and stake our claims in the mountains."

43

Keja bit his tongue. He had almost answered the officer that they went farther than any mere country tavern in their search for the fifth key to the Gate of Paradise. He resolved for the thirtieth time to think before he spouted off.

At the rest for the noon meal, the prisoners had their first chance to talk with each other. The officer went off to inspect his men. He ended up examining the horses enviously.

"He's certainly not opening up, is he?" Petia said, eyeing Brellon. "We don't know any more about our destination than when we left this morning."

"I'm sorry I said anything to him," Keja said. "He thought he was being terribly clever when he concluded that this was the way we had been traveling. I didn't want to give him any information at all."

"Yes, I know," Giles said. "Any fool could have figured out that we were traveling north—even *that* fool. In fact, we told him so last evening. I worry that he's taking us in the direction we wanted to go."

"We can get away, Giles. I know it." Keja's eyes darted from one soldier to the next. "Look at them. Lazy, inattentive."

"Like you, eh?" Petia said. Before Keja could respond angrily, she rushed on. "We don't know whether we're going to march for a day or a week. I say we should watch for any opportunity to get away."

"I'd hate to leave the horses," Giles said.

"Don't forget the equipment and supplies and our weapons," Petia said. "We can't leave all that behind."

"We could, but it'd make things more difficult than I want in the midst of winter-wracked mountains," Giles replied.

"Why not just be agreeable and find out where we're being taken?" Keja asked. "After all, we head in the proper direction, don't we?"

Giles grimaced. He stared at Keja as if he were a small child asking a stupid question, then turned away. The idea of being anyone's prisoner tore at Giles' sense of honor. He hadn't fought against the slavery imposed on the Trans out of repugnance at what was done to them—at first. He had been drafted and fought because his lord commanded it. But over the years he had come to loathe slavery in all its forms. Every gray hair on his head marked a new promise to fight against such oppression.

Although they weren't slaves, Giles cared little more for being subject to another's whim.

The rest came to an end, and the officer prodded his troops into a semblance of formation. The four companions took their places and set off. The officer seemed to have talked himself out; their only accompaniment was the scrunch of boots through the dry snow. Even the wind took a rest from its mournful howling between mountain peaks. Giles marched along as if lost in a soundless bubble, lost in his own thoughts. Keja might be right about going along with their captor—but deep in his heart he knew Petia spoke the truth: at the first opportunity they'd have to make a break for freedom.

Later in the afternoon the squad tired of shuffling through the snow and began to complain bitterly to their leader. Brellon had to encourage them with promises of billeting and beer. Grumblers, Giles thought. And probably insubordinate when the going got tough. Certainly not men he would want at his back in battle.

In spite of the discord, Giles saw no good chance for escape. They arrived at a small village as the day turned to dusk.

"Trenora, isn't it?" Giles asked. He remembered that much from his map. Instinctively, he touched the spot where the map lay beneath his tunic, hidden. At first, he'd been surprised that he hadn't been searched when arrested. In his day they stripped prisoners and looked for messages, briefs, and maps. But he had come to know how poorly planned their arrest had been and how little the officer knew of his job. One more indication of sloppy soldiering.

"That it is," Brellon responded, not even wondering

how Giles had known. He spat into the snowy street as a crowd began to form around them. The people here did not even have the energy to jeer. They stood and stared with empty, dull eyes.

The four companions were taken to the inn and, with a great deal of fussing, the officer obtained billeting for his men and a room where his prisoners could be held. When a meal of sorts was brought to Giles and the others, they saw that two guards lounged outside their door. When the dishes were taken away, they found that the guard had been increased to four. In spite of being weaponless, they might have overpowered two guards, but four guaranteed the failure of any escape attempt.

"We'd best settle down and rest," Giles said. "This is becoming tedious."

Their travels became even more tedious; for two more days they continued marching north. Mornings found Brellon talkative and gregarious. And boring.

The days continued mild and indistinguishable from one another. Each night a trace of light, dry snow fell. The mornings were crisp and the weak afternoon sun brought little real warmth. At times the companions wondered how long this would go on, if perhaps they had not died and marched to the lowest regions of Hell.

Giles' impression of the officer raised a notch when he realized that no circumstances developed in which they might escape. With the soldiers often edging perilously close to insurrection, Giles found this startling.

Even more puzzling to him was the undercurrent of discipline in an otherwise outwardly slovenly squad; it had been a topic of whispered discussion among the four travelers.

Keja expressed it best that night when they stopped at another inn. "How did they send the message so fast? On one night we were given a pass, and the following morning it was revoked and we were arrested. We've been on the road for two days already and haven't reached the place where the message must have come from. What manner of sending must they have?"

"Perhaps we'll find out when we arrive there, if we ever do," Giles said. "We certainly haven't had any chance to escape yet, so just keep trudging along and keep your eyes and ears open."

"The order for our arrest might have come from some place different than our destination," Petia said. "That indicates a control over the country tighter than any I've seen, even in Trois Havres."

"Time will tell, I suppose," Giles answered. "Do you believe in magic?"

"After Bandanarra, yes," Keja said emphatically. "I also believe in sleep, prisoner or not." He stretched out on the hard wood floor, pulled his cloak around him, and gave up thinking about the mysterious sending of messages.

On the third day, the road began to climb, and they moaned at the strain in their leg muscles. When they entered a pass at midday and saw the mountains ahead, the towering peaks seemed close enough to touch. Anji's eyes widened. "Are we going to climb over them?" he asked as the road straightened out and appeared to be heading directly toward them.

Giles laughed. "Let's hope not. We're hardly dressed for a climbing expedition."

On the morning of the fourth day they topped a small rise and looked out across a high meadow that stretched for miles. In spite of their predicament, the companions paused and marveled at the purple-hazed mountains rising from their base at the far side.

"No time for gawking," the officer said. He prodded at them and kept them moving, pressing hard throughout the morning. He gave the impression that their journey neared its end. Their midday stop was short, and he hurried them along. Within an hour the outline of a citadel sharpened and became more distinct through the distant haze.

"It looks as if it grew from the mountain's base," said Keja, awed in spite of his best intentions to let nothing impress him.

"It also looks to be our destination," Giles said, giving himself over to introspection. He didn't know what to expect when they arrived at the prodigious pile of stone. He ran through the possibilities. They should stick to their story of searching for minerals, but they must also agree on their backgrounds. If they were given the chance to talk, they dared not contradict one another.

As they drew nearer, they were overwhelmed by the size of the citadel. "It's as big as Shahal," Anji breathed.

"Yes, nearly so," Petia agreed. "Except that Shahal is vertical, and this hugs the base of the mountain and stretches out. It doesn't have as many floors as Shahal."

"It is huge, big enough to have dungeons." Anji voiced a concern no one had yet spoken aloud: the possibility that they would be imprisoned, for whatever reasons the ruler of this sorry country might have.

The high cirrus clouds parted, and the wan sun lit the sides of the citadel. Huge blocks of a gray stone rose in tier after sloping tier. In some respects it reminded Giles of a story he had once heard about a structure built by the gods and called a pyramid, although he recalled that the mythical pyramid continued upward until it ended in a sharp point.

This building rose from a base stretching along the mountains to a height of more than eighty feet. Crenelations decorated the top of the wall, and Giles suspected that behind it stretched a broad walkway, perfect for sentry duty and defense. From its battlements, guards would be able to look across the grassy high meadow for miles. Attacking such a fortress would be a difficult task.

But even as the thought crossed his mind, Giles began formulating ways to do so. He cursed this futile activity, but recognized it as part of his training.

"To conquer *that*!" he said with a gusty sigh.

As they drew closer, they saw the huge ironwood gate built into the wall. The road ended there, swallowed by the structure. Giles saw sentries walking their stations along the wall and knew that the arrival of their little band would have been announced long ago. As if in response to his thoughts, the doors of the gate swung open. Their thickness confirmed Giles' suspicions that, no matter his feelings about the soldiers who had arrested them, this was a well-built fortress. Inside he anticipated finding properly drilled troops under the command of tough, demanding officers.

And in supreme command would be, ironically, a military man whom he might respect—and who had ordered them imprisoned.

Now within sight of their destination, Brellon showed his nervousness. It was obvious that they were being watched, and he wished to present a troop of something besides stragglers. He tried desperately to form his men into reasonable ranks, to bring them to a semblance of a squad in fighting trim, ready and eager to take orders.

Giles nudged Keja and nodded toward the ineffectual officer. They enjoyed the look of embarrassment and dismay on his face. It might be their last bit of entertainment for a while.

Giles sobered when he realized that any chance for escape had evaporated upon their arrival at the citadel. This had to be the ruler's fortress. No one else in a country would be allowed to possess such a powerful base.

What had the innkeeper called him? Lord Onyx? Giles straightened as he came to the decision that they had been summoned by Lord Onyx.

An officer and troop of guards awaited their arrival at the gate. The solid door was even more impressive at close quarters. The soldiers stood at ease in an orderly fashion, alert and awaiting commands. Their officer stepped forward and said, "I'll take command of the prisoners, Brellon. Take your men to the lower level barracks and, by the gods, see that they bathe and clean their uniforms and weapons. They look disgraceful. I will personally conduct inspection in the morning."

He forced away the look of disgust at Brellon's soldiers, then commanded his guard to attention and form
ranks behind the prisoners. Two men broke rank and
took the animals to stables within the citadel. Then in a
calm voice the officer ordered the companions to follow
him.

Keja tensed, but Petia restrained him. It did no good
to fight now. They all realized that their chance for
freedom lay behind them. They could only go along with
their captors and confront the man who commanded
such grand forces in the otherwise miserable mountain
kingdom. They trudged up wide granite stairs lighted by
torches placed in twisted wrought-iron brackets along
the wall.

Ever the soldier, Giles paid close attention to the
route. They climbed several flights of stairs, each ascend-
ing in a different direction. They took the left, the left,
two rights and a final left staircase before entering a
broad hall.

The officer turned smartly and said, "Remain here.
You may warm yourselves at the fire until I return. You
shan't be waiting long." His guard efficiently fell in
behind as the officer walked away.

"What do you make of that?" Keja asked.

"We do as he says," Petia replied, shivering. "He
doesn't look like Brellon. He'd kill and never miss a
night's sleep over it."

"He's a soldier." Giles counted that as the highest
compliment he could give. He gestured to the others and
they took advantage of a roaring fire in a fireplace along
one wall. Four-foot-long logs sent waves of heat out into
the room from the massive head-high fireplace. Having
marched through the snow for four days, all four travelers eagerly crowded close, hands extended, feeling
warmth crawl back into them.

"What next?" Keja asked. Already the small thief
moved from the fire and appraised the room's furnish-
ings. Back in Neelarna the solid gold candlesticks would
bring a small fortune to anyone bold enough to offer

them to the right buyer. He saw no way of slipping even the smallest candlestick into his tunic without being obvious.

"We'll soon find out," Giles replied. "This is the end of the track in this snowbound country."

Doors burst open at the far end of the long hall. The companions turned at the sound and saw guards bring their halberds to attention. A rustle of activity made Giles uneasy for no reason. Then he saw a small hunchbacked man—a dwarf?—bustle about, shooing people out of his way. Giles jumped when a robust laugh echoed throughout the huge room. A rotund man, magnificently dressed, strutted through the door, then stopped and struck a pose.

He threw his arms wide in greeting, and his voice boomed down the hallway. "Welcome, my friends."

Anji gasped. The boy's eyes widened and he exclaimed in a hushed voice, "The mysterious stranger! The one who has followed us for so long!"

Chapter Five

A CHUCKLE CAME FROM THE MAN'S HUGE FRAME, THEN GREW into a hearty laugh. He threw his entire body into the effort, holding his sides and tossing his head back. When the laugh finally subsided, his baritone voice rolled like thunder down the hall.

"This room has excellent acoustics. I could hear your young friend's whisper all the way from where you stand. Remarkable, is it not?"

The four stood, transfixed by the booming voice. Its owner was dressed in knee breeches of burgundy velvet and a rose brocade coat with a white linen shirt underneath. Gold braid decorated his shoulders, and his shoes bore massive gold buckles. His stockings were tinted a delicate pink.

The man walked toward them, the dwarf preceding him with hands fluttering right and left to clear the way.

"So you call me the 'mysterious stranger,' do you? I like that. I had not thought you would notice me, but it's obvious that you did."

"We only knew that a man in black has been following us," Giles said, frowning. This might be the man he had run into so long ago before confronting the Flame

Sorceress. "You followed us on Milbante, too. Why have you been spying on us?"

"Let us say that it was enlightened self-interest, keeping apprised of a situation that interests me greatly."

"And what would that be?" Keja asked.

"There will be time for discussion later, my friends. You must be tired from your long journey. Please, follow me." He turned and led the way back along the hall. At the doorway, he beckoned to the dwarf. They were amused to see the misshapen creature stand on tiptoe and cup one ear to hear his master's orders. They could hear them well.

"Get rid of these other people. They bore me. And close the doors after us. See that refreshments are brought." The diminutive man backed away and began to turn. "And be sure to bring that wine from Albiado," the huge man roared after him.

He led them into a sumptuously furnished room. Another fireplace burned with the same vigor they had witnessed in the outer hall. A long table covered with a linen cloth ranged along one wall, candelabra spaced evenly along it. Chairs upholstered in brocade faced the fire.

The huge man gestured. "Sit, sit, my friends. There will be food soon. After your meal, you will be shown to your suite. No, no." He held up his hands. "No questions now. Tomorrow. Tomorrow we will talk. In the meantime, please do not consider yourselves as prisoners. Rather, consider yourselves the guests of Lord Onyx."

Giles and the others exchanged glances. This *was* the lord of the region, the Lord Onyx mentioned by the innkeeper.

"Serve them," Lord Onyx ordered as a servant silently entered. "The fire warms without and the wine warms within. Don't be afraid, my friends. It's not poison. I have much to talk about with you and the dead hold little converse. Ah, the lady and the boy grow tired."

Petia stifled a yawn behind her hand, but Anji's yawn

was audible and his eyelids were drooping.

Onyx rose and pulled at a tassled rope near the fireplace. A meticulously groomed major-domo appeared.

"Their room is prepared? Then escort them to it. We shall talk later. In the meantime, be comfortable, my friends. Enjoy the delicate fruits, the wholesome meats, the vintage wines. Food, a hot bath and a good sleep is what you need. You have journeyed long and will find the beds most comfortable here."

They followed the silent major-domo, constantly aware of their escort—a half dozen soldiers trailed. They climbed stairs, walked down long hallways, and rounded corners. Anji's legs began to fold as he was nearly asleep on his feet. Keja scooped him up and carried him in his arms, and Petia gave the man a grateful look. Her own arms lacked strength to hold even one as small as Anji.

At last the servant stopped at a doorway. Two guards stood outside. The servant opened the door to a suite unlike any the companions had ever seen. No common hostelry this, the rooms were large and appointed with rich furniture and draperies. A table that ranged along one wall was set with silver goblets and decorated china, platters of meat and cheese, and bowls filled with ripe fruits. A loaf of bread, neatly sliced, was arranged artistically on a board of polished ironhorn.

The major-domo turned and inclined his head toward a woman standing in a doorway leading deeper into the suite of rooms. Without word, he left.

"Is the water drawn?" she asked.

"Yes, Mistress Oa," four voices rang in unison. Giles jumped at the answer. He hadn't seen the other servants when he'd entered the room. He had been too engrossed in the luxurious settings. The four bowed and silently left, just as the major-domo had. This time Giles paid more attention.

The door closed softly behind them. Giles listened closely for the click of a lock. He heard none.

"All has been readied for you," Mistress Oa said. "If there is anything more you require, please ring. I shall be in attendance." She bowed slightly and floated from the room as if she had clouds instead of feet.

"What do you think of all this, Giles?" Keja said when the door closed.

Giles put a finger to his lips and led the way to the fire. Beckoning them close, he whispered, "Let's leave talk until later tonight. Someone is undoubtedly listening. You heard the acoustics in the main hall. I don't trust these rooms—or Lord Onyx."

Keja raised his eyes in exasperation but complied. "Something to eat," he said. "There's a feast over there."

After he had filled a plate, he wandered into the adjoining room to test the beds. When Giles and Petia had finished eating a light meal, they found him fast asleep, his plate resting on his stomach.

"Not a bad idea," Giles said. He stretched out on another bed, wrapped a blanket around himself and closed his eyes.

The sun was slanting through the windows when Giles awoke. He noticed instantly that their clothes had been cleaned and returned. Walking to the door and opening it, he saw soldiers standing guard outside. One looked balefully at him but uttered no word. Everyone but Onyx seemed taciturn here. With a shrug, Giles turned back and closed the door.

"'Guests,' he said. 'My friends. You're not prisoners, but of course, you can't leave.'" Giles strode to the fire and heaved another log onto it, watching the sparks and ashes whirl upward.

When Anji finally awakened, Giles asked, "I want you to think carefully before you answer, Anji. Is the man downstairs, the one calling himself Lord Onyx, the man whom you sensed when we were first reached Khelora? Is he the one who followed us on the road?"

"I think so, Giles, but I can't be sure," the boy replied.

"I never did see him, but I *know* he's the one in Bandanarra."

"What do you suppose he intends to do with us?" Petia asked.

"I don't even want to guess," Giles replied. He walked to the window and stared out over the meadow. "Sloping walls a couple of hundred feet down. We're not likely to get out that way."

"You can be sure that his friendliness is only an act," Keja said. "A facade as big as his belly."

Giles nodded, stuffing his pipe. When he had it going, he let wreaths of smoke envelop his head while he thought.

"Everything we saw as we traveled here indicates a ruler who brooks no opposition. A ruler who expects to be obeyed, who totally dominates his subjects and turns them unfriendly and suspicious. I fear that our next conversation with him will not be so pleasant."

Giles pointed his pipe stem at the others. "Whatever happens, stick to our story. We're simply looking for minerals, gold specifically."

"But if he's been following us, Giles," said Keja, "he knows that's a lie."

"Onyx obviously knows more about us than we do of him," Giles agreed glumly. "We have no choice but to play a waiting game. We'll see what the fat man has to say and then go from there. Meantime, we scout ways out of this place."

He walked to the windows again. Pale sunlight bathed the snow-covered meadow two hundred feet below. The windows were hinged, and Giles tested a fastening. To his surprise, it released easily. He swung the window outward, and the cold early-morning air gusted into the room.

Bending outward over the sill, Giles examined the sloping wall carefully. The stonework was magnificent, the joining of stones nearly imperceptible. Petia, Anji and Keja came to stand at his back, eager to see if they could hope for escape in that direction.

Giles shook his head. "Nothing, not the slightest toehold. It would be a long slide, probably exhilarating. But the stop at the bottom would be abrupt—and deadly." He sighed. "Hang onto my feet." He stepped onto the sill facing the wall, holding to the opened window and bracing against the frame. When he had gained his balance, Keja held him by the ankles.

Giles found a new grip and leaned out as far as he dared. Immediately above him he found the upper window casement mounted flush with the wall, joined smoothly with the stones. No hand or foothold there, either. Above him stretched more floors of the citadel, some identifiable by windows. Giles could not see the battlements along the top.

He swung back into the room. "It's a marvelous piece of architecture," he said. "It must take an enormous base to support a building like this. If you were to drop a line straight down from the battlements, I'll wager you'd find that the base is over a hundred feet thick."

"Wonderful, Giles," Keja said. "A lesson in architecture is what we need right now. So how do we escape?"

"That's what I like about you, Keja. You go right to the heart of the matter. I don't know how we get out of here. Not by windows and wall, I can assure you. Even if they hadn't taken away our ropes, I don't think they'd be long enough to reach the bottom." Giles glanced out the window again. "And it looks as if there'd be a welcoming committee if we made it."

The others crowded around Giles and stared down. Two guards marched along a wide pathway on the south side of the citadel, their heads swaying alertly from side to side as they patrolled. The companions watched the guards until they disappeared around the corner. Giles caught movement to his right, and said, "Look, here come another pair."

"How can they circle the citadel?" Keja asked, perplexed. "It's built right into the mountains, isn't it?"

"Inside passage," Giles muttered, his mind elsewhere. The soft rustle of silk skirts caused them to turn.

Mistress Oa stood in the doorway, a frown on her face.

"Lord Onyx has summoned you," she said. "Please follow me to the audience chamber."

"But . . ."

Keja tried to engage the woman in conversation, but she turned and left, as if he didn't exist. Giles slapped Keja on the shoulder, then made a mocking bow in the direction of the open door. Few were the women who did not respond to Keja Tchurak's charms.

They were led once again down the long corridors and wide stairways to the chamber in which they had first met Lord Onyx. The portly man stared at them with cold eyes.

"I see you are rested, my friends," Onyx said. "You seem to find my hospitality agreeable and know I am a caring ruler."

"Why are you holding us?" Keja interrupted. "We were simply traveling through this country—"

He was cut off by Onyx's voice, as angry as a growling bear. "Don't give me any of your tall tales. I know who and *what* you are. Keja Tchurak, petty thief. Petia Darya, good over the roofs, but there her thieving skills end. She is also rescuer of Anji, no last name, Trans boy bought in a slave market on Bandanarra. Anji, clever boy, learning quickly what Petia has to teach." He moved away and paced in the front of the fireplace. When he turned back, his anger had abated. "Giles Grimsmate, the only one for whom I have any respect. Twenty years in the Trans War, able fighter, well-liked sergeant, cynical, wearied by witnessing too much death."

Onyx shook his leonine head. "What an unlikely partnership! Searching for minerals, especially gold. An even more unlikely story."

"But it's tr—" Keja began.

Onyx turned fiercely on him. "Remain silent or I'll have your flapping tongue cut out. I don't need your lies, Tchurak. Instead I will tell you some truths. Do you remember being hit on the head in the Temple of

Welcome in Glanport, Giles? You three came together at the Gate of Paradise and couldn't open it, is that not so? Two keys for five locks. Somehow you defeated the Flame Sorceress—I watched you leave Sanustell. Were you cold hiding underneath the docks, Tchurak? I hoped you would drown with the high tide. And you, Trans woman. The Callant Hanse should have demanded your death for trying to rob them. Sloppy work, but then, all your thieving has been sloppy."

He paused to take a ripe plum from the bowl on the table. "Bandanarra almost finished your adventures, didn't it?" he resumed. "The Sand Seas of Calabrashio, the Skeleton Lord and his men? I do hope the poor beasts can bring the economy back to Shahal and the Track of Fourteen."

Giles and the others were overwhelmed by Onyx's detailed knowledge of their adventures over the past two years.

"So please humor me, and don't attempt that sorry story of prospecting," Onyx said, his lips curling into a slight sneer. "It's the final key you're after. I know it, and you know it. There are five keys, one for each lock on the Gate of Paradise. Four of them sit safely in the vaults of the Callant Hanse. An admirable choice, by the way. A well-respected merchant house, eminently trustworthy. Much more than I can say for the four of you. Now, you will excuse me for a moment while I let you digest this information. Please be seated."

He strode away to the opposite end of the room, where the gray-clad dwarf huddled over a stack of papers. The companions sank into chairs and sat quietly, each absorbed in his or her own thoughts. Remembrances of their adventures bombarded them, and behind each image was the thought that they had been watched. This elegantly dressed man *was* the man in black, the mysterious stranger, as Anji had named him. He had watched and chuckled at their struggles, sometimes intervening.

Damn, damn him! Giles thought. They had been used. Onyx wanted the keys and had let them take the risks obtaining the other four. Giles had no doubt that Lord Onyx held the fifth and final key to the Gate.

Onyx ambled back to the shocked companions. As he reached them, the doors of the chamber swung open and a figure entered. If Onyx could be described as stout, this man was obese. Petia stared and then gasped in recognition. "Segrinn," she sobbed. The Trans seemed to shrink in size, cowering down in her chair.

Giles and Keja turned to her. "What? Him?"

"You know him, my dear?" Onyx asked ingratiatingly. "An old friend of yours, no doubt."

Petia's hands knotted in her lap. The man waddled down the center of the room, his eyes fixed on the Trans woman. "You've done it, my Lord Onyx," he bellowed. "You've found my luscious Petia."

Shaking free of her shock, Petia sprang to her feet, baring her teeth and snarling. "Keep that swine away from me, or I'll tear his throat out. I'm not his and never will be."

Anji stared at her, this woman who had rescued him. She had turned into a feral cat cornered by a hunting dog and determined to fight to the death. He had seen Petia fight before and knew that she could be fierce and relentless, but never had he seen such savageness. It frightened him; a small sound came from his throat.

"It gives one pause, does it not, my dear?" Onyx said. He turned to Segrinn. "No farther, good sire. You may return to your rooms."

"But I wish to . . ." Segrinn began. His voice trailed off when he saw Onyx's expression.

"Go. Now." Onyx's bellow echoed around the room.

Segrinn blanched and glanced at Petia. He reached a tentative hand toward her, looked once more at Lord Onyx, then turned on his heel. His shoulders sagged as he exited the room.

"You see, many reins of power rest in my hand," Lord Onyx said as he settled himself in a comfortable chair facing the four. "Now let us get down to some simple bargaining."

"Our four keys in exchange for our lives," said Keja.

"What else?" answered Onyx, smiling wickedly. "You think, no doubt, that you know the location of the final key. That is why you came to Khelora, not for such a ridiculous reason as prospecting in the winter-cloaked Adversaries. You came for gold, that much is true. The gold key."

He paused, as if waiting for a response. None came. Onyx continued. "The key is not where you suppose it to be. Oh yes, I have the final key, but you would never find it, even if I stood aside and watched—with a great deal of amusement, I might add—while you searched for it."

"Why do you want the keys?" Giles spoke up. "You appear to have all a man could want. Wealth, power, a country of your own. What can the Gate of Paradise mean to you?"

Onyx glared at Giles as if he were insane, then moved to the fireplace, warming his hands and staring into the leaping flames. At last he turned back.

"You truly don't know, do you?" He searched each face in turn, finding nothing but puzzlement at his question. Then he threw his head back and laughed.

"What's so funny?" Keja muttered.

"You're looking at a god, and you don't realize it. A minor one in the pantheon, as such things go, but a god, nonetheless. I watched the Gate of Paradise being built, or rather, *placed* on this miserable world. It was no engineering feat, no architectural wonder. It was merely the thought in the mind of one far more powerful than I.

"Once, while I was battling another god, a decree came from an even higher, more potent god that we were to desist. I did not. As punishment I was cast from what you mortals call Paradise. Exiled on Hawk's Prairie, I saw the Gate set in place and listened to the locks click shut. My powers were stripped from me, and I was told that when I found the five gold keys unlocking the Gate, I would be allowed to return to Paradise. You don't know how many centuries it has taken to come this far, nor would you believe the hardships I have suffered. I have not always been as you see me now."

"You want us to hand over our four keys?" Giles asked.

"It is a hard command, is it not?" Lord Onyx's voice hinted at sympathy, but his eyes were colder than steel. "Return to your suite and consider the consequences. For three of you, the alternative is death. And for Petia, my dear Trans, a living death with that odious pig, Segrinn. You may go now."

Onyx lunged out of the chair and tugged on the bell cord. The door opened and Mistress Oa entered, with her escort of guards, to lead them back to their room.

Onyx seemed in no hurry. For two days the companions stewed over the dilemma facing them. At first Giles, Petia and Keja despaired. There followed a period of anger, then at last a quieter discussion of their plight. They knew that they were being given time to come to a decision, and that the only decision acceptable to Onyx was for them to hand over the keys.

But their anger sustained them. They had been through much, perhaps not as much as Onyx had hinted of his own tenure on this world, but they were determined not to give in easily.

"We must escape, Giles," Keja said. When Petia nodded, he went on. "If he calls for us again, it may well be the last time. If we refuse to give up the keys . . ." He drew a finger across his throat. "And Petia is turned over to that waddling beast again."

"I know, Keja, but how do you propose to get out of here? We've examined the wall again. It is not a route to escape, but to death."

"Maybe better death trying to escape than the kind that will greet us when Onyx calls again."

Anji had been listening to the conversation flow around him. He had heard the despair, the anger, the abortive thoughts of escape. He understood the danger, but for a boy almost twelve, he had faced more danger than most grown men.

Suddenly he gasped, clutched at his stomach and staggered from his couch to fall, writhing, to the floor.

Petia jumped to her feet and knelt at his side. "Anji, what is it? What's wrong?"

The boy turned his head and stared up at her. His brown eyes shone like a deep dew pond from which devilment bubbled up.

Petia looked up at Giles, who slowly nodded. Keja was slower to understand, but when he did, he couldn't keep from smiling broadly.

Petia opened the door and darted into the hallway. The guards jumped alertly.

"The boy, the boy," she shouted, gesturing for the guards. "Come quickly. He's got the falling sickness." She wrung her hands. "He's writhing on the floor. I think he's dying."

The two guards rushed into the room, seeing only the boy in convulsions on the floor. One laid his halberd down and turned the boy over.

Keja stood nearby, looking distraught and yelling, "Do something for him. Don't let him die!"

The guard still holding his weapon turned to tell Keja to calm down. Keja seized the guard's wrist and twisted the man's arm behind him. The guard yelled in pain. The second guard looked up to see what was happening just as Giles hammered a blow to the small of his back with two closed fists. The breath went out of the soldier with a whoosh, and he slumped over Anji's body.

"Move carefully and don't make any noise," Keja said as he forced his prisoner to his feet. Giles tied the arms of his man with strips of cloth torn from the window drapes. Petia stuffed the bound guard's mouth with more of the material. When the first guard was secure, they tied the second, then dragged both to the interior room.

For a moment, they stopped and drew a breath. When their heartbeats had slowed, Giles nodded. Petia pulled on the rope pull which would summon a woman servant. They captured her with little effort.

Petia slipped the outer garment from the servant and

63

put it on over her own clothing. Giles and Keja took the guards' jackets and boots, tucking their own trousers into the boot tops, to look as much like guards as possible.

Keja stood at the door, halberd in hand, while Giles and Petia questioned the servingwoman about the layout of the citadel.

"Is there a way out of here besides the main doors?" Giles prodded.

The woman shook her head, fear in her eyes.

Giles put a sword he had taken from a guard to her throat. She saw her death written on the grizzled man's face.

"Yes, yes," she stammered. "Don't kill me. I'll tell."

When she had told them, Giles said threateningly, "If you lie, we will come back and kill you." They tied and gagged the woman and put her in the room with the guards.

Opening the door quietly, they slipped into the corridor. Empty. They went swiftly and silently along it, pausing only at the corners of stairways to check the floors below. Once, they heard voices and waited for a small knot of servants to pass. Petia counted each floor on their way to the lowest floor. At last she touched Giles on the arm and nodded.

"This level?" he whispered. "You're sure?"

She nodded again, and Anji nodded, too, verifying it.

Keja cupped his ear, and they fell silent, listening. The sound of boots echoed somewhere, but from which direction, they could not tell. They were certain, however, that guards patrolled nearby.

Had the alarm been put out for them yet? Were guards already seeking them?

Giles peered around the stair railing, searching for the doorway marking the exit. He spotted it and pointed to it. The boot echoes sounded closer. The guards were certain to round the corner soon.

"Come on, let's run for it." He swung around the banister and broke into a run, the others at his heels.

Behind them they heard a voice. "Halt! Stop where you are! Stop by the command of Lord Onyx!"

Keja glanced over his shoulder to see how close the pursuit might be. Four guards lumbered along nearly a hundred feet behind them. "Keep going," he yelled at the others. "We can beat them."

When next he glanced at the guards he saw that they had not broken into a run. They walked no faster than they had when he had first spotted them.

Giles reached the archway the servant had told them about. Inside it stood a small round door of solid iron with a large ring for a handle. Breathing a prayer, Giles pulled. The door swung open. He motioned the others to hurry through.

Glancing back he saw the guards standing in the corridor, hands on hips. They made no effort to pursue them.

One was laughing and beating a fellow guard on the back. Another cupped his hand around his mouth and shouted, "Go ahead, take the tunnel. Feed the ice demons!"

Giles hesitated as he looked after the others, then ducked his head and stepped through the door. It clanged shut behind with a peal like that of a death bell.

Chapter Six

"Hurry!" Giles urged, pushing Keja by the shoulder. Herding the others ahead of him, Giles pelted down the tunnel, expecting at any moment to hear boots pounding after him.

Only the words of the guards chased him. "Go on, that's right, run. We don't need to pursue you. We'll leave you for the ice demons, demons, demons . . ."

The words echoed down the corridor, turning him increasingly fearful with every step. Had they entered the home of the ferocious ice creatures they had heard about earlier?

Giles skidded to a stop and turned to see if the guards were loosing any hounds, but in the dim light of the tunnel all he saw was the huge iron door, a closed, baleful eye. He jumped when metal slammed against metal. Giles realized that the guards had dropped an iron bar across the other side of the door. Entry back through the citadel had been effectively denied them by that simple act.

"You can slow down," Giles shouted after his retreating companions. "We need to take stock. They've closed and barred the door behind us."

A pale blue light filtered back to them from some-where ahead, giving adequate light for them to make their way. Even though the tunnel proved wide enough to walk abreast, they continued to walk in single file, with Keja in the lead. Walls of dark gray granite glistened with seeping water that puddled in little pools on the uneven floor. Giles' feet grew wetter and colder by the minute.

Adding to their discomfort, the underground coldness began to work its insidious fingers through their clothing.

"Giles," Petia said. "Let's stop for a minute. I want to fasten the blankets." They all took the blankets Petia had brought, and they threw them around their shoulders as cloaks. "When we have time, I'll try to make clasps." Petia seemed dissatisfied with the way the knotted blankets kept coming loose from around her neck.

Giles nodded, pulling his blanket closer and enjoying the warmth. But it would get worse, he knew. If the tunnel led farther into the mountain, the air could only become colder. He had taken a squad of men into a mine once, searching for the enemy rumored to be hiding there. They weren't, but the experience wasn't among his favorites of the war years. He had lost six good soldiers, to cold and gas.

His greatest desire now was that a tunnel would lead off in a direction other than north. He preferred angling to the northwest, in hopes of finding a way out of the underground. If they couldn't, they might come crawling back to scratch feebly at the iron door—only to find that Lord Onyx no longer cared.

Giles almost screamed at the idea of their dying in the closed-in tunnels, tons of rock on all sides. A premature burial. Their own crypt, with them still living.

Morbid thoughts, Giles told himself. He had never liked confined rooms. Surviving the Flame Sorceress' cave had been easy enough—it had been vaster than many cathedrals. In Shahal he'd had no trouble, either. But here? Too tight, too damned tight around him!

"Best we find the source of that light, no matter how feeble," he said, more to hear his own voice than to tell the others something they already knew.

Keja turned and beckoned to Giles. "Tunnels lead off on both sides. Which way do we go?"

Giles entered a tunnel that branched off to his left. Within a few feet, the light dimmed drastically. If they continued, they would soon be groping in total darkness. He came out of the tunnel.

"Without candles, there's no way we can make our way. We'll have to keep going toward that light ahead."

They proceeded down the tunnel, sometimes stumbling on the rough floor, often wading through shallow pools of frigid water they couldn't avoid. From time to time they investigated other tunnels leading off at angles but always found impenetrable darkness.

Time became meaningless. The tunnel stretched forward but the light at the end never changed intensity. Giles wondered if they were getting any closer to it. They plodded onward, heading north directly into the mountain, as Giles had feared.

When they stopped to rest, Petia took some fruit from her pouch and shared it with them. She was the only one with the presence of mind to gather some food before they left the chamber. And without the blankets she had scooped from the beds before they left, their escape would have already ended in freezing death.

Cold and stiff when they resumed their walk, they were glad to be moving again. Giles wondered how they would sleep when their bodies could no longer go on. The prospect of freezing loomed larger and larger to the veteran soldier.

And the walls! They closed in on him so much that he often had to shut his eyes and imagine himself on a vast prairie just to keep his sanity.

Gradually, those tunnel walls turned from hard granite to slick ice. At first it had been a thin coating, but it thickened until the rock eventually vanished beneath it. Just as Giles thought the tunnel would never end, an exit appeared in the blue ice. He restrained himself from racing forward.

"Caution," he muttered to himself. To his surprise he had broken out in a sweat from the ordeal of trooping along the tight, suffocating tunnel. "Let me scout ahead," he told the others.

He slipped forward and gazed out into a large ice cavern, illuminated by no discernible source. It was empty, but he spied tunnels leading off in a dozen directions.

"What now?" asked Keja, crowding beside Giles.

Giles lined himself up with the tunnel back to the citadel and then said, "That one," indicating the largest tunnel to their left.

"As good as any," the small thief said, shrugging. The tunnel was much like the earlier one, with icy walls, sometimes slippery patches of ice. Anji, unable to contain himself, ran at one particularly long stretch and slid the length of it. He would have done it again had not Petia chastised him.

For the others, it was an episode they wished to be quickly over and as quickly forgotten. They plodded on, silent and alert. The sameness bored them and they prayed for escape from this underground kingdom of ice. For Giles, it was the worst experience of his life. He had to continually fight the feelings of suffocation, of having the walls close in on him. All his life had been spent on open ranges, in mountains where he viewed thousands of square miles. Being able to reach out and touch the limits of his cold world wore heavily on him.

Hour followed hour, the monotony broken only by finding another empty cavern. There was no way to tell time, and at last, staggering with fatigue, Petia said, "Giles, we've got to stop. I don't know if it's night or not. Anji is out on his feet, and I'm not much better."

"When we reach the next cavern," Giles replied. He didn't want to share his fears. If they kept moving, he could convince himself the ice walls wouldn't crush him. But to stop? He shivered. "I keep hoping we'll find a stick of wood, anything to try to make a fire, but from what we've seen so far, that's only wishful thinking."

When at last they reached a cavern, Petia sagged to the floor. "We've got to keep each other warm," she said.

Keja laughed. "I've been trying to tell you that for ages, but you've always rebuffed me."

Petia scowled at him as she lowered Anji to the floor. She fussed with his blanket, making sure that he was not sitting on the bare floor. Turning to find Keja sitting beside her, she said quietly, "It would be best to have the boy between us so that he can draw warmth from both of us." She moved to the opposite side of the boy, pulling her blanket around herself and Anji. She leaned wearily against the wall.

Giles checked the tunnels leading from this cavern before he, too, settled against the wall. He rested his head on his knees for a moment. It had been a tiring escape. No longer on the move, he felt the cold more keenly now—and his fears. If they got any sleep at all, it would be a restless one. He knew that they should keep watches, and started to say something, but the others were already asleep, exhausted. Giles gave himself into the hands of the gods and closed his eyes.

He had no idea how long they slept. When they awoke, limbs stiff and knee joints protesting, it took several minutes to orient themselves. Petia pulled out a few pitiful remnants of fruit, saying the words none wanted to hear, "It's the only food we have."

The Trans woman offered it to Giles, who refused. Keja looked at the rinds with some longing, then declined the offer, also. Anji ate what remained.

Giles grew restive. The claustrophobia began to work its terror on him once more. They moved on into the next tunnel and found that it led to the inevitable empty cavern. Giles shook his head. "I've lost my sense of direction. Might as well toss a coin, unless any of you has a better idea." No one answered as Giles went to examine the tunnels leading onward.

A sudden, bitter wind issued forth from a tunnel to his left. Shards of icy crystals blew out into the room and swirled around the walls.

"Get your cloaks over your faces," Petia yelled. "The ice will slice our flesh to bloody ribbons." She grabbed the edge of the blanket and flung her arm up to protect herself.

"At least someone has blood left. More than I can say for myself," grumbled Keja.

Squinting, Giles tried to find the wind's source. For a moment, he saw nothing but the eddying ice. As it fell toward the floor, four creatures stepped out of the tunnel mouth.

"Ice demons!" Keja shouted.

Taller than humans and more massive, the creatures stood with icy legs planted firmly. They ranged themselves across the cavern. Their frozen torsos presented an excellent target, but long arms holding swords of ice told of their fighting prowess.

Giles drew his sword and handed it to Keja. "Give me the halberd," he yelled.

The monstrous creatures stood gazing at them from sockets without eyes. Although Giles knew sight was impossible, it was obvious that the demons knew exactly where the humans stood. Giles waded in.

The demons moved slowly but with a power no human could match. A blow from an ice sword would kill, but Giles easily avoided them. He swung the halberd at one demon's arm. The creature tried to pull the arm back, but Giles' shaft caught the ice sword and shattered it. Shards of ice dropped to the floor, but already Giles was swinging back the other way. The shaft caught the demon's right arm below the shoulder. Giles watched in fascination as the arm fell to the floor and shattered. The creature plodded on, oblivious of missing sword and arm. Giles swept the halberd shaft low, catching the demon at the knee. He jerked hard; the leg came off. The demon toppled heavily to the floor and

71

lay, scratching feebly with his remaining hand.

Keja, meantime, put his sword skills to good use. He ducked the swing of an ice sword and drove his sword point upward into the center of the torso, aiming for what should have been a breastbone on a human opponent. A thin line started where the sword point hit, and quickly streaked down the center of the demon's body from throat to groin. The creature took a step forward, but only half of its body moved. One side of the torso sheared neatly from the other and both sides crashed to the cavern floor.

Giles and Keja combined to slay the third ice demon while Petia raised her sword high and brought it down on the remaining ice demon's crown. The battle was over. The cavern floor was littered with blocks of ice, sparkling travesties of bodies which shed no blood.

"It feels good to be warm again," Giles said, wiping sweat from his forehead.

"Giles, come here." Anji had retreated across the cavern when the ice demons had appeared. Now he beckoned to Giles and the others. "Come here, quick. Feel."

"What are you talking about, Anji?" Giles asked.

"It's warm down this tunnel," the boy said, pointing.

Giles held his palm out, but shook his head. "I can't feel it, but then I'm sweating. You try, Petia."

"Some warmth, but not much," she said. "What do you think is causing it?"

"I have no idea. It could be—" Swirling ice cut off Giles' words. Across the tunnel he saw the vortex created at the tunnel mouth. Hailstones filled the air. They flung their cloaks across their eyes for protection. The ice whipped around the cavern once again, and Giles tried to shout against the rattle it created as it hit walls and floor.

"More ice demons," he shouted. "Quick. Down the tunnel. Petia and Anji first. Keja and I will hold them off."

"No," Petia shouted. "I can fight, too."

Giles spun her by the shoulder and shoved her down the tunnel. "There will be more of them this time."

He shuddered when he realized how right he was. Four shambled out, then four more, and a final four. They stood as if awaiting even more to bolster their rank.

"Stay close to the tunnel mouth," Giles yelled into Keja's ear. "If they're too much for us, we retreat. There's only room for two side by side in there."

The great creatures shuffled toward them. Giles shifted the halberd and charged. Keja followed immediately, aiming for a demon's sword arm.

Soon, shards of ice littered the floor and made their footing treacherously slippery. Giles put his years of combat experience to good use. First he used the haft to break the ice sword off, then swung quickly to fracture the creature's leg. Finally, a thrust would split the demon in two. Giles fell into fighting rhythm and, for him, the most dangerous part became getting out of the way when his opponent toppled. The ice demons backed away, giving Giles time to see how Keja fared.

The demons had forced the small man away from the tunnel mouth and backed him against the cavern wall. Two ice demons closed in for the kill, Keja swinging wildly in an attempt to slow them.

Giles attacked from behind. Against humans he might have shouted a warning, but against these moving blocks of magically animated ice he had no such compunction.

Keja, relieved of one opponent, dealt with the other. Splinters of ice showered the room as he hacked at any limbs he could reach. Pieces of the demon fell to the floor as Keja whittled him down to size.

The ice demons retreated from such ferocity. Giles gave a battle cry and brandished his weapon at them. The demons moved away even farther. But he became too cocky. He slipped on the icy floor and yelped in pain as he pulled a muscle in his groin. Gritting his teeth, Giles planted the halberd and pulled himself erect. The creatures sensed weakness and closed in again.

"Keja, can you take over?" he shouted.

Keja slipped and slid to Giles' side. "What's the matter?" he yelled, as he slashed at the oncoming ice demon.

"Hurt. Better retreat into the tunnel," he said. "There isn't as much room to move around, but they'll only be able to attack us two at a time."

Giles limped toward the tunnel entrance.

Keja slashed once more at the oncoming creature, then followed Giles into the tunnel.

The ice demons hesitated, then two lumbered forward. The sword tip of the leading ice demon found its mark, scoring Keja's left shoulder. The young thief leaped backward, clapping a hand to the injured spot.

Behind him, Giles massaged the aching groin muscle, willing it to stop hurting. He realized he'd have to fight wounded or they'd both die.

Lifting his weapon, he said to Keja, "Step behind me."

Keja retreated, moving around Giles in the narrow passage. He massaged the shoulder, which burned like fire.

The ice demons plodded after them. Giles rushed forward to meet another demon, holding his halberd high to strike with the cutting edge. Before the creature could recover, Giles thrust three times at the crystal blue neck. Ice chips flew back in his eyes, but he kept thrusting until the creature's head fell from its shoulders. It stumbled blindly into the wall and collapsed.

Another took its place, but Giles and Keja retreated fifty feet down the tunnel. Petia and Anji had rounded a corner and were safely beyond their sight. The two men watched in silence, catching their breaths as the demon lumbered forward. Just as they prepared for another fight, it stopped and looked from side to side.

Giles leaned on his halberd, watching in bewilderment.

Water dripped from the creature's arms and body, puddling onto the floor. The demon looked at its feet, as if perplexed. It turned slowly and made its way back along the tunnel.

Giles and Keja heaved sighs of relief.

But why had the ice demon started to melt? They hurried down the tunnel to find the answer to this unexpected reprieve.

Chapter Seven

GILES CLAPPED KEJA ON THE SHOULDER. "WE'VE DONE IT, they're going for good."

Keja fingered the sore spot on his shoulder. "I don't think it was us so much as the warmth of the tunnel," he said.

They found Petia and Anji crouched around a corner, awaiting the outcome of the encounter. "Did you kill them?" Anji asked, eyes shining with excitement.

"The heat did it," Giles answered. "Let's find where it's coming from. If it's a volcanic fire pit under the mountains, we might be worse off than fighting ice demons."

The tunnel became warmer as they walked along. Eventually they removed their blanket cloaks. The ice walls dripped and refroze, creating a clear, glazed surface that glistened in the wan light.

The tunnel sloped downward and Keja commented on it. "We won't find a way out if we're heading for some volcanic center," he said.

"At the moment I don't care," Giles replied. "I want to find the source of the heat and get thoroughly warm. If we have to turn around later, then we will. And we need to look at your shoulder. Your tunic is ugly where the demon's sword touched you. I'm almost afraid to see what's under your shirt."

At last they stopped for a rest. Petia sagged to the floor on one side of the tunnel and Anji collapsed beside her.

"What's that?" Anji asked, cupping his ear with a hand.

"I don't hear anything," Giles replied. He glanced at Petia to see if she sensed danger, but she shook her head.

"What do you think it is, Anji?" Giles asked. "Your hearing must be better than ours."

"I don't know. Just a noise. It's faint and a long way off. I can't make it out."

Giles looked around and shivered—and not from the cold. His fear of enclosed places heightened again. The idea of some unknown beast lurking in a dark side tunnel filled him with almost uncontrollable fear. The old veteran fought this inner battle and won, more for the sake of the others than himself. They depended on his coolness in combat. He didn't dare let them down now.

"Let's go on—cautiously." He motioned and they rose to continue.

In a short while they turned a corner and they all heard the sound. They continued on, stopping from time to time to listen intently.

Giles was puzzled. "There's the sound of metal," he said, shaking his head. "But something else, too."

Anji looked up with a grin. "It's singing—or someone trying to sing."

As they moved closer, the sounds became louder and clearer. Giles made out the melody of a song which had been popular during the War, a song not about war, but about the ladies. He smiled as he remembered some of the words. Whoever was singing did not remember the words, only the melody, and that not very well. They would hear a phrase, then a pause and the clang of metal, then the singing would resume for another half line.

"It's a smith, I'd bet my life," Giles said.

"What do we do now?" asked Keja.

"We can go on and discover who this fellow is or we can turn and retreat," Giles answered. "I'm for finding out, and for getting warm. This is the source of the heat that held back the ice demons. Maybe we can even talk the smith out of a meal."

"What if it's not human?" Petia asked. "Have you considered that it might be a dwarf? They're as famous for mining and smithing as they are for hating humans —and Trans. We might be in greater danger than we were back in Onyx's citadel."

"Caution is the word, Petia," Giles said, feeling as if he wanted to throw all caution to the gods and rush out of the tunnel. "With all the noise the fellow is making, we should be able to get a peek at him without his seeing us. If it's a dwarf, we'll turn back."

They crept along, making as little noise as possible. The tunnel widened, and they felt the force of the heat from the forge fire. They hesitated. The anvil seemed to be around the corner to the right, unless the acoustics of the place played strange tricks.

They moved forward again, and at last looked down a circular staircase. Giles gestured for silence and placed each foot carefully as he negotiated the metal stairs.

The smith was human, tall and well proportioned with muscles that rippled and sweaty arms like the trunks of small trees. Long, gray hair that had once been black hung down his back.

He lifted the hammer and brought it down on the sword blade he fashioned. Sparks flew from the red-hot piece; the smith raised the hammer and struck again. Between blows his voice rang out, sometimes grunting, sometimes repeating a few bars of the song. At every blow the man changed keys, as if he had never learned to carry a tune properly. Tone deaf, from the noise of his trade perhaps, Giles thought.

Keja, Petia and Anji followed Giles down the hand-crafted stairs and now peered around him to see into the smithy.

The smith held up the ragged blade and studied it, plunged it into the coals of the fire, then returned it to his anvil. Again the hammer rose and fell, shaping the metal, thinning its edge, working in the essence of sharpness that would later be honed into perfection.

There was beauty in the man's work and his own satisfaction with it. Occasionally, his face turned to the side so that the companions could see it. They saw delight for his creation, a bit of smugness that things went well, and above all, contentment.

For a final time, the smith held the blade aloft and examined it critically. He held it out and sighted down its fiery length. He gave two final taps of the hammer, almost love taps, and plunged the blade into a barrel of water. Steam billowed into the room as the smith placed his hammer atop the anvil and picked up a towel begrimed with charcoal.

From behind the towel, his deep voice growled at them. "Well, don't stand there, come in and keep me company the while."

Giles stepped into the room. "How did you know we were here? You never turned around." Perhaps the man's hearing wasn't as bad as Giles had suspected.

"When you've spent as much time alone as I have, you can always tell when someone is near," the smith replied. His huge hands cleared shavings of metal from a bench and several stools. He gestured. "Sit, sit. You must be tired. You've come a long way from the citadel."

While the four of them sat, turning to the forge fire and soaking up its warmth, the smith bustled around the room. He hung his worn leather apron on a hook on the wall and wandered out of the room.

Giles watched him go, a puzzled expression crossing his face. "I know this man," he said. "I've seen him somewhere in my wanderings. Can't remember where."

Several minutes later the smith returned, carrying a board covered with apples and cheese, a thick, round loaf of bread, and bowls of steaming stew.

Using one foot, he pulled a stool over and placed the

banquet board down on it. "Eat, eat," he said. "There's plenty of time for talk later."

When they had finished their first real meal in what had to be two days, the smith cleared it away and returned with goblets and a pitcher of wine. He poured, sprinkled spice, then thrust a poker into the fire and then quickly mulled each of the goblets.

Giles settled back and lit his pipe. Wreathed in a cloud of smoke, he waited for the inevitable questions.

"You've escaped from my Lord Onyx, then?" the smith began. "He's a cruel one, my lord is. By the way, I'm Bellisar."

Giles introduced himself and the others, then sat back to let Bellisar continue.

"It's a favorite trick of his, you know, to let prisoners escape down the tunnel. He lets the ice demons do his dirty work for him. The tunnels are tricky, as you no doubt learned. It's only sheer luck you've found me."

"We were attacked by ice demons twice," Giles said. "We fought them off, and Anji found the tunnel leading here. But I don't think we were *allowed* to escape, we worked hard at it. Onyx won't be pleased since we still have something he wants."

"Ah," the huge man sighed. "You were something more than criminals exiled into the tunnels, then. Well, you can thank the lad for discovering the warm tunnel. Smart boy. Got your wits about you, haven't you?" He beamed at Anji, and the boy responded in kind.

"But what of you?" Giles asked. "I've heard of communities of dwarves living underground, mining, smelting, smithing. But you were a surprise. When we saw a human pounding away, we thought our senses had left us."

The smith looked keenly from face to face. "You three certainly were caught up in the Trans War. Perhaps not the boy. Giles, you would have been involved longest. Beggin' your pardon, Petia and Keja, but you're too young to have endured it for many years. The gods be thanked it finally ended."

"Not so," Petia interrupted. "You have no idea. I was only a five-year-old Trans kid when the War broke out. I may not have fought, but that doesn't mean I escaped the War. I'd rather not talk about it. You wouldn't like the stories."

A look of anguish crossed Bellisar's face. "My apologies, lady. Those of us who went off to fight came home with a peculiar view of what happened elsewhere. I'm sincerely sorry."

He paused, gazing into the fire, then went on. "I don't like to talk about it, either. I was sick of it by the time the War ended. There were battles—Kelter Plain, Malden, Chevin—where I saw men die by the hundreds, bodies piled up, and a stench you could smell for miles. I reeled away, retching, more than once. Never got used to it.

"When it was over, I tried to settle down. Various places along the Nerulta coast. All I found was the constant pettiness of man. Lord Onyx saw my work and liked it. He's an evil man, no question of that, but insidiously perceptive. He examined my soul, so to speak, and offered me the only position I couldn't refuse: all my needs taken care of and a place where I no longer had to deal with people. I didn't even stop to consider."

"And now you spend your time hidden underground, forging more weapons," Giles mused. "Weapons kill people, or have you forgotten already, Bellisar?"

Bellisar gave him a black look. "Don't preach to me, old man. I know what I do, but I'm beyond caring. If I don't provide a sword, someone else will. My pleasure lies in creating works of functional art."

He reached behind him and took a polished sword from the wall. He placed a cloth across his lap and laid the weapon reverently on it. The guard was of filigreed silver and the hilt intricately engraved. The pommel had been fashioned in the figure of a raven's head. Along the blade in Granarian script ran the quotation from Tenera I, judged guilty by his court and sentenced to death: "Is this justice, and in a rightful cause? Then I answer, yes."

Cryptic questions, Giles thought. I hope that whoever

owns the sword thinks on them before using the weapon.

"Onyx's invitation allows me to create. No one has been given such time and materials as I have. I've perfected a new steel process, and I make weapons that are *art*. It is my hope that they will live after me. Be not so harsh on me, old man. It tells too much of your own thoughts."

Silence filled the room. Was Bellisar the enemy? Or had he only taken the first opportunity to escape from a world he no longer fit into?

He's right, Giles thought. Who am I to question him? But since Bellisar was Onyx's man, could they expect any help from him, even the barest information?

Carefully putting aside the finely crafted sword, the smith refilled their goblets. Giles returned from his thoughts when Bellisar resumed his seat and said, "Now it's your turn. Tell me of yourselves."

They took turns giving him their backgrounds. Bellisar nodded often as Giles told of his long years at war. He understood. His eyes held true sadness when Petia related how the War had affected her, the loss of her husband, her indenture by her mother for a paltry few coins, her escape from Segrinn's father, Ambrose, and her turning to thievery.

Keja actually made him laugh a time or two with tales of his roguery, but afterward Bellisar realized that the man had revealed nothing of his own ancestry or childhood. He simply nodded as Anji told about his life as a Bandanarran slave until his rescue by Petia. "Exactly," Bellisar murmured. "From people like these I am able to exclude myself."

When they had finished, he asked, "Why did you come to Khelora?"

Giles looked from one to the other. Petia frowned and shook her head negatively. Keja shrugged and studied the weapons hung about the wall.

"Have you heard of the Gate of Paradise?" Giles asked, making the final decision. They had revealed much of themselves to this solitary man. Giles had the gut feeling they would not go wrong revealing their quest, too.

"Of course. You're after the key." The big smith brought his palm down on his knee. "I should have guessed."

Jaws dropped and they stared at Bellisar in amazement.

"The key," Bellisar mused. "You're as discontented as I was before coming into the tunnels. Can't any of you find peace in your lives? Do you think you'll find peace behind those gates? I doubt you will."

Petia spoke up. "Whatever I find will be small repayment for what has been done to me. I'll find a better life for Anji and myself. The War may be over, but we Trans are still treated like garbage. Money will buy us respect. It may be only to our faces, but I don't care what happens behind our backs. Anji will have an education, and I'll have some security for what remains of my life."

"Let us hope," Bellisar murmured.

"I like the challenge," Keja said. "I've seen more in the last couple years than I ever dreamed of. I've stayed out of gaol, thanks to Giles more than anyone. But this is no thievery for small coin. The reward is immense and the adventure, while it hasn't always been fun, will be something to tell my grandchildren about." He laughed quietly. "Providing I ever stand still long enough to find a wife and have the luck to sire a child. They say that children have to come before you can have grandchildren. If I have none, then I will spin tall tales in taverns and live to the end of my days a hero!"

Giles listened with as much interest as Bellisar did. They had started the quest for the keys two years ago with little discussion. They had neither found the time nor had the inclination to discuss their reasons since then. They had simply plunged on, with only the keys as a goal. Interesting answers, Giles thought. Revealing. He would have to think about this some more. But now it was his turn, he realized, as Bellisar turned toward him.

"I'm somewhat like Keja," he said. "This has become a quest, and I'm afraid that the quest has become more important than the result. Truth to tell, I don't know what will happen when we find the final key and go to open the Gate."

Giles puffed thoughtfully. "It will be all over, won't it?" He asked the question as if only now realizing the answer. And what then?

"I think I understand," Bellisar said. "Probably better than you. In your own way you're doing the same thing I am: turning your back on society. I've hidden, you've run off on the great adventure. A boy again, playing a more dangerous game. Do you have any of the other keys?"

"Four of them. This is the final one," Keja blurted, and blanched at Giles' scowl.

"What if I told you that the final gold key had been melted down? That I did it myself?"

"Nooo!" Keja wailed.

"You're lying," Giles said. "Onyx told us that he had the final key. He wanted us to exchange our four for our lives. That's why we ran."

Bellisar held his right hand in the air. "I swear. I melted it down right there." He pointed at the forge fire. "Later I made it into the medallion Onyx wears around his neck. You must have seen it. It's his little joke, tells you something about his humor."

Giles jumped up and paced. "It can't be. We've come too far. No, I won't believe it. If it were true, why would Onyx want our keys? They'd be no good to him without the fifth one."

He stopped and stared at the others. Their eyes held a stricken look, and Giles knew that they did not want to believe any more than he did. They had been through so much together.

Maybe too much.

Then he clapped his hands together. "Of course!" he cried. "You're a devil, Bellisar. You made a copy of the key before melting the gold one down. Come on, confess."

The smith threw back his head and roared with

laughter. When he could breathe again, he gasped, "You're a clever one, old man. I wish I had known you during the War. Indeed, that's exactly what happened. The gold key is now Onyx's medallion. But he took a steel key of my own making, a duplicate of the golden one."

"So, in spite of all, there is a final key."

"Yes," Bellisar replied. "For all the good that does you. Are you happy now?"

"We're happier now than we were a few minutes ago," Giles said. "At least there's still hope of finding it—if we ever find our way out of this forsaken mountain."

"It's not so bad," said Bellisar.

"How can you stand it down here?" Keja asked. "Alone, no one to talk to. If I were in your place, my own thoughts would drive me crazy."

"I'm content. Must every man be alike? Then it would be a dull world. Besides, I sing the old songs. I love to sing."

"Yes, we know," Petia murmured, but Bellisar went on, either not hearing or ignoring her.

"I have much to think on. I packed more into my life than it would seem from my age. I am grateful to be away from people, although I must say I am enjoying your visit. It's been years since I had unannounced visitors, other than a few criminals and the occasional foolish ice demon. Neither lasts for long near my forge."

Giles sat down again. "We can hope again. But the duplicate key is obviously no longer where the map shows it."

"May I see the map?" Bellisar asked. Giles pulled it from his tunic and handed it to the burly smith.

He unfolded it carefully and laid it across his lap. With a grimy finger he traced places that he had nearly forgotten from his days on the surface of the land. The thick finger edged up the page, stopping for a moment here and there as Bellisar smiled at some remembered incident. At last he stopped. "I don't see any mark. Where do you think the key is hidden?"

Giles pointed to a spot north of the Adversary Mountains.

Bellisar thought, looking up from time to time to stare into space, then returning to the spot. Finally he shook his head. "The key is not there, I can guarantee that. I once heard Lord Onyx murmur something about the Mountains of the Lions. And this"—he jabbed it with his finger for emphasis—"is nowhere near the Mountains of the Lions."

"Where are these mountains?" Giles asked, not expecting an answer.

"Somewhere in this area." The finger jabbed again. "There are two immense peaks. If viewed from the right spot, you can see the outline of two lions, lying down and facing each other. I'm told it is a magnificent sight. The mountains go up and up and your eye follows them. And there on the heights, splendid in their majesty, are two lions couchant." Bellisar sighed, as if considering how isolated his life had become. "It would be like Onyx to hide the key there, guarded by two such regal animals. It would appeal to his twisted sense of humor."

"You don't know the exact area, then?" Petia prompted.

"No, only what I heard Onyx say. For all I know it could lie between the paws of one or the other. And there is a pass between them. Now, don't go running off all excited. I only said that by way of example. I truly don't know, my lady."

"Onyx may have said that in your hearing only to conceal the real hiding place, so that even you, should you decide to go looking, wouldn't know where it was truly hidden."

"Yes, I suppose that's so," Bellisar replied, rubbing the harsh stubble on his chin. "Never gave it much thought. Even if I were interested, what good would only one key do?"

Bellisar glanced at an hour candle burning in one corner of the room. "Ah, best we be making some preparations. Up with you."

The companions stared at him for a moment, but he heaved himself from his chair. "Come on, come on, they'll be here shortly."

Shock struck the four. "Who?" they echoed with one voice.

"Guards. Every week they bring supplies. Today is the day, this is the hour, and you wouldn't want to be found, would you? You'd be dragged back to Onyx. I gather that's one thing you wouldn't like."

The four shot out of their chairs. "Where can we hide?"

"Don't get upset," Bellisar cautioned. "There's no problem, if you can stay quiet. No sneezes now." He pointed toward a ladder made of small tree trunks. The limbs had been trimmed, but the bark had been left. It led upward onto a platform in one corner of the cavern.

"I like to sleep there, near my forge fire. Keeps me warm. You just climb up there, crawl under the skins I use for covers and try not to sneeze. And no giggling, either, young man." He mussed Anji's hair and swatted him on the bottom to hurry him along. "I'll call you after they've gone."

As he waited at the bottom of the ladder, Giles watched Bellisar pull the skin curtain aside and leave the room. He wondered what lay beyond this room, and not for the first time, whether the man could be trusted. Their lives were now in his hands.

There were skins aplenty on the platform, and more than enough room for the four of them. They pulled the skins over them, and immediately realized that they were going to have a sweaty time of it. The heat and smoke from the forge fire rose to the ceiling of the cavernous room and hung there, dissipating slowly through a tiny vent hole.

"Petia, I'm hot," Anji whispered.

"Quiet. A day back you were complaining of the cold. And remember, no sneezes."

Giles heard Bellisar's voice from beyond the curtain. "Come in and sit where it's warm." Had they been lulled

87

into a sense of security by the smith? Were they about to
be sold out? After all, Lord Onyx had brought Bellisar
here and was, nominally at least, his ruler. What loyal-
ties did Bellisar have to the man in black?

From all Giles could discern, Bellisar owed his very
existence to Onyx.

Giles' pounding heart slowed when he heard the
guards speak. They sounded like the lowliest recruits,
assigned to the job because of their newness. They told
Bellisar the latest news from the citadel and warned him
to watch for a group of four "very dangerous" people
who had escaped into the ice tunnels.

When the guards had gone, Bellisar called the four
down and laid out more food and drink for them. He
laughed when Giles told him that he had suspected that
they were about to be turned over to the guard.

"Why should I do that?" Bellisar asked. "I care
nothing about what Onyx does, or you four, either, for
that matter. I am my own man, doing what I enjoy
doing."

"For your sake, I hope that it always remains so. I trust
Onyx no farther than I can throw him."

"Then you might look over your shoulder for his
guards when you leave my forge," Bellisar said, walking
to his anvil and picking up the heavy hammer. Giles
jumped a foot when the smith smashed it down into the
hard surface.

Chapter Eight

"ARE YOU SAYING WE'LL BE GOING INTO A TRAP?" ASKED Giles Grimsmate.

Bellisar shrugged. He pumped the bellows a few times, and watched the coals come to life. "Nothing's safe within these ice caves. You know that. All I want's to be left alone." He thrust a bar of metal into it, then turned to Anji. "How'd you like a knife all your own, young fellow?" he asked, and nodded at the smile that lit the boy's face.

Giles studied the smith and wondered at his intentions. Then the gray-haired man's thoughts turned gloomier still. He had to face the end of their quest. Only he knew that only one would be allowed through the Gate of Paradise; the runic inscription on it told this. What of Keja and Petia and Anji then? Giles felt a dozen years older in that instant, almost unwilling to continue the path he now followed. When he had told Bellisar that the road meant more than the goal, he'd meant it.

Life, since the War, since the death of his beloved wife and children, had been a concatenation of barely endurable days. Seeking the keys to the Gate had brought back a vitality to his arthritic limbs. Giles didn't kid himself into believing he felt as good as he had twenty years earlier, but he felt better.

The final key would rob him of even this. The thrill of the hunt would be gone. And a decision had to be made concerning entry into Paradise. The weight of years slumped his shoulders even more with that thought.

"Giles, look!" exclaimed Anji, holding the shiny blade forged by Bellisar. "Never have I seen one so fine."

"Nor I," said Giles, examining the knife but not taking it from the boy. He remembered his own first knife and knew Anji would be loath to part with it for even an instant. "Best get some hide to wrap the handle."

"A moment, then," said Bellisar. He bustled through the curtain and returned with his arms full. He tossed Anji a cut strip of hide. The boy sank down and began winding it about the knife handle. To Giles, Bellisar said, "You can't stay here," he said, "but I can't send you off without food."

"It's time for us to go," Giles agreed. "But we can't take the food. It will leave you short of supplies for the coming week."

Bellisar dumped the food on the table. "Nonsense," he bellowed. "You ever hear of fasting? It's good for one with a bloated belly like mine. The body gets too accustomed to being filled. Deprive it once in a while, show it who's boss."

Giles looked at the smith and failed to find even a hint of fat anywhere on his muscular body.

"We'd be grateful," Petia said, shooting a dark look at Giles. She fetched her pouch and began to pack the food.

"Thank you, Bellisar. But even more than the food, we could use directions out of this godforsaken mountain."

Bellisar fetched a piece of paper and the stub of a crude pencil. On one side of the paper was a drawing of a beautiful weapon. Bellisar drew a large X across it. "It wasn't a good design," he said. He closed his eyes for a second and his head bobbed and turned as he mentally traced a route through the complicated tunnel system.

Finally satisfied, he opened his eyes and began to draw. "This will get you to an exit on the west of the mountain. But there are several tricky parts. See here . . ." For the next fifteen minutes he went over his drawing, describing certain places carefully, and occasionally writing notes with arrows drawn to the points where special care must be taken. Finished, he looked to Giles for any questions. Seeing none, he rose and tugged on the bellows rope, bringing the forge fire to life and preparing to spend more time at his solitary craft.

Giles rose and fetched his pouch. Keja nodded behind Bellisar's back and mouthed, "I don't trust him. It's too easy. Why should he give us a route away from our enemy, who also happens to be his lord?"

Giles shrugged and touched Petia's arm. He nodded toward Bellisar.

Petia closed her eyes, concentrating on any emotions emanating from the smith. She found only delight at beginning a task he truly enjoyed. Bellisar had already dismissed them from his thoughts. His work, whether craft or art, was all that was on his mind.

Petia shook her head at Giles and motioned that they should depart.

The twisting tunnels and dim light had long ago confused them. They gave their trust to the map and Bellisar's notes and only once did they come to a juncture which gave them pause. They debated the meaning of the note, and finally agreed which tunnel to follow. Keja, only partly trusting the map, made a large X on the cavern wall in case they must retrace their steps.

When they grew tired, they slept, keeping watches. But time ceased to have meaning. For Giles, after it became apparent Bellisar's route avoided the ice demons' lairs, all that existed was the gnawing fear of the tight tunnels. At last the light became brighter, the tunnel walls changed gradually from ice to solid rock, and they knew that they were nearing the exit. They emerged blinking

91

into a mid-morning sun reflecting from a valley. Immediately below them the snow slope was darkened by the shadow cast from the mountain at their backs.

Giles muttered, "At last." He didn't quite run out into the freedom offered by the valley, but the pressure lifted from him, and he allowed himself to relax for the first time in what seemed an eternity.

Three days later the companions followed a rapidly descending river valley to a broad plain. They saw the river rushing in many directions and finding its own pleasure in carving myriad paths through the gravel surface. It was a strange delta-like vista, several miles across, and Giles wondered how close they were to the coast.

They staggered, leg-weary, onto the riverbed. Logs lay scattered, torn up by the roots and brought down from the slopes above by previous spring floods. They sat and rested.

Giles pulled out his maps. He folded the sketchy map that Bellisar had drawn and was about to toss it away when he thought better of it and slipped it back inside his tunic. The other he flattened onto his lap.

"Is this where we turn north?" Keja asked.

"I've been giving that some thought. I wonder if we should reconsider," Giles said.

"What? Quit?" Petia glared at Giles, and Keja leaped to his feet.

"You misunderstand. The more I think about it, the more I'm convinced that the key isn't in the Mountains of the Lions. We know that Onyx retrieved the original, the one Bellisar melted down. Now, I believe Bellisar when he says he made a duplicate. I don't think Onyx would take that back to the mountains."

"Why wouldn't he?" Keja asked, finally sitting down again.

"He obviously knew that we had the other keys. He told us so and wanted to bargain our lives in exchange for them. He knew about the Callant Hanse,

Bandanarra, everything. I don't know if he's a god or not, even a minor one. But he has immense powers. That is unquestionable."

"So?" A "prove it" tone tinged Petia's question. "Why does this convince you that the final key isn't where Bellisar says?"

"Think about it," Giles said. "If you had found the key, would you put it back in the same place? Might not someone have a map, like we do, and come looking for it? I'd hide it somewhere else so nobody could find it if they had the map."

"So where would he hide it?" Keja asked.

"Ah, good question, Keja. Where would he hide it? He knew that we would come looking for it. He intended to capture us and bargain for our keys. He knew we'd all have to travel to Callant Hanse if we agreed. He'd have his own key, the fifth, somewhere close by."

"At Callant Hanse?" asked Keja.

"Somewhere in the citadel?" Petia suggested.

"Exactly," Giles said. "At least, that's what I think. Why don't we stop here for the rest of today and tonight? You three think about it and see if you can tell me where I'm wrong. If you persuade me otherwise, we head north. Otherwise, we have to head back to the citadel."

The others agreed and each of them spent the afternoon alone. Keja and Anji had their knives out, Keja whittling sticks away to nothingness, and Anji concentrating on his first attempt to carve with his new knife. Petia, tired of sitting, paced catlike along one path of the river. She threw rocks, trying to fathom answers in the showers of water that splashed up.

By morning they had come to agree with Giles. Keja glanced at Petia, who nodded. "You're right, Giles. Nothing else makes sense. But what do we do now?"

"Follow the river. Down to the delta, find a boat and sail to a sea town and do our planning there. Even with the map, I'm not absolutely sure I know where we are."

They set off, braving the frigid spray from the river. Only when night fell did they stop to rest. Warmed by the fire and with food in their stomachs, all felt better.

"Petia," Anji said nervously. "Are there huge dogs over there?" He gestured with his head.

"Wolves," she told him. "I sensed them earlier today, but now it looks like they're getting bolder. We'll have to be careful tonight." She raised her voice. "Giles, wolves approach."

Giles looked up from staring into the fire and brooding. "They won't give us any trouble if we have the fire and keep watches. They're interesting animals, have a society of their own. Look at them pacing back and forth. They're curious, but unless they're absolutely ravenous, they won't attack us."

"What makes you think so?" Keja asked. He moved closer to the fire, hand on his knife. Keja preferred the city—and its human wolves.

"I've had some experience with them. On Bericlere during the War."

"By the gods, is there anything you haven't done or experienced?" Keja asked. "You must be a thousand years old."

"I feel like it," Giles said glumly. "I'm getting too old for these adventures. I wish they'd end. It's too late now, but I could give you a good argument for leaving this search for the last key until spring."

"That doesn't sound like the Giles we know," Petia said. "What's bothering you?"

"Sorry, Petia. I'm tired and getting old, and I don't feel like wandering anymore. What are we doing out here, anyway? Wading through water, fighting ice demons, running from some black lord. For what? Some wealth hidden behind gates on another continent. Why don't we just go home and take up thievery with style?" Giles hunkered down before the fire and warmed his hands.

"You don't mean that," Keja said. "Tell me you don't. Not after everything we've gone through to get this far."

Giles sighed. "I don't know, Keja. Ask me again in the morning." He turned to warm his backside.

Petia looked at Keja and shook her head. Turning to Giles, she said, "Meantime, O downcast one, what are we going to do about the wolves? It's too dark to see them any longer, but they're prowling out there. You may have had some experience with them, but I haven't. And remember, Anji and I are part cat. They make us uncomfortable."

"How many are there?" Giles asked.

"About a dozen, I think. Four or five big ones and some smaller ones."

"Probably two families running together, with cubs. We'll watch tonight and keep the fire built up. No sleeping, not even nodding off. Wolves are discerning. They know when you're not on watch and they can attack swiftly. Keep a burning brand close to hand. They don't like fire. Not at all."

"Something else's out there," Anji said. "To the left and upstream."

Petia looked at him, disconcerted that he was aware of something she had missed. Her thoughts had been elsewhere. Now she concentrated, facing upstream and closing her eyes. "Anji's right," she said. "There are deer grazing up along the bank. They've come out of the forest into a clearing."

"Can you influence them?" Giles asked. "If you can steer them down to where the wolves can pick up their scent, we wouldn't have to worry about ending up as wolf meat."

"I can't communicate with animals, but I'll try, no guarantees."

The others remained silent while Petia put her empathic powers to work. Giles and the others watched, wondering what went on in Petia's mind at a time like this. They were puzzled when, after a long time, Petia turned her face in an entirely different direction. At last her body relaxed, her rigid concentration ebbing away.

"Well?" Keja asked.

"I don't know. At first the deer became uneasy when my emotions touched theirs, but soon they settled back to grazing. I think they may be heading this way, but I can't tell whether they'll come within scent of the wolves. We'd better post watches to be safe, Giles."

He nodded. "What else is out there, Petia? We saw your head turn and look in a different direction."

"I don't know. I can't tell if it's human or animal, if it's intelligent or not. It's out there, but not thinking, almost as if it can't."

"Another good reason for keeping watch. Is it moving?"

"It's not doing anything. Or they aren't, oh, it's all confusing. I can't tell if it's one or a dozen." Petia shook her head in desperation.

"Don't worry about it," Giles said. "We know it's out there, whatever it is. We'll be extra careful." He turned and checked the wood supply that Keja had gathered. "Looks like plenty for the night. Wolves still pacing?"

Petia peered off into the dark, as if trying to penetrate the blackness that lay outside the firelight. In a moment, she nodded. "Yes, although one has gone off. Let's hope it's to investigate some faint scent. Like deer, maybe. I've always said that venison is much tastier than human flesh."

Keja made a disgusting face. "Petia, do you have to?"

Giles chuckled. "Don't you agree with her, Keja? I do." He threw a few more sticks of wood onto the fire, and laid one stick carefully so that only one end would burn. It was a brand to pick up quickly in case of attack. "I'm for sleep. Keja, take the first watch."

For once in his life, Keja stayed fully alert during his watch. Sometimes he had been known to nod off, but tonight he determined that wolves and some other unknown were enough to keep him alert. He tended the fire and thought about Giles, how the man seemed to be growing older and more tired with every passing day. He wondered if they would ever collect all the keys. Keja snorted. Beyond that he didn't want to think about the Gate of Paradise and the hardships reaching it.

These thoughts disturbed him, and he turned to daydreaming of settling down with his hard-earned wealth and entertaining the ladies in a respectable manner. He'd own his own house, dress fashionably, serve special wines and rare viands. A stable with beautiful horses, perhaps even a carriage. A respected gentleman of the town, that's what he'd be.

He added wood to the fire and stepped beyond its light to peer into the darkness. Starting upstream, he saw nothing but the blackness of the sky and a star or two where the clouds parted. He turned and cupped his ears in the direction of the wolves. He heard nothing.

Turning downstream, he was startled to see dancing light motes against the night sky. A column of sparks erupted skyward, and Keja knew a fire similar to their own burned. He grew uneasy and spent the rest of his watch staring downstream. He still faced that direction when Petia relieved him.

She came up to him and touched his arm. Keja pointed and Petia hoisted herself up on the log for a better look. "I don't feel any danger in that direction. Probably natives. They're not hostile, I'm sure."

"Should we wake Giles?" Keja asked.

"I don't think so. He was so tired tonight. And depressed. I'm worried about him, Keja."

"I was thinking about that earlier. Maybe we should wait until spring."

"No matter, for the moment," Petia said. "Let's not wake him. I don't think we're in any danger. But we'd better be on our way again in the morning." She shuddered. "Wolves and humans and something else. How do we get into these situations?"

But Keja was already wrapped in his cloak. Within minutes Petia heard his snores. She sat staring, wondering, beginning to fear what lay out there awaiting them.

Chapter Nine

Daylight climbed slowly over the mountains they had left several days before. The dawn showed little of the alluvial plain, but to the west Giles saw morning light reflecting from the sea.

Petia had told him about the fires farther downstream, but he saw no sign now.

"Giles, I'm not easy with this place," she had said. "Let's go now." Her earnestness convinced him.

As he turned, four tall, young men appeared with drawn bows in their hands and four arrows aimed directly at Giles' chest. He turned to grab the halberd stuck in the river's sand and saw four more of the natives standing to his left. On his right were four more.

Giles dropped his hands and said, "Wake up, Keja." He nudged Keja and Petia with his toe. "Come up easy. We have company."

Keja rolled, caught in his cloak, straining his neck, and saw the natives and their weapons. He waved halfheartedly, hoping the men would not take his gesture as threatening. He disentangled himself and sat up.

"I didn't do a very good job of standing watch," Giles said. "Or these people are good stalkers. I didn't hear a thing. Better wake Anji."

A middle-aged man stepped forward, motioning them to stand in a line facing him so that they would have their backs to the arrows. The natives had the advantage, Giles admitted ruefully. He still didn't understand how they had been able to sneak up without his hearing. "You *are* getting old," he muttered to himself.

The older man spoke. "So Lord Onyx now sends spies to dog the Brada. Do the steel warriors follow in your footsteps?"

Keja, always quick to take offense, stepped forward. "We weren't sent by Onyx. We're not spies and we don't know anything about any steel warriors."

The man gestured slightly; Keja winced at the arrowpoint in the middle of his back. He stepped away cautiously.

Giles warned him to control his tongue, and said to the leader, "We're not from Onyx. In fact, we escaped from him and fled through the ice tunnels."

"You lie!" the man snapped. "No one escapes from Lord Onyx—not through the ice tunnels. The ice demons would get you."

"But we did escape," Giles said. He was determined to keep secret Bellisar's assistance. "What are Brada?"

The man drew himself up, and Giles saw that the others stiffened as well. "We are Brada." The leader hit his chest with a closed fist. "We will not be harassed by Onyx. You will come with us, but first we will tie your hands. You must not escape and tell Lord Onyx of us."

He gestured to the four young men on his right. They stepped forward, pulling the arms of the companions behind them and binding them with rawhide thongs. When they were bound, the leader pointed for others to pick up the captives' packs. They set off at a brisk pace.

"What are we going to do, Giles?" Petia asked between breaths.

"Wait. They're obviously taking us to their leader. We've got to convince him that we weren't sent by Onyx. If we can do that, we might find some valuable allies."

For two hours they marched, with only one rest. Giles tried to wriggle loose from his bonds but found them too tight. Neither asking for them to be loosened nor promising that they would not attempt escape brought the slightest response.

They had not yet reached the sea coast when the leader led them up the southern riverbank and into a forest of scrubby, wind-blown conifers. A trail led south and skirted a salt marsh. As they passed it, Giles saw long-legged birds, frightened by their appearance, explode upward and wing their way north across the river.

At last they stopped. The leader yelped several times like a wolf cub, then repeated it. When he heard an answering call, he urged them over a rise and down into a village. It was a temporary affair, Giles saw, with the dwellings made of beach driftwood, their roofs of tree boughs.

Giles and his companions were hustled to an open shelter in the village plaza. People dropped their tasks and came to stare at the prisoners. An older man sat on a stool in the center of the building, and the war party leader shoved Giles forward until he faced the man. The man examined Giles silently, before turning his attention to Petia, Keja and Anji.

Finally he spoke to the man who had led their capture. "Who are these?" he asked.

"We took them prisoner along the river. They are spies sent by Lord Onyx to scout for the steel ones."

"We are *not* spies," Giles interrupted. "We tried to explain, but he wouldn't listen."

Keja said, "We were prisoners in the citadel. We escaped down the ice tunnels and don't like Onyx any better than you do."

The man looked at Keja with expressionless eyes. "Only the older one will speak."

"We're equals; he's not our leader."

Keja's words were cut short. The sitting man made a small gesture, and a native seized Keja from behind, thrust a piece of leather into his mouth and tied a thong behind his head. He hauled Keja away and threw him into a nearby hut.

Petia started to protest, but a look from Giles stopped her. She snorted, angry at their captors and at Giles, but she held her tongue.

Giles faced the village leader. How could he convince the older man that they were not spies for Onyx? Would the leader believe him if Giles told the truth? When at last he spoke, he told their story carefully, leaving nothing out except their assistance from Bellisar.

There were many questions, and Giles answered them truthfully. He was pleased that the questioning never got around to their reason for being in Khelora. When the questioning got to Petia, she answered for herself. She wasn't surprised that most of the questioning involved the feline qualities the Trans blood gave her and Anji.

At last the leader held a conference with other village elders. They spoke rapidly in their native language and Giles had no idea how the discussion was going. The leader smiled at Giles.

"We hear truth in your words," he said. "Excuse our caution. We have been harried ever since Onyx came to our land and captured many of our people for slaves. Many died during the construction of his citadel."

The old man straightened proudly. "Khelora is Brada land. The Brada have always lived here in peace with those who farmed the valleys. We are a simple people, hunting, fishing, doing some small agriculture. Onyx does not even allow us to do that. His soldiers and his steel beings push us from place to place.

"Now we hide our villages, but when we are putting in our supplies for the winter, we live in these temporary huts. We build these huts knowing that they will be destroyed whenever we are found."

"We know of Onyx's cruelty," Petia said.

"He tries to beat us down," the old man replied. "But Brada were here before he came and we will be here after." A rustling sound caused Petia to look up and see the natives slapping their right hands on the knuckles of their left hand. It was a curious applause, but she knew that his people agreed with the old leader.

"Then we are of one mind," Giles said. "He has hounded us, too, even in other countries. We did not always know it, but we have found that he has injured us more than once. We intend to pay him back and to get something from him which we need badly." Giles did not intend to relate the story of the Gate of Paradise and the five keys. The old man's next question surprised him.

"What can we do to help? We have offended you by doubting your honesty. We must repay this debt."

"I don't know," Giles replied, taken aback. "Maybe nothing more than food and drink. Perhaps you would release our companion now?"

Keja cursed loudly when he was brought from the hut and his bindings cut. He spit the taste of leather and scowled at the serene old man, ready to charge him. It was all Giles could do to restrain him. "Easy, Keja. We've found allies. Don't do anything to upset that."

"They had no right to—"

"Neither did Onyx."

Keja's face flushed red, then he scowled at the old man once more and turned away.

A scout ran into the village, came up and bowed to the old man, who signed to him to speak. "The steel ones have been seen. They march along the river plain." He described the location to the elders, who nodded.

So did Petia. "Giles," she whispered, "that's where we were when we camped. Before we were captured. The steel ones must be what I sensed in the dark. Find out what they are."

Giles waited patiently while the discussion went on around him. When they paused, he asked, "What are the steel ones?"

The leader's eyebrows shot up in surprise at Giles' ignorance. "Special troops of Onyx made of steel, but they look like men. They walk upright and cannot be killed. Sometimes they do not move at all, as if they sleep on their feet. We think that they have no minds of their own, or perhaps only tiny ones. They do not have a leader but get orders during combat. We do not know how."

"If they are Onyx's creatures, I say attack," Keja said. "I'm tired of being hounded."

Giles was cautious. "We haven't seen these creatures. We don't know what we're up against. Petia, can you sense them?" She shook her head. "Well," Giles continued, "this poses a problem."

"And I don't think that we'll get back to the citadel until we remove these steel ones, whatever they are," Keja snorted. "Caution is the hallmark of old age, I'm told. You said you were getting old, and I'm beginning to believe it."

Giles frowned, but Keja continued on. "This whole trip, ever since we left Bericlere, you've been holding me back. I'm getting tired of it. You don't seem to have the drive anymore. Perhaps you don't want to see our adventure end. Are you afraid of being wealthy, is that it? Or don't you want to lose the only friends you've got? Damn, Giles, I say *let's get on with it*! Get what we came for, and if it's where you think it is, then the steel ones are going to be in our way." He stopped finally, breathing hard, pleased that he had finally expressed his feelings.

Giles stared at the small thief, taken aback by what Keja had said. He would mull it over when there was time. Before he could respond, a Brada ran into the village shouting, "They come! They come!"

"Do you not stand and fight?" Giles asked when he saw the Brada beginning to flee. "Are there so many of them?"

"We move away," an elder said. "They are slower and cannot catch us."

"Would you give us some help?" Giles asked the

leader. "Would you lend us some of your bravest young men? We wish to go and take a closer look at these steel ones."

"I don't know." The leader rubbed his chin.

"Please, Father." The voice came from a young man standing to the rear of the shelter. He was tall, slender and well muscled. The old man stared at his son. He saw eyes pleading for a chance to go with the strangers against the steel ones. "We will take great care, Father. I will not endanger lives without need."

The leader turned questioningly. Giles nodded approval. "We would welcome his assistance, and four more young men of his choosing."

Keja was still muttering to himself, and Petia was attempting to mollify him. Giles went to the leader's son.

"Giles Grimsmate," he introduced himself.

"I am Natabor, son of Veldon." Pride rang in the young man's voice, pride of self, of father, of the Brada.

"Choose well, as your father directed," Giles said. "There must be a way to fight these steel creatures, rather than running away. If so, we'll find it."

Natabor's eyes narrowed, and for a moment Giles assumed he had offended the young man. "For long years we have sought a way—and failed. Yet there is something about you that inspires faith."

"I've seen a considerable number of good men die," Giles said, his thoughts returning to the War years. "Choose well, Natabor."

The leader's son picked four, then motioned to the runner who had brought the warning. Natabor knew the information Giles needed and interrogated the scout. From time to time he made gestures, while the other man nodded. Once they squatted and the scout drew a rudimentary map on the ground. Finally, Natabor, confident that he knew where the beings had been seen, rose and faced Giles. "We are ready," he said simply.

"You might be, but I don't think we are," Giles

replied. "We had a long run this morning after we were taken captive, and we need a bit of a rest. Unless those steel beings move fast, I think they can wait. Tell us of them."

Natabor sent a man to fetch food, and while they ate, Natabor answered questions about the steel ones.

"They are like men but are not men," Natabor said. "While man-shaped, they move slowly, as if uncertain of their actions—or have no control of their own bodies. But they are made of steel, and it does no good to fight them. Arrows bounce off their bodies, and a spear will not go through them. We have found no way to kill them."

"Strange," Keja said, forgetting his anger in the intensity of his listening to the description. "Do they think? Do they have a leader? How do they attack?"

"They do not appear to have a leader," Natabor answered. "They simply move forward as a group but not in a formation. Sometimes they change directions together, but sometimes one or two of them continue, as if they didn't hear the order. Then finally they straggle along behind."

"Mind control," Petia said. "Someone tells them what to do. Are they good fighters?"

"We have not fought them. When we found that spears and arrows could not stop them, we always ran from them. When they find our temporary villages, they tear them apart with their hands, tipping over the huts, scattering the wood around."

"There may be a way to disable them," Giles said, wiping his hands on his trousers. "Ready?" As they rose, he touched Natabor's elbow. "Go slowly or we'll never keep up."

They skirted the marsh once more, sending up a cloud of wildfowl. Soon they entered the alluvial plain and moved along paths through the trees on the southern riverbank. Snow covered the tree boughs, but for the most part, the path was clear. Giles had to remind

Natabor that he and his companions needed to rest occasionally. While the pace was slower than in the morning, it was considerably faster than they were accustomed to.

When Petia sensed the steel ones, she cautioned Giles, who ordered the group to a halt. "They are near," he told Natabor, and saw the young man's consternation.

"How do you know?" Natabor asked. "We have seen no sign."

"Petia is able to sense people and animals. She is Trans and part cat."

Natabor nodded, but Giles knew that the young native did not understand. He wasn't sure that he did himself, but he relied on Petia's ability.

"First we'll take a look," Giles said. "Then we'll see about setting a trap for them." He turned to Petia, and she pointed the direction to the steel creatures.

"Quietly now," Giles cautioned Natabor.

They set off along the path. Natabor ducked to one side and under a bush. The others followed and Giles found a hidden path that opened out into a forest clearing. He nodded to himself as he passed under the great trees.

"You've got an idea hatching, haven't you?" Petia asked.

Giles only smiled.

Anji, paying close attention to what his senses told him, touched Giles' arm. Giles gave a low whistle and the natives halted. "They're close now, according to Anji."

Natabor frowned. "Him, too?" he whispered.

Giles nodded. "Let's take a look. Great caution is needed now."

They crept ahead slowly until the forest ended at the riverbank. Lowering themselves onto their stomachs, they peered out between dried grasses with seed heads covered with snow. Keja gave a small cry as snow dropped down his neck, but Giles' angry look made him smother any further sound.

In the center of the riverbed, a dozen of the steel beings moved west toward the sea. They seemed oblivious of their surroundings, plodding ahead through water channels and gravel bars alike. They were truly as Natabor had described, creatures of steel, mechanical beings with metal joints instead of knees and elbows. The unclothed structures looked obscene.

Their shape was more or less human. They even had a rudimentary head atop a slender neck. Giles looked quizzically at Petia. "What do you sense?" he mouthed. She studied the creatures, opening her mind to them, and then shook her head, holding up her hand to forestall interruption.

After a moment, she put her lips close to Giles' ear. "Someone directs them. Their own minds are so elementary that they merely get by, but they take orders from someone else. It feels like Onyx, or perhaps that dwarf advisor."

Giles gestured to the others to retreat into the forest. When they reached the clearing, he called them around him. "Can we lure the steel creatures here?" he asked Petia.

Natabor spoke up. "They follow easily. Often we send runners out to lead them away, while the villagers escape in a different direction."

"Can you lead them in here?" Giles gestured at the clearing in which they conferred.

"Yes, but why?" Natabor asked, clearly puzzled.

"I have an idea," Giles said. As he outlined it, he saw smiles crease the faces of the Brada.

In a half hour all was ready. Natabor explained carefully to his companions and cautioned them that they must go slowly to insure that the steel ones followed.

"Good luck," Giles whispered and sent them off. He turned to his own companions, and they made ready to spring the trap.

They waited silently, hidden so they would not be noticed by the pursuing steel beings, or, Giles hoped, by whomever was directing them. Soon they heard the Brada youths coming noisily along the forest trail. Behind them sounded the rustling of metal against the low bushes. The Brada broke into the clearing, turning as if looking for a way to escape. The steel ones plodded into the clearing after them. For a moment it seemed as if all the steel soldiers would follow only one youth. Giles groaned inwardly. Then, haltingly, the steel beings sorted themselves out so that three of them pursued each Brada.

The youths turned and backed slowly across the clearing. The steel creatures plodded after them, raising shining steel swords which Giles recognized as Bellisar's work.

Natabor shot an arm into the air and shouted, "Now!"

Giles, Keja, and Petia along with Anji tugged hard on ropes in their hands. Loops enclosed the feet of the steel beings and yanked them off their feet. A loud clang echoed as they fell heavily to the ground. Giles and Keja pulled on their ropes, and Natabor and the other Brada rushed to assist them. They hoisted the beings into the air, wrapped the ropes around the trees and secured them, then ran to help Petia and Anji. The third group of steel soldiers was lifted into the air, twirling upside down at the end of the rope.

Natabor sent several of the youths to climb the trees and secure the ends of the rope farther up, where they would be more difficult to reach. When done, Giles gestured to Natabor, and the party faded back along the path.

"Onyx is not happy," Petia said. "I can feel it."

"I didn't expect him to be, but at least he gets a taste of defeat for a change," Giles said.

"I think it's all-out war now, Giles," Petia said. "I've never felt such rage in my life." She looked at Anji. The boy felt it so strongly that he put his hands alongside his head to ease the pain.

Lord Onyx would not let them live after this, keys or no keys.

Chapter Ten

THE BRADA VILLAGE REJOICED WHEN THEIR WARRIORS RE-
turned with Giles and his companions. Natabor's eyes
shone as he told his father about the trap and its success.
The young men who had been left behind, though
jealous, pounded the backs of the heroes from their
village.

The villagers stored their belongings back in the huts,
and by dusk life had returned to normal. Veldon ordered
a feast in celebration. Fish from the sea broiled on
planks set aslant around the fire, and waterfowl roasted
on spits above. Giles, Petia, Keja and Anji were treated
as heroes and allowed to do nothing but enjoy the
adulation.

"Quite honestly," Giles said, "I'm thankful for a
chance to sit. I wonder how many miles we've covered
today."

"I don't ever want to run like we were forced to this
morning," Keja said. "These people are a marvel when it
comes to running. When Natabor sent one with the news
of the steel ones, he disappeared down the trail faster
than a hare. By the time we returned, the news of our
success had spread throughout the village."

"It's not over, though," Petia said. "Onyx will cut the steel men down from the trees. We should have tried to smash their limbs and put them out of commission permanently." She sipped at a warm drink. "The Brada are foolish to stay here. Onyx won't accept this easily."

"I'll talk with Veldon," Giles said. "They know where the citadel is and can lead us back. Either the key is there or it isn't. If it isn't, we'll have to find out where Onyx has hidden it." Giles subsided, the day's events finally enervating him. He slept through most of the festivities and still found it difficult rising at first light.

Veldon embraced each of the companions as they prepared to go, saying, "You are always welcome at the Brada fire. When your quest is at an end, come and spend time with us. You have given us new hope that we will triumph over the Black Lord."

The villagers gathered to watch the strange troop leave. Two humans, two Trans, and five of their own young men against the power of Lord Onyx. They stood quietly, neither waving nor shouting, but Petia and Anji felt the villagers' strength pouring out, wishing further success. Petia shivered, impressed at the power derived from the closeness of these people.

For four days the group marched along coastal paths and secret forest trails. Often they turned inland to skirt inlets, and once they walked carefully through a marsh where a false step into the sucking bottom might have meant disaster. Natabor led, and each of his friends guided one of the companions, staking reputations —and lives—on their knowledge of the route.

At last Natabor turned inland. On the afternoon of the fourth day they came within view of Onyx's mighty citadel. From the edge of the forest they stared out across the open meadow toward the vast fortress.

"Well, you've brought us here," Giles said. "Now it's up to us to get inside. When we were prisoners we examined those walls closely. There's no way to scale them. There might be a foothold here and there, but it's much too smooth to climb."

"How about another entrance?" Keja asked. "Another door. Or maybe through an ice tunnel?"

A grimace of exasperation came to Giles' face. "You liked the cold and the ice demons that much, eh? One of these days you are going to learn to think before you speak. Didn't you hear the iron door clang behind us, or the bar being dropped? No, there's got to be another way in." Giles cut himself short of mentioning the irrational fear of being crushed within the tunnels. Petia and Keja didn't share that with him.

Natabor hunkered down, eyes narrowing as he studied the citadel. "A suggestion?" he asked with deference. At Giles' nod, the young Brada continued. "The citadel is supplied from outside. Supply wagons come from the south. They cross the meadow there." He pointed. "They enter the citadel and unload. If we captured a wagon, we might get you inside as part of the delivery crew."

"Wouldn't they recognize us?" Keja asked.

Giles eyes lit up. "They might four of us, especially two Trans. But if we captured the wagon, kept the driver who they would recognize, and hid our two Trans friends, we could disguise ourselves. It just might work."

Watching the sentries parading along the battlements, they withdrew carefully into the forest. Natabor sent one of his men off to scout for the supply wagon along the road, cautioning him to be back by nightfall. The rest settled down to a cold meal and working on a plan.

The scout returned at dusk. "Did you find the wagon?" Natabor asked. The young Brada shook his head and described in detail how far he had gone. Natabor suggested that the next day they work their way along the road. "With one scouting in front, we can be ready to ambush them."

The plan left a lot to chance, Giles thought, but he could think of nothing better. The next morning they followed a path through the forest, finding a perfect place for an ambush within a day's walk from the citadel. There they would wait until the wagon came to them.

An immense boulder, nearly sixteen feet high and twenty feet long, lay on the right side of the road. The opposite side of the road was covered with dense bushes taller than any of the party. They made themselves as comfortable as possible without a fire. Natabor sent another youth to scout and report when the wagon came into view.

A day and a half went by with no news from the scout. When the youth brought word that the wagon was on its way, Giles stopped brooding. He and the others sprang into action. The plan was simple in its concept, and they hoped that it would be as easy to accomplish.

Natabor gestured to one of his friends. "You know what to do, Jella. Wait for the signal and play your part well."

The youth trotted away in the direction of the citadel. Giles and the others took their positions. From where Giles hid behind the boulder, he could see two of the Brada youths. One was in the direction from which the wagon would approach and would signal Giles. The other youth had gone the opposite direction. Each was a carefully stepped-off distance from the place where the ambush was set.

When the wagon passed the first Brada, he raised a hand. Giles passed the signal on to the second youth, then lifted his halberd and made ready. Since the battles in the ice caves, he had become fond of the weapon. He let Petia keep the sword. It was a bit heavy for her, but she knew how to handle it.

The wagon drew near. Two horses pulled it, and the wagoner seemed in no great hurry. Two guards sat idly on the tailgate of the wagon, their feet dangling above the muddy road.

Giles heard the wagoner call his team to a halt. The snuffling and blowing of the horses carried to him easily on the crisp winter air. "What's this?" the wagoner said. "A Brada seeks help?"

Keja jumped from the boulder, rushed to the center of the road and grabbed the horses by their bridles. Giles followed him and placed his halberd at the wagoner's throat.

The two guards, hearing the wagoner halt the team, had turned and climbed to their feet. They were facing forward when they felt sword points in the middle of their backs. The attack lasted only seconds.

After the Brada hauled the guards from the back of the wagon and tied them with ropes of braided rawhide, they dragged the two behind the huge boulder.

Giles looked at the wagoner, a bearded man getting on in years, the glitter of his eyes showing intelligence. Even with a spearpoint at his throat, he was thinking. "Don't do anything foolish, old man," Giles said. "Follow our orders and you'll get out of this with your life."

"If it's the supplies you want, take them," the wagoner said.

"No, it's not the supplies. We want to get into the citadel."

The wagoner stared. "You must be mad. Nobody wants *into* that awful place. They usually want *out*." He cackled at his own joke. "But if that's what you truly want, it's you who should be worried. You go in there and you'll never come out alive."

"We think not," Giles said. "What you're going to do is deliver your load, just as you always do. You simply will have two new guards. Explain that any way you like, but don't give us away. The Trans woman and boy will be hidden in the load."

The wagoner turned his head carefully and studied Petia and Anji standing at the rear of the wagon. His eyes widened. Obviously he had never seen Trans before.

"There will be a knife at your back the entire way," Giles continued. "Your life is in your own hands. We don't wish to hurt you. Go gently and you will have no trouble. You can pick up your companions on the way home. We'll leave them secured but comfortable. A little hunger is all they will suffer."

"We'll watch along the way until you come to the meadow," Natabor said. "We'll wait at the edge of the forest for two days. I don't know how we could help, but we will wait just the same." Giles nodded in appreciation. The Brada youth clasped arms with him, then he and his companions melted into the forest, gone.

In a flash, Petia and Anji concealed themselves within the load. After rubbing mud on their faces, Giles and Keja took seats on the wagon, and the wagoner urged his team forward. Keja sat on the tailgate, but Giles sat on the edge of the box, his dagger in his lap, hidden by a cloak. The wagoner had been shown exactly where it was aimed, and he hunched his shoulder blades often as if he already felt the sharp tip piercing his flesh.

By mid-afternoon the wagon left the confines of the forest road and followed the road across the long meadow. The citadel loomed larger, and Giles had more than enough time to wonder if they had made a huge mistake.

The wagon had been sighted by sentries, and as it reached the base of the citadel the huge doors swung open. Only the major-domo and two kitchen servants stood there to welcome them. The steward sniffed when he saw the dirt on the two guards' faces but paid no more attention to them.

With great self-importance, he removed a key and chain from around his neck. He unlocked a large storeroom and swung the doors back, motioning for the servants to begin unloading. The wagoner handed him a sheaf of papers, bills of lading for the delivery. The steward glanced briefly at it and handed it to a menial. He turned without another word and disappeared up the stairway.

Giles motioned for Keja to keep an eye on the wagoner. He stood at the back of the wagon and watched the kitchen servants unload the supplies. One was a Brada youngster, and he touched him lightly on the arm. The Brada looked up, fear in his eyes. Giles smiled and

115

whispered, "We come from Veldon. Natabor waits in the woods. Can you hide us? Four?" He held up his fingers.

The youth gulped and hefted a sack of barley onto his shoulders. He staggered off under the load, but when he returned his eyes shone. He nodded and smiled, and Giles trusted that the young man had a plan. While the unloading went on, Petia and Anji slipped over the side of the wagon and crouched out of sight.

The Brada's plan was amazingly simple. He timed it so that he was alone with the four while the other servant worked in the storeroom. He pointed to the corner near the huge doors where a guard cell stood empty. They hurried into it and crouched against the wall. The other servant seemed not to notice. When the unloading was finished, he locked the storeroom door and tucked the key inside his shirt. He waited while the wagoner turned his wagon and drove out of the citadel, not noticing the absence of the two guards. He and the Brada closed the door and lowered the bars on the inside. Then he hurried up the stairs to report to the major-domo.

The Brada youngster poked his head into the room. "Stay here until I come for you. It will only be a short while. I'll find a place for you to hide."

A half hour later Giles heard stealthy footsteps on the stone stairway. He slid his fingers along the halberd shaft and readied himself for whoever approached. He roused the others from their drowsy mood.

"It's me. Helleon."

Cautiously Giles rose and edged to the door. The young Brada saw the speartip and gestured with his hands wide. He whispered that the way was clear, but that they must hurry.

"Where are you taking us?" Giles asked.

"Kitchen. No time for talk. Hurry."

They followed the Brada swiftly and silently up the stairs. He paused briefly at the first landing, then led them up a second flight of steps. At the top he turned left down a hallway, motioning them to be quick.

They slid through an open archway into an enormous kitchen and pantry. Giles took in the entire room at a glance. They saw no servants, yet a huge fire blazed in an open pit, with a quarter of a beef spitted over it. Around the room, food being prepared for various dishes awaited chefs. He threw a quizzical look at Helleon.

The young man beckoned. "No time. I'll explain later." He led them to a small alcove in the corner of the room. Boxes were stacked helter-skelter, some filled with fruit, others empty. "Quickly," Helleon said. "Move some of the boxes and hide behind them. No one will look in here until tomorrow. We will move you before then. Just be quiet until I come for you again."

They heard voices in the main kitchen. Helleon held a finger to his lips and disappeared around the corner.

The four companions were alone again, but they knew that they had entered the heart of the citadel and that they had at least one ally there. The boy had said, "We will move you." Giles wondered how many other Brada captives in the citadel might be counted upon. Was there a way they could be used? He felt a twinge of conscience. Was there a way to free them?

Silently he and Keja lifted empty boxes and stacked them carefully until they built a cubby hole where they could sit with their backs against the wall and their legs stretched out. Warmth from the kitchen seeped into the alcove, and they removed their cloaks to provide padding for the stone floor.

Occasionally, they could hear the major-domo's voice roaring in disapproval at one of the kitchen staff for some misdemeanor. As kitchen noises filtered through to them and preparations for the evening meal went on, Giles and the others began to relax. No one entered the alcove. Through the late afternoon they dozed, warm and comfortable in their hiding place.

They awoke to a great bustle during the serving time for the evening meal. When the noise finally ceased, Giles knew that the meal was over. He heard the servants settle down to their own meal in the kitchen, followed by the desultory conversation of the weary. Then suddenly all was quiet. What now? Where had they all gone? Giles was tempted to investigate, but he remembered that Helleon had said that he would return for them.

Petia touched his arm and whispered, "Someone's coming."

Giles gripped his spear, but the young Brada's voice spoke. "Quickly now. There's not much time."

They rose and came out into the kitchen. "Where is everyone?" Giles asked.

"They'll be back soon to wash up and start tomorrow morning's meal. But we have a little time to rest after the evening meal. Hurry now."

"Where are you taking us?" Keja asked.

"A better hiding place," the youth whispered back. A young Brada woman stood at the door, checking the hallway. "This is Linnia. She'll lead you while I bring up the rear."

The hallway was empty and Linnia led off quickly. Halfway down the hall she unlocked a storeroom door and ushered them in. It was a larger room than the alcove in which they had hidden. Helleon slid into the room behind them and closed the door quietly. He pulled a candle from a pocket of his tunic and lit it, the flame casting eerie shadows on the walls. "You'll be safe here for tonight. Maybe for a couple of nights."

"The first thing we want to do," Giles said, "is to help you and the other Brada escape. At least as many as we can. Natabor and some others are waiting in the forest across the meadow. We promised him we would try. He said he'd wait for a signal at midnight."

"Why are you here?" Helleon asked. "Surely not to rescue us."

Giles shook his head. "It's too long a story to tell. It has nothing to do with the Brada, except that Veldon helped us. With Natabor and four others we defeated a troop of Onyx's steel men, and that has embarrassed the lord terribly. He's angry and brooding, and you Brada will bear the brunt of his wrath if we don't help you escape."

Linnia spoke up. "I can alert the others and bring them to you. But how can we get out? At night, guards keep watch at the doors where you entered."

"Can you get me rope, a lot of rope?" Keja asked. Helleon nodded. "Good. Is there an open window where we won't be seen? I can lower people down the wall if we can work undisturbed."

Linnia said, "There is a storeroom used to—"

Keja cut her off. "Never mind, if you know where we can do it. Just bring plenty of rope. Enough that it will reach the ground."

The two Brada left to carry out Keja's instructions. Petia saw that Linnia had provided food for them and, while they waited, they ate their first full meal of the day. When Helleon returned with the rope, Keja put down a drumstick and went to work. He examined each length for weaknesses, then carefully began to knot the lengths together.

Meanwhile, Giles questioned Helleon about the citadel. The youth was unable to describe it to Giles' satisfaction. As a slave who worked in the kitchen, he had access to no more than a few floors and then only at one end of the vast building. But Giles got an accurate enough picture of that part of the citadel and, by patient questioning, learned what Helleon had heard from others. Linnia interrupted at times to add what she knew.

When Giles had finished, he retired to a corner to think about the plan taking shape in his mind. Petia took up where he had left off. "How many Brada are there?" she asked. Linnia counted them off on her fingers, Helleon nodding in agreement. There were only four others besides themselves. "Six all told," Petia said. "Good. If there were more, it'd be difficult for you to escape without being noticed."

Giles stirred. "Can you meet us in the middle of the night when everyone is asleep?" He sketched out the location for the Brada.

"Not everyone sleeps," Helleon corrected. "There are guards, always. But we will be there. Linnia will take the others to the place. I will come for you."

Giles was pleased with the young man's confidence, and his own grew with it.

The hall where they met was dark and empty; Helleon led them up two more flights of stairs and down a hall. Flambeaux at each end of the hall cast a sputtering light along the corridor. Helleon scratched at the door, and Linnia, eyes wide, opened it slowly. The companions slipped in and set to work at once. Keja loosened the rope and cast it through the open window. Slowly he paid it out, watching as it descended the sloping wall. Satisfied that it reached the ground, he retrieved it and tied one end around his waist. He coiled the rest carefully on the floor, tying a loop at the other end.

It was a long drop to the ground, nearly eighty feet, but Giles was convinced that these were a brave people. For their own sakes, they would not cry out and alarm the guards.

He lit a candle and moved it across the embrasure three times. He did not expect any answering signal from the Brada in the forest, but he was confident that they waited there.

Keja gripped the rope, passed it around his back and over his shoulder, and placed one foot against the sill of the window to brace himself. "Ready," he said quietly.

"They will come after us," moaned Linnia, eyeing the dark drop to freedom. "Always before, they have hunted down or killed with the steel creatures."

"It'll be different this time," Giles assured her. "Natador and the others will protect you until you rejoin the villagers."

"But then?" Linnia protested, fright growing.

"Let us worry about that." Petia's calmness soothed

the Brada more than Giles' assurances.

Giles explained how the Brada would be lowered. He scanned the sky. The moon shone clear, but clouds drifted from the west, casting occasional shadows on the wall below and across the meadow. "When you get to the ground, step out of the loop but stay close to the wall. Make your way to the right until you come to the end of the building. Watch carefully at the west end of the citadel. We don't know if there are any guards there. If not, work your way along the base of the cliff until you are well away. If there are guards, you'll have to run for it across the meadow." He put a hand on the shoulder of the first Brada woman and said, "Good luck." He nodded to Keja, who braced himself to take the weight.

Petia thought the job went slowly and worried that someone would discover them. She whispered to Anji, "Help me sense if anyone is in the hallway. Turn your back to what's happening and ignore it. Concentrate on the corridor." But they sensed nothing, and the operation behind them continued smoothly.

When Keja had finished lowering two Brada women, he stepped back, flexing his back and shoulders. Giles suggested that he take over, but Keja shook his head. "I'm always making mistakes, but this is one thing I do right. Me and my ropes." He grinned and stepped back to the window. The third woman descended the cloud-shadowed wall.

When the last woman was lowered, Giles gestured to Linnia to go next. She shook her head. Tears glistened in her eyes, but she looked directly at Giles and said, "Helleon and I are staying. To help you however we can."

"You can't," Giles said. Petia's voice was nearly an echo.

"We must. Onyx is our enemy, too, and we don't know exactly why you came here. But we must stay and help you."

"We can't guarantee that we'll get you out of here if

121

you don't go now," Giles said. "We don't even know if we'll get out ourselves. You had better go while you have the chance."

"We will stay." Helleon's voice carried such determination that the others knew it was useless to argue. He dug into his tunic pocket and pulled forth a key. He handed it to Giles. "This is the key to the storeroom. I'll tell them that I lost it. You can't lock the door from the inside, but you can keep it locked while you're gone. It might be useful to you." He clasped Giles' arm and nodded at Keja.

"You might attract Onyx's wrath—for the others who have already escaped."

"We've suffered at his hand. We know how to endure the lord's anger."

Giles went to the window and watched the Brada women make their way along the wall to the end of the building. He saw them hesitate, then turn the corner and disappear. Keja had pulled the rope up and coiled it neatly. He slipped it over his shoulder and said, "I'm ready."

Petia looked up with relief on her face. "I didn't think they could do it. Nothing moving out there." She nodded toward the hall.

They opened the door and silently left. Linnia and Helleon disappeared around a corner and were gone. Giles and the others moved down halls and stairways until they arrived back at their storeroom hiding place. They collapsed onto the floor, pleased with their double success at getting into the citadel and helping most of the Brada captives escape. They were well aware, however, that they may have created more trouble for themselves. By morning Lord Onyx would learn of the escape and his rage would be unparalleled. They had to think, also, that Onyx might order a careful search of his fortress for the escaped slaves.

To be found during such a search meant immediate death—or worse. Onyx might carry out his threat to hand Petia over to Segrinn and kill the others. Giles slumped down, bone-tired. They had only a few hours before they'd pass beyond even the gods' help.

Until then, though, he wanted nothing more than a few hours sleep. He was tired, so tired.

He slept.

Chapter Eleven

GILES AWAKENED TO A STRANGE SMELL. HE SNIFFED ONCE and remembered that they hid in the kitchen supplyroom. He opened his eyes and saw cured meats hanging from the ceiling. He glanced at the others, still sleeping.

He sat up, already worrying about their situation. The Brada women would be reported missing this morning, and Onyx would be furious when he found out. But that wouldn't be soon. The major-domo would make every effort to find the escaped slaves before reporting their absence. His head would be on the block.

Giles wanted to act before the guards centered on the kitchen quarters. Until Onyx was certain that the Brada women had escaped the citadel, Giles and his companions were in great danger. He hoped desperately that Helleon or Linnia would come to the storeroom soon. The foursome had to move as soon as possible, and he thought how foolish they had been last night to return here.

Still, he hadn't been able to act effectively. His body betrayed him more and more with tiredness, with aching joints, with shaking hands and blurring vision. Giles had needed the rest, and that had offset the risk.

He roused the others, and they munched on apples they found in a nearby barrel. They heard a scratching on the door and opened it cautiously. Helleon slipped into the room.

"Are we glad to see you!" Giles said. "Have they discovered that the women are missing yet?"

"Yes and no," Helleon replied. "The major-domo knows that they didn't appear for morning duty. He sent others to get them and is threatening extra kitchen duty for not rising on time. It is only a matter of minutes before he will know."

"Can you find us another place to hide?" Giles asked. "Guards will search this area of the citadel as if their lives depended on it—and they might. Unless you can move us, we'll be found."

"I've thought of that," Helleon replied. "We talked about it last night and have chosen another storeroom farther away. Linnia is making sure that the door is unlocked and that it's empty."

Another scratching came at the door. Petia jumped to her feet, eyes wide. She strained her senses but heard only footsteps continuing down the hallway.

"It's all right," Helleon said. "That was Linnia letting me know that the room is safe. Now listen carefully." He described how to reach the room, and Giles repeated the directions. "You're on your own," Helleon said. "Linnia and I have a story that we've found something strange far from here. We'll lead the guards away, but be careful. When Onyx hears about his missing slaves, he'll launch a full-scale search. Once you get to the new room, stay there until we come again. No wandering around."

"You can depend on that," Giles said. "It's going to be dangerous out there for a while. We'll do our exploring after things have quieted."

Helleon slipped out the door and vanished.

The four sat in silence, wrapped in their own concerns. Giles tried to keep time in his head. Five minutes, Helleon had said. Finally, he signaled to the others. They opened the door and crept into the hall, making sure to close the door fully behind them. Giles urged the others to follow quickly, then set his mind to remembering Helleon's instructions.

They arrived without event, wondering what Helleon and Linnia had done to completely empty the halls of guards. Bright young people, Giles thought. If we ever get out of here alive, we owe them a debt that will be hard to repay.

It was mid-afternoon when they heard a scratching at the door, Helleon's signal.

The young man slipped in and set down a sack.

"What's the news outside?" Giles asked. "This room was an excellent choice. No one's bothered us."

"Onyx doesn't think that the four have left the citadel," Helleon replied. "He thinks they will still be found inside, but they're not considered very important. He's called off the search for the time being. He thinks they'll get hungry and come out of hiding."

"Good, they'll be well away," Giles said. "What about you and Linnia? Aren't you suspected of helping them?"

"That's what we need to talk about." Helleon settled to the floor, facing the others. "Linnia and I discussed that, too, last night. We'll help as best we can, but don't expect too much from us. We're only lowly kitchen help. We'll be watched. Anyway, we don't know what the rest of the citadel is like."

"Then we're pretty much on our own, Giles," Keja said.

"Yes," Giles said, "but do you realize how much we owe these two? They've done more than enough."

"There's another thing that you should be aware of. Onyx has a counselor, a little dwarf of a man. Did you see him when you were here the first time?"

Giles nodded.

"His name is Ulinek. We hear stories about him in the kitchen. He's said to be a crafty one. And it's rumored that he has powers of the mind." Linnia and Helleon glanced from Giles to Petia and Anji.

The Trans became more alert. "What powers?" Petia asked.

"I'm not sure," Helleon said. "I don't know much about that sort of magic. We hear that he can probe minds, sometimes even direct people to work against their wills. He's someone to be extremely careful of. When things are upset, like this morning, it disturbs him. His mind powers fail then, and Onyx shouts at him. That just upsets Ulinek more. It's when things are quiet that he's most dangerous. At least that's what people say.

"He came to the kitchen this morning, poking his nose into everything. Linnia and I were scared to death, but we made ourselves think of home on the coast. He dithered so much that I don't think he could read anything. Anyway, I thought I had better warn you about him."

"Thank you, Helleon," Petia said. "Anji and I are sensitive to such a presence, and we may be able to do something about it. I'm glad you warned us about him. When I first saw him, I sensed something—but mostly I thought him the court fool."

"I must go or I'll be missed. We'll try to stay in touch with you, but I can't promise." Helleon left as quietly as he had come.

Late in the afternoon they heard the scratching again. This time Linnia slipped into the storeroom. She brought the news that Onyx had ordered a large detachment of the guard to leave on an expedition to punish the Brada.

"The rumor is that there are only a few guards left in the citadel. Helleon and I don't know what that means, because we don't know how many guards there are altogether." She wrung her hands and said, "I just hope that the women are a long way from here."

127

"Do Brada women run as fast as the men do?" Giles asked.

"Nearly so," Linnia said. "We race with them." She smiled shyly. Giles guessed that this somehow was part of their mating rituals.

"Then don't worry about the women. They cover twice the ground that poor mortals like us can in the same amount of time. They've been gone since last night. They're probably a day ahead of the guard. They'll get away." Giles spoke with such assurance that her face brightened.

Linnia's news lifted the mood of the hiding companions. "When we go exploring tonight, we have fewer guards to avoid," Giles said. "But we may as well get used to being the hunted until we get the key." Giles silently added, even after that. If Onyx were a god, he wouldn't permit them to walk away with the key and not be pursued.

Could a god—even a deposed one—be killed? Giles frowned. They'd have to find out.

"And we have no idea if the key is here or not," Petia added. She toyed with the end of her belt. "What if we've made a mistake? What if it really *is* still hidden in the Mountains of the Lions?"

"We can't think that way, Petia," Giles said. "It won't be the first time we've made a mistake. I can almost guarantee that it won't be the last." He shrugged. "If we learn that it's not here, then we get out and go back on our trek. Either way we've got to stay out of Onyx's clutches. That's the most important thing."

Late in the evening Helleon and Linnia slipped into the room again.

"We didn't think we would see you again today," Giles said.

"We've brought some paper and a stick of charcoal," Linnia said. "We thought we would give you as much information as we can about the citadel."

Giles nodded. He took the paper and smoothed it out

on the floor, moving a candle closer. For the next half hour the six of them huddled over the paper, while Giles sketched the directions Helleon and Linnia gave him.

When at last Helleon and Linnia had exhausted their knowledge, and Giles, Keja and Petia had asked their last question, they sat back. "Any more news about the guards leaving on their expedition?" Keja asked. "I'd like to know how many we have to avoid in our midnight wanderings."

"When the major-domo gave orders for preparation of the evening meal," Linnia said, "we tried to figure out what it meant in terms of people. There are still plenty of people in the citadel, but many are servants. We don't know how many are guards."

"The only thing we can say," Helleon added, "is that you must take care. The commander of the guards thinks that the women are still inside the citadel, but he's becoming less sure as the day wears on. A lesser officer led the troop to the coast." Helleon and Linnia exchanged glances. "We'd better go. They'll check our quarters tonight, and we must not violate curfew. There would be too many questions, and we would be of no further use to you."

After the two Brada left, Giles studied the map again before folding it up. "Are we ready to go?" he asked, glancing at the others.

"Off to confront Onyx!" cried Keja.

Petia put up a hand, asking for a moment. She clasped Anji's hand, staring into his eyes and nodding her head. "You can do it, you'll see," she whispered.

Once again Keja felt uncomfortable when Petia concentrated on that part of her which was truly Trans, and took on catlike characteristics. She had been working with Anji, and Keja shuddered as the boy, too, set his mind to becoming cat-Trans. Giles simply watched in fascination, knowing that the two would be even more helpful in that guise. He didn't know how they accomplished it any more than Keja did, but he knew that it was a valuable characteristic they would put to excellent use this night.

The hallway was empty, but somewhere ahead Petia picked up the sound of pacing feet. She shot a warning look back at the two men and stalked ahead. The hall stretched forever. Its sides were resplendent with arrases, and the moonlight occasionally glinted from golden threads. Giles reached for the edge of one tapestry and pulled it away from the wall. He was surprised to find a niche behind it, one large enough to stand in. He hoped that they were all like that, ready-made places to hide.

Giles slid behind the tapestry and examined the niche, expecting to find a spy hole overlooking some interior room. There was none, and he wondered at their purpose. He heard Keja call softly to Petia. "Giles has disappeared."

When he stepped back into the hallway, he saw a look of relief flood over Keja's face. "By the gods, man, don't do that to me!"

"Might come in handy," Giles replied.

Twice they heard guards, but Petia and Anji warned them in time to elude them. Once they hurried back to an intersection of the hall and hid in a doorway. A second time they slipped into a niche behind a tapestry, and blessed Giles for having discovered it.

The guards patrolled in pairs, rather than standing stationary duty. "That makes it easier for us to explore," Giles said. "Just keep alert and warn us." He motioned Petia and Anji to a cross hallway. When they came to the end of it, Giles thought he recognized where he was. They overlooked the main hall. The doors to the room where they had been questioned stood open. A guard slouched before it, leaning on a pike.

"Can you two draw him off while we get inside?" Giles asked. Petia nodded and for a brief second Giles saw the image of two very different cats. One was long and sinuous from Petia's home, while Anji's figure appeared

130

to take on the characteristics of a Bandanarra sand cat.

They began descending the stairway, but Petia turned and hissed Keja and Giles back. Startled, they watched in awe as two phantom cat figures crept through the shadows and crossed the main hall. A yowl sounded and the guard leaped to attention. Two cats scurried past, and the guard lifted his pike and followed.

"Now." Giles and Keja hurried down the stairs and into the room. "There'll not be much time," Giles whispered. "You take that side. Look for any places Onyx might have hidden the key. And pick up some of the fruit from the table when you pass it." Without waiting, Giles went to the fireplace, searching the mantel first. He touched anything looking even remotely like it would reveal a secret hiding place.

There was none, but Giles wasn't discouraged. He knew that their search might prove long and arduous. One look into Keja's eyes when they met at the end of the room told him that the small thief had failed, too. He jerked his head toward the door, and they tiptoed down the room. The guard hadn't returned; Keja and Giles ascended the stairway quickly to hide in the shadows and await the two Trans.

"How did you get up to this floor?" he whispered when Petia and Anji padded up on silent feet.

"We eluded the guard," Petia answered. "He was too slow. We took the stairs up, hiding in the shadows, and found our way back here. Cats have a good sense of direction, you know."

"Did you see anything interesting down that hallway?" Keja asked.

Anji's eyes gleamed. "There's what looks like a throne room on the lower floor. The door was open as we went past. There's a huge throne and rich tapestries. Maybe the key is hidden in there, Giles."

"Can we get there without going past the guard again?" Giles asked.

"Yes." Petia and Anji led off in the direction from which they had come. No guard stood at this end of the

long hall, but one passed the foot of the stairs they
intended to descend. They waited in the shadows until
his footstep faded. "Turn right when you get to the
bottom. Anji and I will go ahead and see if the way is
clear."

"Spooky!" Keja muttered as the pair vanished from
sight.

At the bottom Giles saw no sign of the Trans. He took
this as a sign that all was safe. He turned right, came to
an intersecting hallway and turned right again. He felt
confident that he knew his directions. He saw Anji
beckon from a doorway down the hall. With Keja on his
heels, Giles hurried down the hall, making as little noise
as possible.

The richness of the room surprised them. The immense throne looked more than capable of holding
Onyx's bulk. Carved of an ebony wood, it was inlaid
with intricate designs of white birch and *jaffro* pine. The
stark white of the inlays contrasted beautifully with the
jet black. Each of the arms ended with carvings of lions
couchant. Giles prodded Keja. "Look, lions."

"Do you suppose . . . ?"

"We'll have to look," Giles answered. "I'm past making guesses. It just gets me in trouble."

They rushed to the far end of the room and examined
the throne. Keja ran his hands over every inch of the
back, seeking anything that might open to reveal the key.
Giles searched the arms, and Petia reached her slender
arms under the throne, feeling with sensitive fingers for a
hiding place. There was none.

Anji, meantime, looked behind every hanging tapestry. He found nothing but a spy hole that looked into the
room where they had first met Lord Onyx. There was
little else in the room. Some chairs were scattered
around, and stools stood along the walls. It was evidently
used for ceremonial occasions and would have held a
large contingent of the guard, perhaps all quartered in
the citadel.

Giles shook his head. "Not here, I'm sure. There must

be a treasure room somewhere in the citadel. That would be a more likely place, if we can find it."

Petia pulled at Giles' arm. "We're spending too much time searching for the damned key. We intended to make this night an exploration, and we're spending all our time running our hands over things, expecting the key to leap out at us. We're supposed to be scouting the layout of the citadel."

Giles stepped back and bowed to the Trans lady. "You're absolutely right. I always jump at opportunities to search when no one is around. I stand corrected. Lead on."

For the rest of the night they kept to the task they'd set for themselves. Giles grew more confident at every turn of a hallway, every stairway that they ascended. Petia and Anji did an excellent job of alerting them to the roaming guards.

"We couldn't have chosen a better time to explore," Petia said when they stopped to rest. "With most of the guard gone, the others are forced to roam around the building. We could never have avoided them if they guarded their regular stations."

Once, they crouched behind a railing to watch Ulinek pacing a long hallway, muttering to himself. Petia pointed to her forehead in warning that they should block their own thoughts or Ulinek would detect them. They closed their eyes, as Petia had taught them, and thought only of a blank wall. Petia watched as the frowning dwarf paced the length of the hall. He turned, as though he were a citadel guard, rocking on his stubby feet. Then he paced back again. As he neared Petia, he closed his eyes in concentration. Ulinek raised his chin and, had his eyes been open, he would have looked directly at the companions.

Petia closed her own eyes and concentrated on an image of two guards walking down either side of the hall, looking carefully behind each arras. She sensed a mood of security come over the dwarf. She opened her eyes to see him nodding to himself, then he walked away purposefully and disappeared from view.

As morning approached, guard activity died down. The night watch tired of roaming the citadel, and occasionally the companions came across guards asleep at their posts. Giles had measured the length of the citadel, and except for the precise configuration of rooms and hallways, he was confident that he knew where they were in the structure as they ascended to each new floor.

"Time to get back to our hidey hole," Giles said. His voice, though weary, contained a resonance that showed his pleasure with their success. It had been a night well spent. They had not only learned the plan of the citadel but had examined two rooms thoroughly.

Petia and Anji led off, taking an unused side staircase they had discovered earlier. Giles counted the floors as they descended, wanting to verify the number he had arrived at previously. On the fourth floor he paused, and the others went on, not aware that he had stopped.

He looked around, then back up the stairway. He continued down and paused again, puzzled. Something niggled at the back of his mind, something not right. He shook his head and glanced over a banister at the open hallway below. Exhausted, he shook his head again and hurried to catch the others as they arrived at the storeroom. Something was wrong, but he was much too tired to try to puzzle it out now. Maybe when sleep had refreshed him, he would give it more thought and it would make sense.

Giles Grimsmate fell into a fitful sleep, the stairway haunting his dreams. It ran upward to the sky—and down into a pit filled with leering faces all shouting for his death.

Chapter Twelve

GILES AWOKE WITH A CATCH IN HIS LOWER BACK. HE STARTED to turn over and grimaced as the pain shot across his waist. Gingerly, he got to his knees and finally stood, cursing under his breath. "Too old for this nonsense. Oh, for a bed again."

The morning he expected was really mid-afternoon. Giles had enjoyed a good sleep except for the pain in his back. He massaged it with one hand and wiped the sand from his eyes with the other. "Anyone been out?" he asked. The others shook their heads. "Umm," he grunted. "Helleon or Linnia been here?" Again a negative response.

Giles grumbled as he worked out the stiffness in his joints. Petia was explaining to Anji how to improve his ability to turn catlike and to project images misleading to their enemy. The boy concentrated, nodding from time to time as Petia emphasized a specific image which she had found useful.

Keja sat in a corner of the room, his ropes spread out before him. He inspected every inch of them, searching for frayed spots. He wished that he had his triple hooks, wonderful devices for hooking the tops of walls, ledges, windowsills and tree branches, but they had been taken away by Onyx's guards. He had been so distrustful of Bellisar that he had not thought to ask him to manufacture some during their stay in the smithy's quarters. Now he kicked himself and envied Anji the knife that Bellisar had given him.

Giles rubbed his eyes again as he saw the desert of Bandanarra appear where the wall ought to be. The scene changed to a pillar of *lirjan* skulls that had marked the Track of Fourteen, then shifted to the swirling, moving sands of the Calabrashio Sand Seas. Giles shook his head, wondering if he was becoming ill, and felt his forehead. When he opened his eyes again the wall was solidly back in place.

"It's Anji practicing," Keja said, looking up from his ropes. "It's been going on all morning, well, afternoon. Since he awoke. The boy is becoming good. Petia won't be able to teach him much more—all she does is sense emotion. Anji can project mental images. I've tried to avoid looking, but I've been treated to the slave cages, the temple in Kasha and an attack by the desert tribesmen. It's uncanny."

"Thank the gods," Giles breathed. "I thought a fever stole my senses." He chewed on a piece of meat left over from the day before. "Petia, have Anji turn down his newfound power. There's something I've got to puzzle out, something that wasn't right last night."

Still chewing, Giles sank down facing the wall. He closed his eyes, bringing back images of the previous night, all the halls, corridors and stairways they had examined. For a long time he remained lost in his own thoughts. At last he came to the end of their long night of exploration. He remembered that it was only when they were returning to their hiding place that something had felt wrong.

Giles strived to make the picture clear in his mind. They had been on an upper floor when the dawn light began to filter into the citadel. They had hurried down many flights of stairs, but somewhere between the third and fifth floors he had hesitated. The images of stairways came and went. One stairway looked like any other. Walls covered with tapestry on either side, a flight of stairs going down.

Then a thought came to him. The relationship of stairs to the rooms seemed wrong. Giles thought back to the rooms they had been in. The room where they had been questioned, the throne room they had examined last night, the suite where they had been kept when they first arrived. He leaned back and stared at the ceiling of the storeroom. Yes, even this room. All the rooms they had been in were of the same height.

And the staircases they had come down were of the same length. But Giles realized that on the fourth floor there were no doorways into any rooms. Certainly there was a corridor running the length of the building—but not a single doorway along it.

"Something secret there," Giles muttered. "Something hidden behind those walls." He uncrossed his legs and stretched them out before him, moaning as his hip joints protested. Old men should remember not to sit that way, he reminded himself. The pain subsided.

He lay back, staring at the ceiling. Petia threw a cloak over Anji, who, tired from his practice, had closed his eyes and was napping. "Giles," Petia whispered.

"Hmmm?" His mind still turned over the problem, not content to stop where it had.

"I'm going to go out and see if I can examine Onyx's bedchamber. It will be empty at this hour, and we don't know when the guards will be coming back. It's an opportune time." She obviously expected an argument, but all she got was another "Hmmm."

She slipped out of the room and Giles returned to his problem.

No guards patrolled in this hall, but when Petia ascended two floors, she saw them standing at either end of the corridor. She crouched down and cast images of a scrawny tabby before and behind. Then, staying close to the wall, she made for Onyx's bedchamber. The guards took no more notice of her than they would have of a servant bearing a message down the hallway.

The door stood ajar. For airing, Petia supposed. She slipped inside, and stood in wonder at the sumptuousness of the quarters. The room was dominated by a four-poster bed large enough for a zuulan of the farthermost eastern regions of the world and all his concubines. What a romp that would be, Petia thought. He could chase them all night and never catch a one. A brocade awning stretched between four ornately carved posts. Cushions of silk clustered near the headboard.

Petia scanned the room. One wall held a fireplace large enough to roast an ox. A small fire burned in it now, and she knew that she would have to search quickly. Someone might return to check the fire and add logs.

Wall tapestries depicting gods at play festooned all four walls. Petia wished that she had the time to study the beautifully woven arrases. An extraordinary artist had wrought them.

A voice startled Petia. She looked around, fearful that she had been discovered. The room was still empty. The voice faded away, then came back more strongly. ". . . to the coast. These Brada . . ." Onyx's voice faded in and out, as if he were pacing first one direction, then another.

Petia frowned. She searched for an airshaft or other opening in the wall which might carry the words to her. Then she noticed a door half-hidden behind a tapestry in the wall opposite the fireplace. She walked across the room and tugged gently at the handle. The door did not budge, but Onyx's voice came more clearly once again.

"When they return, we will turn this citadel upside down."

A second voice cut in, "My lord, it would not be seemly to be overconcerned. The guards will bring back Brada prisoners, be assured. They will compensate for the loss of the Brada women."

Petia wondered if this was Ulinek, the dwarf counselor. They're just on the other side of the door, she

138

thought. At the same time, she realized that the two rooms Onyx would most likely occupy during the day, the throne room or the room where she and the others had been interrogated, were a long distance from the bedchamber.

In the next moment, Giles' voice overlaid Onyx's response. She couldn't understand the words of either man, but this was followed by a silence before Keja's voice came through clearly. "Ho, Anji, did you have a good sleep?"

Confused, Petia stood listening by the door. Voices came from the kitchen, the major-domo's loudest of all. She heard a captain of the guards snapping orders, a woman berating a maid for making up a bed sloppily and not replenishing a fruit bowl with fresh grapes.

Keja's voice came through again. "What will we do tonight, Giles? Now that we know the layout of the building, will we begin searching in earnest?"

By the gods! Petia thought. Keja's words rang as clear as a bell. They were all in incredible danger if Onyx came to his room and overheard their conversation from the storeroom. She spun to hurry back and warn the others.

Giles eyes went wider than Petia had ever seen them. She continued to nod her head vigorously, her lips pursed. "Yes," she said. "When your voices weren't interfered with by others, I heard you as plain as if I were in the same room."

They whispered now. Giles felt apprehension crawl along his scalp, thinking of how their voices might have trapped them before they got any farther. "Repeat it again," he said, gesturing with his hand for her to start all over.

Petia crossed her legs and sketched with a stick on the storeroom floor. She drew the dimensions of the room, then the placement of the fireplace, the bed, and the door through which she heard the voices.

"You didn't hear the voices coming from the fireplace, or some vent near the bed?" Giles asked.

"No," Petia whispered. "I heard the voices from other places in the room, but the closer I got to the door, the better I heard."

"What was on the other side of the door?" Keja asked.

Petia grimaced, exasperated. "I told you. The door was locked, so I don't know."

"It fits what I've been thinking since last night," Giles said. "Something's funny about this building, and I'm sure it's a room or rooms inside the walls, and probably passages we don't know. The voices certainly could carry through air shafts, but I think there's more to it than that."

"If that's true," Petia said, "how do we find our way in? That's the next step, isn't it?"

"Don't know," Giles said. "I hope Helleon or Linnia come by before dark. They might know something about it. If there are passages and we can get into them, we should be able to explore at leisure. We still have to be quiet, or Onyx will hear us, but, with any luck, we'd find out whether there is a hidden room."

"Behind the door in Onyx's room," Petia said positively.

When the sun set, they prepared to spend another night in exploration. Neither Helleon nor Linnia had come during the late afternoon. Keja was in the process of wrapping one of his ropes around his waist when a scratching came at the door.

When Petia opened the door, both Helleon and Linnia slipped inside, pouches slung over their arms. "Food," Helleon said, setting his bag down.

Giles dismissed all thought of food. He took Helleon by the arm and whispered, "You don't know how badly I wanted you to come today. Are there any passages inside the walls?"

"Passages?"

"Crawl spaces, air vents, even narrow hallways inside the walls, anything like that?" After urging them to keep their voices to a murmur, Giles explained about the voices that Petia had heard.

"No passages that I'm aware of," Helleon replied.

The look of disappointment covered Giles' face. It left with the next words.

"Wait!" Linnia said. "In the cold room!"

Helleon nodded. "Go ahead, you tell them."

"There's a small space in the cold room. Some slaves bring ice to keep things cold, and there's a special storeroom set aside to hang whole oxen and pigs. In one corner there's a hole. It lets water run away when the ice melts. That's the only one I know."

"Describe where it is," Giles requested. He listened carefully, asking questions when he did not understand. When they had finished, he asked, "Is it locked?"

They shook their heads. "There's no reason for it to be. The cooks send people there all day to fetch meat for the spit."

"Can you leave us some candles there?" Giles asked. "We've run low." When they nodded again, he said, "All right, you'd better go now before we all get caught."

When the Brada had left, Giles pointed at the pouches. "We'd better eat, now that there's food. Then we'll go take a look at this storeroom."

No one prowled the lower levels of the citadel, not guards, cooks, servants, slaves, or even the bullying major-domo. They made their way swiftly along the halls. With every step, Giles felt more confident of his sense of direction within the vast building.

The ice room door fit tightly but opened easily. Cold air hit them in the face and Anji pulled his cloak around him. They stepped into a large room filled with hanging meat, skinned and gutted but not yet quartered. Along the walls stood boxes of fruit—apples, pears, plums —being kept cold to stave off spoilage.

Keja started to pull the door closed behind him and said, "A joint of roast ox wouldn't taste too . . ."

Petia put her hand over his mouth. "The walls have ears, and maybe eyes, too."

Giles only glared and motioned for Keja to leave the

door open until he found if the Brada had been able to leave candles. He found them between the fruit boxes, a half dozen long white tapers. He lit one, watched it gutter for a moment before the flame burned steady, then nodded for Keja to close the door.

Quickly, he walked to the four corners of the room. At the corner farthest from the door, he found the space Linnia had spoken of. Water from the blocks of ice ran down to a grating and disappeared beyond the wall. The hole was large enough for them to crawl through on their hands and knees.

"Want me to go through and see where it leads, Giles?" Anji asked, eyes shining. "I'm the smallest. Maybe it doesn't go anywhere."

"Only five feet. No farther," Giles whispered in his ear. "Look around, then come out immediately." He handed the candle to the boy. "Only a quick look," he repeated.

The boy took the candle from Giles' hand and ducked his head. He flung the front of his cloak back over his shoulders and, dropping to his knees, disappeared, leaving the cold room in darkness.

Good at his word, and afraid of what Giles might do to him if he disobeyed, he returned almost immediately. "A passage that leads off that direction." He pointed. "The water runs off the other way. It's mucky for a few feet. You'll get your hands and knees dirty."

Giles looked at the others, questioning them with his eyes. "Let's give it a try," he said.

Keja shuddered and Petia said, "I'm the one who's supposed to do that."

"Not you," Keja said. "You're a cat and can see in the dark. I'll bet it's like a tomb in there."

Anji spoke up. "It's not bad once you get through the hole. You can stand up and the candle gives a pretty good light. Come on, we're wasting time."

Giles bowed to Anji, and with an impish grin the boy disappeared through the hole again. The rest of them were left standing in near darkness. Giles stepped toward the feeble candlelight and dropped to his hands and knees. Keja and Petia followed, blinking as they came into the light again.

A passage ran ahead in a westerly direction. Giles had to close his eyes and pause for a few seconds to recoup his courage. This was worse than the ice tunnels. He took the candle from Anji and stepped out ahead of them.

The candle threw its light against crudely finished gray stone. The passage was low, the ceiling only a few inches higher than Keja's head. It was cold, but Giles thought perhaps that came from the ice in the cold room. No water dripped from the walls; their dryness complemented the rough surface.

They walked forty feet to the passage end. The candle showed metal rungs affixed to the wall ahead of them, a ladder which disappeared upward into the dark. Giles tested the bottom rung with his foot. It appeared sturdy and he stepped up, putting his weight on it. It was solid and, holding the candle in one hand, he reached for the next rung.

"I'm going up. Wait here." His voice rumbled in the hollow passage, but he was certain that, no matter how strange the acoustics of the citadel, it would only be one more rumbling voice in the myriad which must reach Onyx's chamber.

The rungs remained solid, and Giles climbed twenty feet into the darkness, the candle showing only the sides of the shaft. At length Giles reached the top and stepped cautiously out onto the floor of another passage. It appeared to be much like the one they had entered: dry gray stone, high enough for the party to walk through. He examined it for several feet, then returned and motioned with the candle for them to come ahead.

When the party had assembled again, they discussed lighting a second candle but decided against it. Giles looked for a second set of rungs to take them to a higher floor, but there was none in sight. He led off down the passageway, intent on exploring to the west.

At the end of the passage they found not only another

ladder set in the stone, but a passage leading to the right.

"We haven't gone high enough to be at the level to find any hidden room." Giles moved the candle about, intently studying the walls and ceiling. He motioned at the rungs. They climbed again, this time finding two passages and a ladder.

Giles felt comfortable that they were now at a proper level to explore seriously. He suggested that they turn right and, with the candle held high to light their way, led off down the passage. They walked quietly, but to their own ears their footsteps sounded like the rumble of thunder.

A soft breeze blew through the passages. Sometimes it was in their faces, sometimes behind them. Occasionally a gust made Giles wonder at the cause. They closed their eyes to keep out dust picked up from the floor.

From time to time they heard voices of guards giving the nighttime challenges as they made their rounds of the fortress. They sounded edgy tonight, probably from lack of sleep on the previous night, Giles thought. He remembered such nights himself, nights during the War, when everyone knew that men like themselves sat on the opposite side of a meadow or at the edge of a forest, waiting for the dawn. Perhaps the testiness they occasionally heard would be of some assistance to them, though he couldn't conceive how.

They came to a spy hole in the wall. Giles was astonished at the thickness of these interior walls. The spy holes angled downward through the stone, to enable looking down into hallways and passages. Once he watched a young officer in discussion with an even younger guard. The guard's face showed apprehension, if not fright, at having no older companion with which to share his watch. The officer patted him on the shoulder before continuing on his rounds. He'll have enough to do before this night is over, Giles thought. He had done the same to many a young recruit.

They came to the end of yet another passage and halted. Petia pulled a farmer's sausage from her pocket, took a bite, and passed it on. "Does anyone know where we are?" she asked around a mouthful of the meat.

"I do," Keja replied, passing the sausage on to Anji. "We're on the fourth floor, at the intersection of the farthest east hallway and the long main corridor."

"I don't think so," Giles said. "That hallway that we looked down on is not the main hallway."

"The point I'm trying to make is," Petia said, "do we know how to get back to where we entered this maze? We've been turning corners right and left, and I have the feeling that not one of us has been keeping track."

Giles said, "I can get us back from here. Don't worry." But the Trans saw that his attention lay elsewhere.

"I'll be the one responsible from here on. I don't want someone stumbling across our skeletons a hundred years from now." She pulled out a piece of string from her pocket. "An old Trans trick." Petia smiled. "Nothing to worry about from here on," she said as she knotted it once.

Chapter Thirteen

THE CITADEL MUST BE HONEYCOMBED WITH THE HIDDEN passages, Giles thought, perhaps reaching to the top of the many-storied building. More important, might one of them provide a vantage from which to look down into the throne room, the private chamber, or even the bedchamber of Lord Onyx?

The candle had burned to a stub, dripping hot wax onto Giles' fingers. He handed it to Keja and pulled another from his pouch, lighting it. When it was burning well, he blew Keja's out, warning him, "Keep that stub. We may need it before we're through."

With the new candle lighted and confidence in Petia's ability to keep track of the twists and turns, they pressed on. The bite of sausage had relieved their hunger, but Giles wished they had brought provisions. The gigantic citadel might take days to explore. There was hope now of reaching parts of the complex which they would never have attempted during nighttime forays through the main hallways and corridors. They couldn't stay for long, however, without food. They would need to return to the kitchen area during the night to steal provisions. Giles' stomach knotted at the closeness of the passage;

146

while he trusted Petia's skills, he wondered if he would be able to win free of this maze.

But for the final key, anything could be endured.

They came to another spy hole and gathered around it to peer down into a darkened hallway. Light flickered from a flambeau and Giles heard boots echoing, but no guardsman came into view. They moved on, finding more spy holes. This part of the citadel had many spaced evenly along the passage. They looked down from both sides of the passage into both the hallway and the interiors of rooms.

The overall structure of the building was complex, but there was a pattern to it, the genius of a master builder. He might compare with the great Alvarious Teneclif, whose masterpiece, the palace at Yetmifune, Giles had once seen during his wanderings.

Petia looked down into a suite similar to the one in which they had been held when they first arrived. Voices carried on the air, faintly at first, then louder and with a great deal of clarity.

"It's Maida that I want," a young male voice said. "Have you watched her hips when she walks away? She holds herself so straight and her figure is delicious. Oh, for just one night with her."

Petia turned bright crimson. "That's what I get for spying," she whispered. "That's how the sound must travel. Through the spy holes and along these passages. The problem is that you can't tell where it's coming from. But a great deal of it reflects back to Onyx's chamber, at least from what I heard when I was there."

Giles nodded. "It's a potent weapon hold to have over his people. He must get great satisfaction out of hearing secrets that no one would suspect him of knowing."

The four moved on, descending to the level that contained the throne room. They moved quietly, Giles checking through the spy holes to reassure himself of their position. Finally, they looked down into the room. Petia clapped Giles on the arm in appreciation of his growing knowledge of the citadel.

The room stretched empty before them, dimly lit by a torch at either end of the room. In the darkness, the throne stood massive, its intricate designs barely visible. Even the deep lion design of the back was veiled in shadow. They examined the room as well as they could, but inky black hid all but a small portion of it.

Disappointed, Giles slid to the floor and sat, holding his head. The others sat, too, taking the opportunity to rest. He looked up at them, shaking his head. "I'm not sure that we're getting anywhere. This place is so vast that we could roam these passageways forever. They run everywhere, floor after floor of them. We'll need incredible luck to find the key. If we could find a treasure room, perhaps . . ." He shook his head. "I don't know. I just don't know."

"Sometimes you seem to know exactly what you're doing, Giles," Petia said. "And other times, you're as confused as the rest of us."

"I know. I get my bearings when I can look down into a hallway, then we go off at an angle and I'm confident. When we get to the next turning, I find myself lost again, until I find a spy hole that looks out on something I'm familiar with. It's frustrating."

Keja slapped at his trousers, raising a cloud of dust. "Thirsty, that's what I am. Confused, tired, and thirsty and hungry. Got any more sausage, Petia?" When she answered negatively, Keja hung his head. A mood of depression settled over the companions.

Giles needed to use his head rather than his feet if they were to find the key. But confusion blurred his thoughts and all he wanted to do was sleep.

Ulinek sat hunched over a stack of papers, muttering as he sorted them into stacks. Being advisor and counselor to Lord Onyx proved no easy task. So much to attend to, and he was never certain where Onyx wanted him to expend his energy. A secretive man, Ulinek thought, not quiet, but he keeps his plans locked inside him. A hard man to advise.

A hard man to rob.

He moved another piece of paper, placing it onto a stack that did not need his immediate attention. He had learned long ago how to separate the urgent from the less important. A shouting fit from Onyx taught him to be ready with advice of some kind, even if it were never taken.

Never time to do anything right, always time to do it over. Ulinek snorted in disgust at the necessities involved in running the citadel for such a capricious lord.

Candlelight threw shadows of Ulinek's squat figure across the floor and onto the wall. The dwarf measured his age by his service to his lord, and he could hardly remember the time before Onyx. Once, Ulinek had traveled dusty roads from one fair to another, setting up his small booth to tell fortunes in exchange for copper coins. He sighed. Such a fine life it had been—until at a fair in Karlile when a robust man, dressed completely in black and, to Ulinek, huger than life, had sat across from him. He had asked such a simple question that Ulinek nearly laughed out loud and did not answer it. He couldn't remember what had prompted him to give the question more consideration than it deserved and to answer it seriously. That had changed his life, even though he sometimes wondered at its lack of pleasure. By the standards of most men, he had accumulated enormous wealth, but he found no great joy in it. Putting up with Onyx's frequent rages was what he was paid for, or so it seemed.

Ulinek sighed and climbed down from his tall stool, striding across the floor to arrange the papers on a lower table he could reach easily. He straightened the stacks and paused, cocking his head to one side. Strange noises in the citadel tonight, he thought.

He had been unsettled these last few days, since the escape of the Brada women. He had told Onyx time and again that he was of much more use to him when things were quiet in the huge building. If Onyx had not immediately summoned the guard and set pursuit in motion,

Ulinek might have been able to tell him something substantive about the escape.

"I've got powers, yes, I have," Ulinek muttered to himself. "If he'd listen to me, there's lots more I could tell him. Quiet is what I need, but he won't remember that. Gets guards running up and down the halls, fetching provisions, readying the horses, breaking out weapons. So much activity, so much noise, I can't think, the brain won't work. If he'd order silence throughout the citadel, I'd tell him quick. Ferret out those responsible, send my mind searching the rooms and corridors."

Ulinek brightened. Silence ruled a citadel again bathed in moonlight from clear winter skies. Sleeping, everyone sleeping, and quiet so the mind can once again be calm and creep from room to room, testing, searching, probing.

"Give me another day of quiet, and I'll hand you the culprit. Already I have suspicions. Two young Brada from the kitchen staff. Oh, yes. Why didn't they escape with the other Brada at the same time? A good question, yes."

Ulinek paced the floor, stopping to warm his hands at the huge fires burning at each end. Finally, his blood circulating, he reached for a large book, bound in the leather from an unborn calf. He carried it to his work table and climbed the rungs to perch on his stool.

Settled, he turned the vellum pages, pages he had written or transcribed himself. Ulinek chortled. This was the chief work of his life, a work he would finish one day, the gods willing—and Onyx one of them, or so he claimed. Ulinek wrote the record of Onyx's constant quest to return to his rightful place among the gods. It was an important position, so Onyx averred, but Ulinek knew better. If Onyx did not lie, he was a minor god, indeed. Yet powerful enough, the dwarf told himself. Don't forget that, old son.

The reward for helping Onyx return to those paradisial fields, however, was enough that Ulinek never spoke of Onyx's rank in the pantheon. If they succeeded, the citadel became Ulinek's—a worthy prize for half a lifetime's work. Meantime Ulinek was warm, dry, well fed and held a position of power in Onyx's earthly realm. He kept his complaints to himself and did whatever he could to keep from upsetting the Black Lord. When he chastened Onyx for the pandemonium he caused, he did so humbly, waiting cautiously for the proper moment.

Ulinek hunched forward and studied his last entry. Complex, he wasn't even sure it applied to Onyx. However, better to write it down and give it some thought than dismiss it out of hand.

He closed his eyes and another image came to him. His eyelids popped opened, and he stared into the orange, dancing tongues of fire. His thoughts raced, rejecting, ordering, searching for any flaw in his own abilities.

He let his mind roam the citadel. Yes, *they* were here. Inside the building. The four escaped prisoners. In spite of the obstacles in their path, all the reasons they should be dead by now, frozen or killed by the ice demons, he had no doubt that *they* were back in the citadel. Perhaps they had something to do with the escape of the Brada women? Why? What did this gain them in their hunt for Onyx's precious key? Ulinek pushed these questions aside.

He must find them.

It was the sort of task in which Ulinek reveled. A problem with a finite answer and a logical way of exploring it. He had often done it for practice, searching out the guard captain or a pretty serving maid at odd hours. As vast and complex as the building was, patterns existed. He could explore the entire building with his mind, never missing a corner. His mental quest moved to the main gate, and he commenced his exploration.

A half hour later, perplexed, Ulinek rubbed his eyes and swore. It showed the depth of his frustration. The four hid in the citadel, of that he was convinced. But his probe had failed to locate them. He cursed again and climbed down from the stool. Onyx must be told. Ulinek knew that he would once again bear the Black Lord's wrath because of the failure.

Ulinek dashed water from a basin onto his face and wiped his eyes clear with a towel. Silent halls led to Onyx's bedchamber. He cast his mind here and there at random, still hoping to find where the companions hid.

Onyx awoke with a start as guards opened the chamber door for the advisor. Ulinek bowed and said, "My lord." Onyx sat up, blinking. He looked foolish, coming out of his sleep, Ulinek thought, especially wearing that night cap with black tassles on the end.

"What is it, dwarf?" Onyx bellowed.

Ulinek bowed again, hiding the hurt that came each time Onyx addressed him in such a slighting manner.

"My Lord Onyx," he began, "I have reason to believe that the four prisoners who escaped earlier are back within the citadel."

"What? You woke me to tell me that four useless Brada women did not leave? I should flay you, dwarf."

"Not the Brada, my lord." That's twice he's called me that, Ulinek thought, growing wroth. "Grimsmate and his companions, the two Trans and the thief."

Onyx's eyes smoldered. "Where?" His voice filled the room. "The guards, summon the guard captain!" Onyx tugged at the bell rope beside his bed. "The hall, the hall, you idiot. Call for the nearest guard."

Ulinek shuddered and held up his hands, supplicating Onyx not to destroy everything he had accomplished. "My lord," he pleaded, "please contain yourself and I will find them. I know only that they are within the walls. Excitement and commotion in the citadel counteract my abilities."

But it was too late. Onyx, in his black silk night shirt and the tassles of his nightcap flying, plunged across the room. If Ulinek would not summon the guards, he'd do it himself. He flung the door open, bellowing, "Guard, summon the captain. Tell him to rouse the men. Prepare to search the citadel. And send for my valet." He turned to find Ulinek covering his ears. "Where are they? Take your damned hands away from your ears and speak, dwarf."

Giles felt a hand on his sleeve and he awoke with a start. He must have been napping. He closed his eyes again and thought, I must be getting old. Shaking off the sleep, he opened his eyes again and saw Petia, her face close to his ear. "What is it?" he whispered.

"Someone's probing us. I feel another mind. I'm sure that whoever it is knows that we're here."

"The dwarf!" Giles said, now fully awake. "Remember? Helleon and Linnia told us of the rumor. Does he know our exact location?"

"I don't think so." Petia reached over and shook Anji. The boy shuddered in his sleep, not wanting to wake, fighting as children often do. Petia shook him again.

The boy's eyes opened. He scowled at Petia. "Leave me alone. I was asleep."

"I know you were," Petia said. "I need your help. Please."

Anji struggled, rubbing his eyes. He stretched his arms and yawned. "What do you want?" Indignation still tinged his voice.

Petia, somewhat exasperated herself, took Anji's ear and pulled it close to her mouth. "Listen carefully, bratling. I think someone probes for us. Trying to find out where we are. Do you feel it, too?"

The boy's eye opened widely. Awake now, fear showed in his face. Petia nodded solemnly at him, and urged him to see if he sensed the same thing that she did.

The boy concentrated, then nodded without looking at Petia. He sensed the other's thoughts, but they were unfocused, confused. He turned to Petia. "He's unsure —he's certain we are here, but his mind looks hard for us. What can we do?" Finally wide awake and eager to help, he was too unskilled to know the next step.

"We've got to create a diversion, something to further

confuse. He may know we are here, but if we can keep him from finding our exact location, we may be all right."

"He'll tell Onyx, nevertheless," Giles broke in. "There'll be a search, but we may be able to avoid them. Why not imagine a roaring fire in another part of the citadel, Anji? That should create chaos to keep them all busy for a while longer. I'll think of something else as we go along."

"Wait," Petia said. "His probing is all muddled now. His mind runs everywhere, agitated. I have no idea what's happening." She paused, head cocked to one side, as if listening. Then she said, "It's gone now. Completely. I don't know what's going on."

"Stay alert," Giles pleaded. "If it happens again, let us know."

"Believe me, I will," Petia said. "You, too, Anji. Keep your mind tuned to anything that doesn't feel right." The boy nodded.

"Are we going to stay here or go?" Keja asked. "I'm for moving on. They can't hit a moving target, that's an old motto of mine."

"I think you're right, Keja," Giles answered. "Let's see if we can get up another level." Giles led off down the passageway, praying that Petia and Anji could give them at least some warning. He wanted his weapons out when the soldiers came for him.

Giles found a stairway, swept cobwebs aside and peered upward in the dim light. They had blown the candle out when they came to the spy holes, the light filtering through the slits in the stone sufficient for them to make their way. Giles lit the candle again to climb the darkened stairway. He made his way to the top and held the candle high so the others could see the steps.

At the top, Giles said, "Petia, describe again Onyx's private chamber."

Petia knelt and drew a map in the dust of the floor. Giles nodded and blew the candle out, stuffing it into his belt. "If we cross this passage and turn left at the end, we should come out above it. Let's hope there is a hole we can watch from. Maybe we'll find out something that will help us."

He turned and led the way down an even narrower passage, then moved into a wider one. Within a few steps Petia caught at his arm. Giles stopped.

"For a moment," she whispered, "I thought I felt the probe again, but it's gone. Listen."

Giles heard shouting ahead. While unable to make out the words, it sounded like Onyx's roaring voice. He put his fingers to his lips and tiptoed toward the sound. Within ten steps, they heard the voice more forcefully and made out the words. "The guards, call the guards, you idiot."

They gathered around the stone slit and stared down into Lord Onyx's bedchamber. Anji, the shortest, stood in front, and the others peered over him. He turned with a look of astonishment on his face and pointed at Ulinek. "What?" he mouthed.

The dwarf sat on the edge of a hassock by Onyx's bed, his hands over his ears, his eyes shut so tightly they crinkled at their corners. Giles shrugged, not understanding either. Petia gestured to her head, waving her hands in circles to communicate Ulinek's confusion. She wasn't sure why, but if it stayed that way she was pleased.

Onyx disappeared from their view; he shouted for guards. He appeared again, shouting at the dwarf to find the intruders. Pain showed on Ulinek's face as he looked up, pleading with the Black Lord to give him the quiet he needed to do his best.

Petia pursed her lips. Now she understood. She touched Anji's arm and said, "Smoke and fire." To Giles and Keja she made a singular gesture. She cupped one hand in the other, placed them on her forehead, then slid them outward, trailing her fingers across the skin, telling them to blank their minds.

She pulled Anji away from the hole and sat him on the floor, sinking crosslegged to face him. "Smoke and fire," she whispered again, then closed her eyes, conjuring the image in her mind, a roaring fire, flames leaping along the edge of the citadel, thick, black smoke pouring from the windows and down hallways.

Keja fidgeted, trying to blank his mind, but it filled continuously with the scene playing out below them. He saw the dwarf again, pain obvious on his face, the sinister Onyx standing over him, berating him. He shook his head and tried to empty his mind of all thoughts and images. He looked again down into the chamber. He saw the fireplace on one side of the room, the rich tapestries Petia had described to them, the four-poster bed—and the doorway with mountains carved on them, the profiles of two lions clear.

Desperately he tried to erase these thoughts from his mind, knowing that he might give away their location and place them all in jeopardy. He closed his eyes, and images came of endless dusty passages and corridors, climbing rungs in stone walls. He pressed his hands to his forehead, trying to push his thoughts away.

The dwarf's cry reached them. Petia and Anji had been sitting motionless, concentrating on smoke and fire. Their thoughts were shattered by the cry.

"They're somewhere in the tunnels!" The shriek was one of desperation, a shrill shout to get Onyx to remain quiet so that Ulinek might pinpoint the intruders.

A sigh of relief came from the huge man striding up and down the bedchamber in his black nightclothes. Onyx drew a key from a drawer and walked to the door with the mountains carved upon it. Unlocking it, he flung it open. Giles glimpsed only a shadowy entrance into what he supposed was yet another tunnel.

"I know you're in there, Grimsmate, you and your companions, coughing dust in that honeycomb of tunnels. *I deny you escape!* Before you can retrace your steps, all the entrances will be sealed." His hollow laugh reverberated through the tunnels. It took a long time to fade, and Giles thought that he heard echoes of the laugh meeting each other from opposite ends of the citadel.

Giles shook his head and pantomimed to them that there was no way that Onyx's men could seal the entrances and close off all passageways. He beckoned to them to leave their vantage point over the bedchamber. He led the way but had to go back when Keja did not follow. He pulled a depressed Keja to his feet and gave him a shove down the hallway.

At the next intersection, Giles turned left to find another spy hole above Onyx's bedchamber—and over the door with the mountains carved on them. He paced off the steps he had calculated, keeping his eyes on the left-hand wall.

When he reached the spot, he ran his hands over the wall but found nothing. Anji, behind him, began to jump up and down. Giles started to curb the boy's enthusiasm; the boy pointed to the opposite wall.

There, at the level of Giles' head, was an ornate bas relief. A shelf protruded from the wall, and above it was an exact replica of the mountains, the Mountains of the Lions, with their magnificent profiles cleanly etched in the sculptured stone. Giles stared at it, but Anji, delighted in his find, leaped up and curled his fingers over the edge of the shelf.

It fell away, pulled by his weight, and Petia stepped forward to admonish the boy. A section of the wall crumbled with the shelf. At floor level a smaller passageway was revealed.

The entrance was too small for the adults but large enough for the Trans boy to enter.

Chapter Fourteen

"I'LL BE CAREFUL," THE BOY PLEADED AS GILES' HEAD emerged from the hole. "Just let me go in for a few feet. I'll come right back and tell you what I see. If there's any danger, I'll crawl right back out."

Petia shook her head, not wanting the boy to put himself in danger. "We can't let him go in there, Giles. If something happens to him, there's no way we can rescue him. It's not worth it." She raised her hand for quiet. "The dwarf still probes for us. I can feel him."

"What do you think?" Giles whispered, looking at the others. "Anji is eager to see what's in there."

Keja shrugged. "It can't do any harm. I doubt that the key is in there, but we should take a look. Then we'd know for certain."

"Let's think about this for a minute. There's something that Bellisar told us when we were in his smithy. By the gods, that seems like such a long time ago! Onyx retrieved the key from the mountains, which is where the map placed it. Bellisar melted the gold key but made a duplicate. We've assumed that Onyx wouldn't take the steel key back to the mountains to hide it. We've spent several days inside the citadel, learning the layout.

discovering the hidden passages." He picked up the bas relief from where it lay amid a mound of crumbled plaster. "This may be the best clue we've had. I don't think we should ignore it."

He turned to Anji. "Are you willing to take the risk?"

Anji had been quiet during Giles' rumination. He lifted his earnest face. "I'm part of this company, have been ever since Petia rescued me in Bandanarra. I may be only a little boy, but little is what you need right now. You're all too big to get through the tunnel. I'm just the right size to squirm through. I can make the right decisions; I won't do anything stupid." He turned to Petia and took her hand. "Please, Petia," he pleaded.

She took Anji's hands in her own and forced him to face her. She looked closely into his eyes and whispered, "Promise?"

Giles watched as Anji nodded and said, "Yes." A single tear threatened to spill from Petia's eye. She became more of a mother and less of a thief every day. It would be good for her when this adventure ended. He didn't intend that Petia would ever reach the Gate of Paradise before him, but he would somehow see to it that she and Anji shared in whatever treasures were there. They could never pass—only one could, and he'd be that one—but there would be enough for them to settle somewhere, buy a dwelling, hire a teacher for Anji, perhaps. By her own admission, Petia had not been a good thief. She got caught too often.

Giles smiled without humor. She hadn't even been able to figure out the runes on the Gate telling that only one could pass.

Petia let loose of Anji's hands. The boy turned and dropped to the floor. Giles handed him a newly lighted candle. The hole was too small for Anji to crawl on his hands and knees. Wriggling forward on his chest, he disappeared headfirst into the hole. Almost immediately the tunnel turned to the left and Anji struggled to make his body do the same.

"Anji," Petia whispered. "Send back images."

Giles grinned wryly. She's still afraid for him, he thought. What will it be like when he's a little older?

Giles, Petia and Keja stood alone in the dark. The only sound was their breathing. Then, from Petia, "He's turned another corner to the right. Wait, the tunnel is getting even smaller."

Silence descended again as they waited for Anji to send an image back to Petia. "He's still able to make it, but only by hunching along with his elbows. A tight squeeze."

Keja folded himself to the floor and made himself comfortable with his back to the wall. He reached idly for something to keep his hands busy and touched the bas relief. He pulled it onto his lap and ran his fingers over the sculpture, lightly touching both mountains and lions. Somehow it gave him sardonic comfort. The others seemed unaware that he was culpable for the dwarf's finding out that they were within the hidden passages.

Time slipped away slowly in the darkness. When Petia received an image she relayed the information. Sometimes she said only, "He's all right."

Nearly five minutes had elapsed when a voice booming down the passage startled them. It was unmistakably the voice of Lord Onyx, and Giles sensed the satirical pleasure he took in their predicament.

"Hear me, my friends. Are you enjoying yourselves in the dark passages? A bit dusty, are they not? Forgive me for not knowing that you would be visiting them. I would have had them cleaned for you. But I shall make amends for that. I'm sending something to you now —something which will clean those passages of unwanted filth. It will be there soon, oh, yes. It is deadly and swift, this cleaner of tunnels. And it's coming for you, my friends. You'll not escape this time."

The hearty, bellowing laugh that the companions had come to despise followed the message through the hollow passages. It twisted and turned, as their stomachs were beginning to do.

* * *

Anji's nose pressed close against the floor, and his elbows ached from scraping the floor. He ignored the pain and struggled on. He had the opportunity to prove himself, and he didn't intend to let Giles or the others down. Most of all, he had to prove his capabilities to Petia. He was tougher than she thought, and sometimes she coddled him too much.

He thrust the candle out at arm's length and peered ahead. The restricting tunnel made it difficult to see past the halo of light. There was little headroom, but the tunnel appeared to slope upward. He scrabbled forward a few more feet and felt the surface begin to slant. He drew a deep breath and inched forward. His elbows slipped on the surface, and he put his fingers down to feel a surface different from that which he had been crawling over. That had been rough stone; this gave the impression of polished steel.

From the corner of his eye Anji noticed that the ceiling of the tunnel also appeared to be different. Handholds! He reached up with one hand and cupped his fingers, straining to pull his body along. Then he realized how they were meant to be used.

He relaxed again, thinking it through. The candle posed a problem. He needed to turn onto his back and use both hands. One step at a time, he thought, and began to turn over. Rolling was impossible in the tight quarters, but bit by bit he got onto his back, without losing the candle flame. He thrust the candle ahead of him and tried to make it stick to the polished stone. He puddled a little of the hot wax, then pushed the end of the candle down into it. But the slope of the tunnel defeated him.

Frustrated by the attempt, he took the candle in his teeth, the flame to one side, and reached overhead for the handholds. He pulled himself along the smooth surface with only minuscule effort. When Anji had covered twenty feet, he noticed only emptiness under his head. He reached backward and found that there was no longer a ceiling close above his head. The tunnel ended abruptly.

Anji removed the candle from his mouth and twisted his head to one side. He stared down into an open room. A narrow ledge ran around the edge of the room where Anji had emerged. He stood cautiously, his back against the wall. Holding the candle high and to one side, he saw the ceiling far above him. Below him stood a room empty but for a single pedestal in the center. Atop the pedestal lay a steel key.

He drew a breath and held it. Petia's mind searched for him. But all he could think of was that he had been right! The bas relief of the mountains was more than a clue. It was the device that revealed the tunnel and led to the key. All he had to do was jump down into the room and retrieve the key. Their quest would be over!

He sent back an image of the room to Petia. The emotion she returned was one of concern. He expected, and had become accustomed to, that. But the concern was not only for him. He wished that they could communicate better. He saw the image of the tunnel where the others waited. Petia and Keja had their swords drawn and Giles stood with the halberd ready to thrust. Then an image of himself, peering cautiously before he jumped down into the room. She was urging him to be careful.

Anji examined the walls of the room as well as he could with the light from the candle. There appeared to be no door to the room, but he realized that one might be concealed. In the dim light, the floor appeared to be covered with a thin layer of white sand. The pedestal itself was of a white stone, perhaps alabaster. It was a simple column, square and unadorned, flat on top. The key rested in the center of the surface.

Anji searched the room twice. He saw nothing dangerous. He could make the drop to the floor easily. He sat on the ledge, found a place where the candle wax would stick and made sure that the candle was steady and giving adequate light. He pushed off from the ledge and let his knees bend when he hit the floor. The bottoms of his feet stung a bit, but otherwise he had succeeded!

162

He picked himself up off the floor, dusting his hands of the white sand which covered the floor. Perhaps it had been placed there so that some watcher could see if the room had been disturbed. The gods forbid that they looked now, Anji thought. The marks he left were plain to see, even in the dim light.

He walked to the pedestal and, standing on tiptoe, plucked the steel key from the top. Highly polished, it gleamed in the candlelight, sending reflected light dashing around the walls. Anji held it in his hand, admiring the cleanness of Bellisar's work. The final key, Anji thought, and flashed the image back to Petia.

He was too excited to realize that no image came back. He lifted the key, pleased with his achievement. In his glee, he danced about the room, leaving more marks in the sand. He wanted to whoop, but he remembered the need for quiet in time and contained himself.

Finally, his delight exhausted, he tucked the key in his pocket. He checked it three times to be sure it was secure. He walked to the side of the room and looked up at the ledge. Checking the key once more, he bent his legs and sprang into the air, reaching for the ledge. He fell short. When he landed, he slipped on the sand, his feet going out from under him.

A sharp pain shot through his ankle. He rubbed it ruefully and picked himself up from the floor. He brushed away the sand, finding a wooden floor underneath it. When he had a large enough spot cleared so that he would not slip again, he made ready for another try. His ankle still hurt, but he ignored it.

He leaped again and fell short. The ankle protested the abuse. Anji looked around the room for something to help him. The pedestal! If he could drag it over to the side of the room. He tested it. Whether the stone was too heavy for him or was attached in some way to the floor, Anji could not budge it.

Several more tries convinced him that he was trapped in the room. He was neither tall enough nor strong enough to catch the ledge. He sent as powerful an image as he could to Petia. Then he sat, rubbing his sprained ankle.

Anji went cold all over when he realized that Petia was much too large to come through the tunnel. He was a prisoner in the room and couldn't expect help. With tears in his eyes, he picked up handfuls of sand and flung them in frustration.

Onyx's words froze the three companions. They sounded so close that Petia was sure that he stood next to them. They might have been better off if he had been present. Onyx had loosed some terrible beast into the tunnels, and she had little doubt that it would find them.

"Bluffing," Giles said. "Onyx may know that we're in here somewhere, but I think he's only trying to frighten us. Still, it's always good to be prepared." He handed the sword to Petia and took a firm grip on his halberd. Keja took the hint and pulled his sword from his belt.

A blood-chilling howl echoed through the passages. It started with a roar, deep and robust, and ended in a high-pitched shriek which set their teeth on edge.

"By the gods," Petia breathed.

The howl began again and came at them from every direction. Petia grabbed Giles by the sleeve. "What about Anji?" she asked.

"We'll have to take one thing at a time," Giles said. "Just remember, we defeated the ice demons and Onyx's steel men. Don't lose your courage now. It's only another obstacle to overcome. Whatever this thing is, we'll kill it."

"You're a mountain of confidence," Keja said sarcastically.

Giles grinned. "Why shouldn't I be? With stalwart companions who have been through so much together, what's one more little beastie to worry about?" He turned his head, trying to sort the real voice of the beast from the echoes reverberating through the endless tunnels.

The howls confused them, coming from every direction. Keja turned to face the way they had come, while Giles took several steps forward in the direction they had been walking when they found the bas relief. In truth, he thought, I don't know if there's one or a dozen nor from what direction they are coming. Where's Anji? If the boy were here we could retreat. In spite of his outward calm, his apprehension mounted.

He glanced at Petia. Although she clutched the sword, her mind was on Anji. She crouched by the hole in the wall, shouting his name. She wasn't going to be of much good in the coming battle, with her mind torn between her own preservation and the boy's predicament.

Giles went to her. He had to shout in her ear in order for her to hear over the roaring that surrounded them. "What of Anji?"

Petia held down panic as pain showed in her eyes. "I don't know. I don't get any images. I don't know what's happened to him."

Giles put his hand on her elbow. He glanced back at the passageway. In the distance two red eyes glowed in the dark. They moved closer, and another roar shook the tunnel. At Keja's end, he saw nothing but Keja's startled face, looking back over his shoulder and staring down the tunnel.

"You've got to reach Anji," Giles shouted. "Concentrate." He turned and gripped his halberd. "Never mind the battle. Keja and I . . ."

The beast attacked.

The roaring ceased; all they heard was snorting and pawing. Unseen claws rasped against the stone floor. Keja came to Giles' side and stood, his sword ready.

"Giles, Anji is trapped," Petia cried. "He has the key, but he can't get out." Giles turned one ear to listen, not taking his eyes from the red eyes which glowed ever closer in the darkness. "He jumped down into a room and now he can't jump high enough to reach the ledge and get back to us."

Giles cursed beneath his breath. "Concentrate on Anji. You've got to figure out some way to rescue him.

We'll do what we can with Onyx's little friend." He shook Petia's arm. "You can do it. Never mind how the fight is going. Just put your mind to getting Anji out of there."

The sound of claws against stone came closer. The red eyes looked larger than saucers. A deep-throated growl sapped at Giles' faith in defeating this unseen creature.

"Come on, beastie," he said. "We're ready for you."

He hoped that proved true.

Petia crouched by the hole, ignoring the snorting and pawing from the other end of the passage. She followed Giles' advice and cleared her mind, focusing on Anji and the room into which he had so foolishly jumped. She went back over his route to the room, remembering the pictures he had cast back to her. It was impossible for her to follow him through the twisting tunnel. It had been difficult enough for a skinny cat-Trans boy.

"Think, Petia," she murmured to herself and pounded her fist on her knee. A memory flitted through her mind. She recalled one of her less successful attempts at thievery. She had been careless enough to wake the owner of a house she was burgling and had left hastily through a window. Not hastily enough, as it turned out. She had found herself trapped by the nightwatch in a narrow passageway between houses. She had stood frozen, then remembered the feline part of her Trans nature. Catlike, she had escaped while the watch stood scratching their heads.

"Rope, Keja!" Keja's head swiveled. He tugged at a rope around his waist. He pulled the end free and unwound it quickly, handing it to Petia and resuming the grip on his sword.

Quickly Petia rewound it around her own waist so tightly that it hurt to breathe. Then she dropped to the floor, closing her eyes and focusing on the hidden part of her nature. She felt the changes and waited. Patience and impatience warred within her. The rope become looser. Never had Petia gone this far with physical transformation. Always before she had adopted cat traits, but never the physical aspects of a true feline.

She saw Keja glance at her, close his eyes, and shake his head. Petia knew that he was still uncomfortable with this part of her Trans heritage.

She took one last look at Giles and Keja, standing ready for battle, murmured, "The gods be with you," and disappeared into the hole, her sleek cat body easily fitting the tunnel.

Ulinek cowered in the corner of Lord Onyx's bed-chamber, his head throbbing from his attempt to locate the intruders. An impossible task, he knew, but Onyx insisted that he keep trying.

Soldiers filled the chamber. The guard captain arrived, accompanied by two lesser officers. Young recruits stood ready to act as runners, carrying messages from one end of the citadel to the other. How could he concentrate on a probe with so many people, talking, running here and there, their minds causing a continual buzz? Feet tramped the hallways, adding their hollow echoes to the din.

The ache in Ulinek's head moved up behind his ears; he rubbed his fingers over the heavy mastoid bones, massaging them in a vain attempt to relieve the pain. If only Onyx would provide him with the silence he so badly needed. He switched to rubbing his temples and forehead, then inspired, he sent a recruit for Actina, a serving maid.

When she arrived, Ulinek explained his distress and asked her to rub his neck and head. She had done this many times before and set to work with good will. Ulinek groaned with relief as Actina's soothing fingers massaged the cords at the back of his neck, brushing upward behind his ears. Of all the servants, only Actina seemed not to notice his diminutive stature.

At last Onyx issued orders for all who remained in the citadel. Ulinek waited until he subsided, then lifted his hands in a plea for silence. "Please, my lord. No intrusions for a moment, I beg of you."

Onyx scowled, then stomped to a chair near his bed. He sat, frowning, chin in his hand, but he remained silent.

The serving woman continued to massage Ulinek's neck, and a measure of tranquility filled the dwarf. He closed his eyes and probed again, for the first time in nearly an hour able to focus his mind. Up and down the passages, quickly now, before another disturbance.

He found the companions and knew that one of them had the key. "My lord?"

"What? I thought you wanted quiet."

"I have found them, my lord. One has the key."

Onyx threw back his head and laughed. "Have they found it, then? I never would have believed it possible. But never mind. I have sent the beast for them. There is no escape this time. As for the key, a small enough matter, for a small enough advisor. Is that not right, my dwarfish friend?"

"I do not take your meaning, my lord," Ulinek said, but already fear of Onyx's next words was upon him. He knew what the Black Lord meant and dreaded what he was about to hear.

"I think you do, Ulinek. You, my little one, are small enough to recover the key for me. Is it not so?"

Ulinek fell to his knees, and Actina drew back, embarrased for the little man. The dwarf touched his forehead to the floor, groveling toward Onyx. Ulinek's muffled voice pleaded, "No, my lord. Please. Not the *passages*!"

He looked up to see Onyx's black eyes fixed upon him. He found no pity in them. He could plead forever, but in the end he would be sent into the passages—the *passages*—for the key. He closed his eyes, shuddered once, and collapsed.

Chapter Fifteen

GILES HAD TIME ONLY FOR A GLANCE AT PETIA AS SHE disappeared into the hole in the wall of the passageway. The glowing red eyes commanded his full attention. He did not know what foul creature Onyx had sent against them, but he had no doubt that the Black Lord intended that it should rid him of the intruders forever. He chuckled.

Keja gazed at him in the dim candlelight. "You're crazy, aren't you? Death stares us in the face and you laugh."

"Exactly," Giles answered, continuing to watch the luminous eyes in the dark corridor. "If we die, Onyx will have an impossible time getting the other four keys from the Callant Hanse. He'll never do it without destroying that ancient merchant house. Sometimes our mysterious man in black, god or not, doesn't think too well."

The beast roared again, then grew quiet. It stopped pawing and scratching at the floor.

"Watch for it, Keja. It will pounce soon."

Giles heard the sound of the beast churning toward him out of the darkness. The feet drummed faster and

169

faster as they came. The eyes glowed larger and redder. Giles thought fleetingly of runaway wagons. "Back against the wall, Keja!" he shouted. He flattened himself against the wall as the beast charged past.

The candle flame wavered in the breeze stirred by the charging beast. Please don't go out, Giles prayed silently. In a pitch-black tunnel, there would be no battle at all.

The beast turned at the end of the tunnel and ambient light from the intersecting tunnel showed Giles and Keja what they fought. It spun on all fours and reared onto its hind feet, standing as tall as the two men. Lizardlike with short, massive forelegs and a thick body, it reminded Giles of an ocean amphibian he had seen from the ship that had carried them to Bandanarra. The captain had told him that the beasts were vicious and had been known to kill and eat humans.

Its flat face, long and slender, contained wickedly sharp teeth. A harsh rattle came from the beast's throat. The eyes blinked, then opened to glare at Keja and Giles. It dropped to all fours and pawed once. "Here it comes again," Giles warned.

The beast did not charge, however, but lumbered toward them, an unstoppable juggernaut. Giles heard the talons of its claws scratching the stones with every step. Its thick tail, saw-toothed along the edges, lashed back and forth.

He sized it up quickly. "Watch the tail and the claws, Keja," he said quietly. "Can you build a loop with your rope?"

Keja immediately caught the sense of Giles' question. He loosened a second rope from his waist and awkwardly worked it.

Giles took several steps toward the beast to give Keja the time he needed. He held his halberd ready and watched the lizard creature advance. Several feet away from him, it reared onto its stubby hind legs. Talons seemed to grow longer before Giles' eyes, and he knew that he faced a dangerous weapon.

He stepped quickly toward the beast, thrusting the

170

axe-edge of the halberd at the palm of one claw. Feeling the cutting edge bite into the flesh, he turned the shaft in his hand, withdrawing to use the point. Blood gushed onto the floor. The creature snorted in pain and swung its claws wildly. Giles stepped back quickly and the blow met only air.

The beast gave a hoarse grunt. Giles smelled the beast's foul breath and wrinkled his nose. There was little room for him to move—except back. He stabbed again at Onyx's pet; the creature retreated. Although Giles' weapon did not reach the animal, it gave him time to maneuver. He glanced over his shoulder at Keja and saw that the loop was nearly ready.

The beast extended its arms once again and attacked Giles. The man's world filled with the grime of its claws, dirt and the filthy decay of meat ground between pad and talon. If those claws drew blood, Giles knew, his death would be a slow one. He had seen disease run rampant during the War from lack of sanitation.

Keja joined Giles, laying the loop on the ground. The beast balanced on its tail, confused by two people. Its small brain decided both might die as easily as one. It lunged forward. Keja brought the flattened loop up in an overhead gesture. The loop fell short but settled over one outstretched scaly limb. Keja pulled the loop taut and planted his feet solidly on the floor. He leaned back against the rope, straining to contain the creature.

The beast struggled against the rope, then fell to all four feet to pull against the restraint. Its tail lashed from side to side. It opened its mouth, changed direction and rushed Keja.

The small thief leaped into the air but kept a hold on the rope. He came down on the beast's tail. The tail lashed once and threw Keja against the wall. Stunned, he gripped the rope and staggered aside in time to avoid the tail once again.

"Pull, Keja," Giles shouted.

His head throbbing, blood running down his side, Keja planted his feet. He pulled the beast's leg off the

171

floor, exposing a soft spot underneath.

The creature turned its head toward Keja; Giles seized the opportunity. He planted the halberd and, with the force of his entire weight, lunged with all his might. The point disappeared into the fold of flesh and sank several inches up the shaft. Giles shoved hard against the butt of the halberd and saw it sink even deeper into the beast.

The giant lizard roared in pain and struck once again at Giles. He let go his grip on the shaft and backed away, weaponless. He retreated down the hallway, and the beast, dripping blood, followed after him. Keja was pulled along behind.

"Use your sword!" Giles yelled, searching desperately for something to use as a weapon.

Keja wrapped the rope around his wrist, then used his free hand to pull his sword loose. He took aim at the base of the creature's neck and thrust. The tip found the spot, but the blade bent and the sword slipped away harmlessly.

But the sword had done its work. Distracted again, the beast twisted its head, looking back at Keja.

Giles leaped toward the huge lizard and grasped the halberd shaft, twisting and turning it as he pulled it loose. The creature snorted and hissed. As it opened its mouth, Giles thrust the point into the back of its throat. The hiss turned to a gurgle and gouts of hot blood rushed from the creature's mouth. Its tail lashed feebly once, but the spear had taken its toll. Bleeding internally from the first thrust and choking on its own blood, the beast's head lowered.

Giles and Keja backed away and let it die. They stood, breathing heavily. Giles moaned, aching all over. His joints seized up on him, even though he had escaped unscathed. Keja's wounds were minor and quickly bound. Only then did Giles turn to the hole in the wall and wonder how Petia was doing. He wiped his face with the back of his sleeve, then froze as Onyx's voice echoed through the tunnels.

"Having fun with my pet? No? Then you can thank me. I have something else. But I won't send it yet. As host, however, I must see that you don't lack for entertainment, am I not right?" The laughter turned Giles' blood into a frigid river.

Petia crept catlike along the tunnel, first to the left and to the right. Unable to carry a candle, her feral-eyed pupils dilated to capture any available light. The dim light from the candle in the corridor faded within a few feet, and she made her way in total darkness. Every sense alert, she followed the tunnel to the right. Then she saw, many feet away, a faint ray of light.

Realizing that the light must be Anji's candle, she crept toward it as quickly as possible. When the tunnel sloped upward and her hands clawed at the slippery stone beneath her, she couldn't find a purchase. There was little need for caution now. Onyx, warned by his dwarfish advisor, knew that they explored the passages.

She called to Anji. "Are you all right?"

Anji's small voice echoed as if it came from a barrel. "Yes, Petia, but I can't jump high enough to reach the ledge."

"I know. I'm at the slippery stone. How did you get through?"

Anji explained about the handgrips in the ceiling of the low tunnel. Petia told him to be patient, turned onto her back and felt along the upper surface until she found the holds. In a few minutes, she looked down into the room and saw a subdued Anji standing morosely on the floor below.

"I'm sorry, Petia. I was so excited about seeing the key that I jumped down before I even thought about how I'd get back."

"Don't worry, I'll get you out." She balanced on the narrow ledge and unwound the rope from her waist. She let one end of the rope down into the room. Anji took hold of the end.

173

"What do I do now?" he asked.

She coiled the extra rope carefully at her feet, then looped the rope over her left shoulder, across her back and to the slack in her right hand. "See if you can climb up the rope. Try to lean back on the rope and walk up the wall."

The boy looked doubtful, but he grasped the rope and put one foot against the wall. He leaned back and pulled himself up. He managed to gain a couple of feet before his arms weakened and he had to jump back down. "I'm sorry, Petia, my arms are not strong enough."

Petia knelt, rubbing the shoulder which had taken the boy's weight. She looked at the leftover length of rope coiled beside her. It was nearly as long as the slippery tunnel she had worked her way through. Quickly she pulled the rope up from the room and knotted a loop in its end. Dropping the loop back to Anji, she said, "Stand in the loop." She explained what she was going to do. "When you get close enough to grab the ledge, try to take your weight on your arms and scramble up."

Anji stepped into the loop and held onto the rope. Petia removed her tunic and carefully made a pad on the edge of the ledge for the rope to slide over. She wound the rope around her waist again and backed into the tunnel. She turned to lay on her back and immediately felt her body begin to slip on the polished stone surface.

The rope tightened around her waist, but her body continued its slide down the tunnel. She held her breath, knowing that for every foot she slid, Anji was a foot nearer the ledge. She felt the pressure on her stomach ease suddenly. The boy had reached the top of the ledge.

She waited patiently until she heard Anji's voice. "Petia?"

"I'm here," she replied. "I'm not coming back up the tunnel. Coil the rope around your waist and follow me out. But be careful. There might be something waiting outside for us."

Petia discovered that she could not turn around in the

174

tight quarters. Cursing silently, she backed her way down the tunnel. Before she had gone more than a couple of feet, Anji slid head first down the tunnel. She reached out and tousled his hair. "You still have the key?"

"I made sure that it was deep in my pocket before I left the room, and I checked again just now."

The final key was theirs!

Giles and Keja stood over the lifeless beast. Blood still oozed from its side and mouth, but its breath was gone. They leaned heavily on each other, glad of the contact with another human. Giles cleaned his halberd as well as he could on the beast's body.

Keja went to the hole in the wall and leaned his head down to the opening. "Petia," he shouted. "You there?"

Petia's voice came from so close that Keja jumped back, startled. "She's almost back," he said to Giles. "I wonder if she has Anji."

"He's right behind me," Petia replied. "We'll be out soon—and he's got the key!"

Petia's legs emerged as she twisted and turned negotiating the tight turn in the tunnel near the entrance. She backed out on her hands and knees and stood, winded from her efforts. She shook all over as her body thickened once more into its normal shape, the cat sleekness leaving her.

Anji's face showed in the opening, a bit grimly, but wearing an angelic smile. He stood and hugged Petia, then dug deep into his pocket and pulled out the steel key, flourishing it dramatically. When he had finished, he held it out to Giles.

Giles examined it briefly, then handed it on to Keja. Keja looked at it and shrugged. "So that's the last one," he said, handing it back to Giles. "Hardly looks worth the effort."

"I haven't seen it yet," Petia said peevishly.

"Sorry, Petia, I thought you had." Giles handed the

key to her, but she gave it only a cursory look before handing it back to Anji. Keja opened his mouth to protest, but Giles warned him with a hard look.

The boy stuffed the key back into his pocket. "What's next?" he said, finished with his task and looking up at Giles.

"Getting out of here. And getting Helleon and Linnia out with us. I hope you and Petia can produce some incredible images." Giles leaned back against the wall and drew a long breath. "Can you project a void at the dwarf? A nothing, no emotion, no action, emptiness?"

"Whatever for?" Petia asked. "What will that accomplish?"

"I want Onyx to think we've been killed, that the beast has done us in. If he thinks we're dead, he'll forget about us and go on to other things."

"You forget the key, Giles. He'll send someone for it, a soldier or maybe the dwarf."

"Yes, but we'll be gone by then," Giles responded. "Keja and I will empty our minds. You and Anji project 'nothing.' Onyx will think he has plenty of time to recover the key."

Keja's face turned white. "I can't do it, Giles. I tried before and I couldn't empty my mind. The harder I tried the more thoughts flashed through it. That's how Ulinek found out where we were. I'll give us away again."

"You can do it, Keja," Giles said. He stepped forward, and before Keja could react, he closed his fist and struck the younger man flush on the chin. He stepped back, rubbing his knuckles, and watched as Keja sagged to the floor.

He turned to Petia. "Do it. Now."

"Better than a nothingness," Petia said, "how about an image of the lizard-beast devouring our bodies?"

"A great idea. Just don't overdo it." He motioned with his hand for her to get on with it.

Petia conferred with Anji briefly, then they sat, facing each other. They linked hands. The two Trans stared deeply into each other's eyes, concentrating, fixing the image, agreeing on the details.

Giles realized how much he was asking of them. For several minutes, Petia and Anji didn't move. Giles propped Keja up against the wall. He felt secure that Keja wasn't thinking anything that would interfere with the success of the image-makers. Petia released her grip from Anji's hands. She leaned back, sighed and nodded at Giles.

"Are you all right?" he asked.

She stood and helped Anji to his feet. "Yes," she whispered, but her voice came out faint and thready.

Giles reached under Keja's arms and lifted him until he was erect and leaning against the wall. He bent and slung him over his back. "Hang on to me," he whispered back. "Both of you." He staggered under Keja's weight, shrugged once to redistribute it, then began to walk down the passage. Petia bent and picked up the candle. She put an arm around Anji, caught up with Giles and clung to his sleeve.

At the end of the corridor, they turned the corner. Giles made unerringly for the steps that would take them down two levels of the citadel.

Anji tugged at Petia's sleeve and she turned, questioningly. "Rats," Anji whispered. Petia paused and concentrated. "Onyx has turned rats loose in the passage above. They've found the lizard's body and are feasting on it." She grimaced. "It's ugly. They're tearing it to shreds."

"As long as it's not us," Giles said, turning the corner at the bottom of the stairs and striding off toward the iron ladder.

At last they came to the narrow shaft leading downward to the storeroom where they had begun their night's adventures. Giles lowered Keja to the floor, propping him up, and stood back to flex his back muscles. He was winded from the exertion and stood, breathing heavily, heart triphammering.

"How are you going to get him down?" Petia asked.

"Wake him up. He's going to have do the rest under his own power. Got to rest." He sat and said, "Have you got any strength left?"

"Not much," Petia replied. "What do you need?"

"We've got to get those two Brada out with us. Can you let them know?"

"I'll try. All I can do is throw images at them and hope they understand."

"Anything. Show themselves carrying the garbage out." Giles leaned forward and slapped Keja's cheek, gently at first, and when he got no response, harder. Keja moaned and his eyes fluttered. "Come on, Keja, time to come back to life." He slapped him again and Keja's arm shot up to grip the older man's wrist. "Ah, good." Giles relaxed and let Keja come awake by himself.

"I think I've gotten through," Petia said. "I wish my powers weren't so simple. I sent them a bit of fear, a need to escape. I'd like to be able to communicate in words instead of hoping that vague emotions will get the message across."

"Be thankful for what you have," Giles said. "It's time to get moving again." He pulled himself up and went to the shaft, peering down and listening intently for any sounds below. There were none. He motioned Petia to go down first. Anji followed.

"You next, Keja. And I'm sorry about the punch, but I had to make sure you didn't spoil things."

Keja grunted and made a face that turned into a wry grin. "I know, but I'll get even with you sometime, just the same."

"I figured you would," Giles said, slapping him on the shoulder. "Down you go."

Two floors below they came to the cold room. As they crawled through the hole into the room once again, Keja spotted a string cheese hanging from the ceiling. He drew his battered sword, cut it down and sliced the strings. Quickly he knotted several strings together, testing to see that the knots held.

"The key, Anji," he said, holding out his hand. Reluctantly the boy fished in his pocket and pulled forth the final object of their long quest.

Keja slipped the key onto the string, measured it against Anji's head and tied a final knot. He slipped the loop over Anji's head. "Tuck that inside your tunic," he said. "We're not about to lose that key now." The boy grinned, happy that they still trusted him with the key.

Giles opened the door a crack, listening cautiously for any sound of guards in the hallway or kitchen area. He closed the door gently. "I don't hear anything except normal kitchen sounds," he said. "Any ideas about how to get out of here?"

"Why not the same way we came in?" Keja asked.

Petia closed her eyes. When she opened them again, she shook her head. "Guards there. But that's the only doorway on that side of the citadel."

"We're on a lower level now," Keja said. "Can we go out a window like the Brada women did when we helped them escape?"

"I'd forgotten completely about that," Giles said. "It seems like that was aeons ago, in some past life. Are your ropes in good order?" He turned to Petia and Anji. "Can you tell anything about our Brada friends?"

"How long do they need to be?" Keja asked as he unwound his ropes.

"Helleon and Linnia are uneasy, but they're not sure why. They act as if they know we've returned, but they don't know what to do."

"We can't wait any longer. We'll take them right out of the kitchen. Come on."

Giles opened the door, checked the hallway and led the others at a run toward the kitchen staff's quarters. Startled faces looked up from their tasks as they rushed into the room. The major-domo rushed toward them to protest, and Keja hit him square on the nose. Blood gushed and the portly man sat down squarely on a sack of potatoes.

"Helleon! Linnia!" Giles shouted. The two came running, Helleon from around the corner, and Linnia from the other side of the huge spit where half a beef roasted.

They left as quickly as they had entered. Keja spotted a meat hook and grabbed it as he flew by. "Where's a room with a window?" Giles asked as they ran.

"This way," Linnia said, and shouldered her way to the front.

The furnished room was empty of inhabitants. Giles rushed to the window and found it locked. Grabbing a chair, he smashed at the window, shattering glass and bending the frame. Keja deftly knotted the meat hook to his ropes. When Giles finished, he threw the ropes through the window, hooking the underside of the ledge with the hook.

"The Brada first, then Anji, Petia, Keja," Giles said. "I'll go last."

They quickly slid down the rope to the ground thirty feet below. Gathered at the bottom, Keja tried vainly to loosen the hook and retrieve his ropes.

"Leave them," Giles said. "They've served their purpose."

The dash across the meadow to the forest seemed to take forever. They heard a warning cry from the citadel and saw sentries on the top battlements gesturing. They had been spotted but ran for the protection of the trees and underbrush.

Just inside the forest they stopped to rest.

"Giles, Helleon, Linnia." Natabor and another young Brada swung down from a tree above them. "No time to talk. Follow us."

They trotted across a clearing, ducked behind a bush and found the Brada's secret path. Giles silently praised the dedication of the two young Brada who had waited for them. They had promised to wait for two nights. This was the third. He wondered how much longer they would have waited. Good people, he thought, and then set his mind to keeping up with their tireless pace.

But Giles began to tire immediately. Within another five minutes, he knew his old body wouldn't be able to maintain the pace. Panting, temples pounding, his breath coming in gouts of liquid fire, he stopped, needing a tree for support.

Chapter Sixteen

ALONG THE SEA'S EDGE, THE BRADA SET UP A TEMPORARY encampment deep in the forest, surrounded on three sides by brackish marshland filled with potholes and ponds. It was a difficult area to search, and not a likely place for the Brada to have disappeared.

Giles and the others arrived, leg-weary and bone-tired. It was a long run with few stops; they had pushed hard to get back to the coast. With every step, Giles was more impressed by the Brada's stamina, intelligence, knowledge of woodlore, and most of all by their determination to hold on to what was theirs. But this did nothing to alleviate the pain Giles felt in every muscle in his body.

He was near collapse when he entered the camp. Giles vaguely remembered hearing a hawk screech, as if on the hunt, and realized only later that it was a warning from a perimeter lookout. He slumped to the boggy ground, not caring about the wet and cold.

"A feast tomorrow," Veldon said. "Tonight, a nourishing broth and a long sleep."

Giles nodded wearily and thanked him before Keja and Natabor half carried him to a temporary hut made of beach driftwood, conifer boughs and chinks filled with moss. The last thing he remembered was the harsh texture of the blanket with which someone covered him.

The late afternoon sun, beaming wanly through the ocean mist, greeted Giles when he awoke. Although he had slept, Giles hadn't truly rested. His body ached all over and his vision blurred and cleared. He had about reached the end of his endurance—and yet Giles knew the hardest part still lay ahead.

He stirred enough to find Keja and Petia. Anji sat with two village elders, excitedly telling them of the part he had played in stealing the key from the heart of Onyx's citadel. Giles let the boy boast. Little enough reward for the risks taken.

To Veldon, Giles said, "Lord Onyx won't stop until he punishes all Brada." He stopped short of mentioning the steel key. Veldon might know of it; whether he did mattered little to Giles. All that counted now was Onyx's wrath and what he'd do to stop them.

"We waited only for you," Veldon replied. "We have endured much at Onyx's hand; but as you see, this is a temporary village. Most of the Brada have gone farther south to avoid Onyx's steel warriors. We can now join the others."

Giles wanted nothing more than to rest but realized the necessity for flight. "Let's leave now," he said. "We may have lingered too long." Giles had developed a sense of danger over the years. Even through his fatigue, he sensed the nearness of death.

Veldon nodded and motioned to Natabor, who came to them and said that canoes awaited them on the beach.

"We intended to walk," Giles said. "You and your people should be on your way."

"Many left during the night while you slept. Speed is your true ally against Onyx." Natabor cocked his head to one side but didn't say what he thought: Giles Grimsmate couldn't walk ten feet, much less the many miles required for escape. Instead, Natabor said, "We'll take you along the coast faster than you could travel on foot. We cannot take you all the way to a port, but we will leave you with others, friends of the Brada, who will take you. From there you must be on your own."

Giles gripped the young man's arm. "You do more than enough. We are grateful."

Natabor shook his head. "No, brother, it is we who are grateful." He shouldered two of the packs and led the way to the beach.

The canoes were long and narrow, only one person wide. Natabor ushered the companions into the slender boat, seating them one behind the other. He pushed the canoe off from the sandy beach, wading through the water to his knees, then leaping aboard to take a seat in the front facing the six paddlers already churning water with their long, powerful strokes.

Natabor grunted once and the six Brada lifted their paddles. He grunted again, and they lowered them into the water. Then he hit the side of the canoe softly with the heel of his hand, and the first stroke took them out toward the waves. Giles marveled at the precision and power with which the young men stroked.

Soon, the shoreline disappeared and Natabor turned the canoe southeast and established a tireless rhythm. For two days they stayed beyond the sight of land. Occasionally, the Brada exchanged places, each taking a turn at navigating. Sometimes the paddlers would switch sides so that their arms would not tire, but always they moved up and down silently in the waves, with nothing to look at but endless water. The Brada took short naps from time to time, but Giles, feeling more tired than he had since the wars had ended, slept often and long.

At the end of the fourth day, Natabor signaled to the navigator to turn landward. When they came within sight of land, a small fire glowed on the dark beach. The canoe made directly for it.

"Giles," said Natabor, "we must leave you now." He started to say more, but emotion choked him. He hugged Giles close, then turned and jumped back into the canoe before the older man could appropriately thank the Brada.

"Some good fella, eh?" said a man lounging near the fire. He coughed and spat into the fire. "We will set you on a beach near Grifield. From there you are on your own. You have never seen us nor will you recognize us if you see us again. Understood?"

A man of few and direct words, Giles thought. "Nor do you know us. We are grateful and we thank you."

"Not for you. For them." The man indicated the rapidly vanishing Brada canoe. Their packs were taken and stored in a kind of dory, much wider than the canoe, with high bow planks. Six men pulled the oars, and they traveled only by night, hugging the coastline. By early morning, the dory slipped into a small cove.

The leader, whose name they never learned, stepped onto a rock ledge and held the dory steady. Giles and the others heaved their packs ashore and followed them.

Immediately the leader stepped back into the boat, and the oarsmen backed out of the narrow channel. As the companions stood, trying to find a path upward from the cove in the faint light, a whisper came across the water, "May the gods speed you."

The Sea Hag was only one of many taverns with accommodations along the docks. It displayed a shabby exterior, but Giles thought it safer than the fancier inn down the rocky road. Petia vouched that the sheets were clean, and Keja pronounced the smells from the kitchen as wholesome and appetizing.

Giles set off early in the morning to enquire about passage to Trois Havres. When he returned in the mid-afternoon, disappointment showed in his face. "They tell me that shipping is limited to Grifield during the winter. Ships do call, but they are few and far between. We could wait a month, they say."

"What will we do, wait?" Petia asked.

"I don't think that would be wise," Keja said. "Onyx is looking for us."

Anji spoke up from the corner where he polished the knife Bellisar had given him. "I was out in the town this

185

morning and heard people gossiping about Onyx. He is expected. Keja is right. We cannot linger."

"It's time to move on," Giles said. "Just like the old ballad says, 'last night she slept in a goosedown bed, tonight she sleeps in the heather.' Keja, I'll leave it to you to find horses for us."

When Keja returned an hour later, he brought more news of Onyx. "The Black Lord's not here yet, but some of his men are. The ostler took me into the stable, and I saw a row of saddles hanging along one wall in the tack room. They all had Onyx's crest in steel on each side of the cantle. Another little project from the forge of your friend, Bellisar."

"How many?" Giles asked curtly.

"Six," Keja replied, "but the ostler said that he expected a full stable by tonight. The ostler's a talkative old man. I played the interested stranger. He told me all about Onyx. He's expected with another dozen men by evening."

"Did he give you any reason for Onyx coming now, in the dead of winter?" Giles asked.

"He didn't know," Keja said. "He said he heard some of the men talking about looking for someone, but he thought they meant some women."

Petia snorted. "Men are all alike," she said, looking scornfully at Keja and Giles.

"How about the horses? Did you get us any?"

"Two was all he had. And jugheads at that. But I figured we couldn't be picky. Anji will have to ride one with you, and Petia and I will ride double on the other."

"I'll ride double with Anji," Petia said.

"No," Giles said more forcefully than he intended. "Keja and I are too heavy together. We need to make the best time we can, and riding double is going to slow us." The strain mounted on Giles. He wanted nothing more than to be back on Hawk's Prairie and through the Gate of Paradise.

Without Keja. Without Petia and Anji. Without the

186

continual pressure of pursuit from Onyx and Segrinn.

Petia gave in with obvious reluctance. They hastily packed and got the two horses an hour after sunset. The fog drifted in from the ocean, covering the town. All was quiet and the companions rode along the edges of buildings, disturbing the eerie setting as little as possible. They breathed more easily when Grifield lay behind them.

A short ways along the road, the fog thinned and the moon tried valiantly to show them the road. Winter had brought mud puddles and potholes to the road to Larra. The fog made it difficult to guide the horses, so Giles let his mount pick its own way. No one had told them that the road dwindled to a one-lane track within a few miles of Grifield.

Before they had gone a mile on the treacherous path, Keja's horse stumbled. When it recovered balance it began limping. Giles slid off his horse to examine the animal and found that it had an old, uncared for cut behind the fetlock.

"How far to Larra?" Petia asked, her eyes glassy and far-focused.

"About fifteen miles from Grifield, another twelve miles perhaps," Giles said. "Why?"

"Because I'm certain that Onyx has found our trail and comes after us. I sense his emotions strongly. Triumph. Hate. It's definitely Onyx."

"That's just fine," Keja said. "We'll never get away from him. He'll hound us the rest of our lives. Or until he gets the keys. How'd he find out about us this time?"

"How does he ever find out about us?" Giles said. "How has he followed us all over the world? Shall we keep asking ourselves those questions every time we turn around, or shall we do something about it? We have to stop him, once and for all."

Keja looked up from examining the horse's leg. "Are you crazy?"

"No, I'm just tired. I'm not getting any younger, and I

187

want to be finished with this whole adventure. We've got the keys, but we also have Onyx after us once again. Until we do something about him, we'll be chevied around the world. He's like a plague. Our lives aren't worth anything until we rid ourselves of him."

Keja shook his head, obviously concerned about the state of Giles' brain. "You have a plan?" he asked.

"At the moment, no. We should leave the road, hide somewhere until we've had time to think. One horse is lame and, even with a head start, they'll catch us if we keep going."

The fog swirled around them, becoming thicker or thinner with the vagaries of an offshore breeze. They could hardly see their surroundings, making it almost impossible to stay on the track leading along the coast.

"Some things are in our favor," Giles continued. "We're ahead of Onyx by a few miles, he'll expect us to continue straight on, and the fog slows him as much as it does us. But we must leave the road and soon."

He tied the horses to a windblown scrub oak and shouldered his pack. "Best we walk. The horses are no good to us now," he said as he strode off.

The others caught up with him in short time, and they felt their way along the track. Each time the fog thinned, Giles stopped, hoping to see enough of their surroundings to make a decision. Once he stopped and cupped his ear, listening to an unidentifiable thundering sound.

A short time later it became clear. Ahead was a waterfall rushing its way over boulders. The force of its passage created air currents that lifted the fog thirty feet into the air. When they reached a narrow bridge spanning the stream, Giles could see a way up alongside the water.

"If we go up here, the rushing water will drown out any noise we make. It will disturb the dwarf, too, if Onyx brought him along."

They climbed steadily, and as they gained elevation the fog thinned. At the top of the cliff a long meadow sloped gently upward. The stream running across it

188

burbled less boisterously before it cascaded over the edge of the cliff.

Giles sat, breathing heavily from the climb. When his heart had slowed, he looked at the others. "Now's the time for thinking. We must rid ourselves of Onyx, once and for all. Tell me everything you think of, no matter how stupid it sounds."

"We can't fight the entire troop," Petia said. "Not with swords. They outnumber us. If what Keja heard is correct, there are at least eighteen of them, plus Onyx."

"You're right. Eighteen against four. It has to be something that gives us the advantage, something devious."

Keja stood. "Excuse me. I've got to relieve myself," he said, walking away along the edge of the cliff. When he returned a smile crossed on his face.

Petia grinned wryly. "Feel that much better?" she asked.

"No, it's something I saw. I don't know if this will work, Giles, but you said to mention everything. When you get to the edge of the cliffs, there is an overhang where the winds have sculpted out the rock. You think you're walking on solid ground, but from the side you can see that there's only about a foot of soil and sod, and nothing but thin air beneath it."

Giles nodded. "Go on," he said.

"Farther down, a huge hunk of cliff has fallen away. It must weigh tons. But it didn't slide far. If we could get it moving again, it might carry right down to the track."

"And bury Onyx, is that what you're thinking?" Giles asked.

"Keja, that sounds—" Petia began, but Giles stopped her with a gesture.

"Let's take a look. Lead on, Keja."

When they reached the place, Keja stretched his hand out. "Stand over here, Giles. See how there's nothing but emptiness under those overhangs? They've got to be dangerous. Now, see where that big piece gave way."

Giles stared down. Twenty feet below the dawn light

outlined a chunk of earth, broken away from the top and still wearing its sod and grass crest. Cracks and crevices around the base of the huge hunk showed that its purchase was precarious at best.

"Rope, Keja," Giles said. He took the rope from the young thief and knotted it around his waist. "Keep a firm grip on that," he said as he disappeared over the side of the cliff. Giles made his way down the landslide to the huge chunk of earth. He prodded the hairline cracks and larger crevices with his halberd point, nodding to himself from time to time. He skirted below the fallen segment, and Petia feared that it would choose that moment to release its tentative grip.

When Giles climbed back up, he said wearily, "It's worth a try. If it lets go, it will be splendid. If it doesn't, let's hope that Onyx doesn't look up and discover us. Keja, we'll have to be roped, and you've got to find something to anchor us. If that goes, the whole cliff could go with it."

An hour later all was ready. The companions waited nervously. Giles and Keja took the outside places, Petia and Anji, the inside. Giles had probed cautiously again and thought he had found the precise spot that would trigger the avalanche. Anji had gathered some thick lengths of scrub oak branches and Keja had tested them for strength. They had placed boulders to provide leverage, and dug warily to reveal wet clay underneath the base of the cliff segment. Giles showed his first optimism in days.

They squatted patiently behind the fallen segment of the cliff, alert for any sign of travelers along the road. Petia occasionally cast for emotional activity back along the road. She could give them ample warning, but still all were tense. This might be the only opportunity to rid themselves of the Black Lord.

Below the fog swirled in from the sea, eddying with the breeze, thinning and thickening as the wanton mistress of the wind dictated. At times they could see the road, and at others it vanished beneath a soft gray layer. Giles worried that the fog might never lift.

Nearly an hour later Petia signaled that she sensed something. "How far?" Giles mouthed, afraid that even the slightest sound would carry over fog and water to warn their enemy.

Petia shook her head slightly and whispered, "Can't tell yet."

Tense now, they waited impatiently, eager for any action. At last the sound of horses snuffling carried faintly to them on the moist morning air. Giles flexed his arms in anticipation, anxiously peering below for sight of the road.

Keja nervously checked the ropes which held them. He had sharpened a branch into a stake and sunk it deep in the ground some distance into the meadow. Each of the companions was held by a rope tied to the stake. If the whole cliff let loose, he was certain they would be safe.

The discipline of Onyx's men was good. They came without a sound. There was no conversation, only the occasional jingle of a snaffle and the creak of leather. Hoofbeats were muffled by the muddy ground.

Giles stood, hoping for a glimpse of Onyx—and that it would come soon enough for them to set the landslide in motion. In answer to his prayer, the sea-borne fog thinned.

Onyx did not ride at the head of his troop. The guard rode single file on the narrow track, and Giles counted heads as they neared. Another and another, appearing out of the mist, heads down and muffled against the wet chill.

The others had risen, too, and taken their places. Eighteen, Giles counted silently and hoped once again that Keja had heard the correct number. He caught his breath when the next head coming out of the swirling fog wore a black casque ornamented in gold. Lord Onyx, the Black Lord.

Giles' arm swept down and the others concentrated their energies on the job ahead of them. Giles' halberd prodded deep into a crevice he had discovered earlier. When he had pulled it out, wet clay covered its tip. He hoped that the moisture beneath would provide the slippage they needed. They would give it all the encouragement they could.

Keja threw his weight against the end of a log thrust into a hole they had dug. A boulder several feet in circumference provided a fulcrum for the log. Petia and Anji each had positions where they added their lighter weights to the project.

Giles leaned his weight against the halberd, probing, urging, goading the tons of earth to release its precarious grip. He felt a tremor under his feet, as if the fallen segment could not make up its mind. Again he probed, finding a soft spot through which the speartip cut. Again and again he worked it back and forth, loosening the soil's hold from the more solid earth below it.

He felt more than the quivering movement. The entire section began to slide, slowly, and he raised an arm to urge the others to greater effort. Keja jumped up and down, throwing his weight against his prying log, thrusting its end up a fraction of an inch farther each time.

When the earth gave, it did so with silence and great dignity. It gave not so much as a groan but began to slide effortlessly, the top collapsing inward as it went. It gathered momentum, and Giles watched jubilantly.

The section pulled great hunks of earth after it, strata breaking away and following down the slope. Petia felt the earth move beneath her feet and tried to scramble up the slope. Her feet were pulled out from beneath her and she fell—but Keja's rope held. She turned, pulling herself to her feet, and headed for the top of the slope before any more dirt gave way.

Keja felt the slide begin and scrambled to get out of the way. The log, loosed from its mooring, slid off the boulder and banged his ankle. He leaped away to avoid further injury. Anji jumped the other way and scrambled up the slope.

Giles simply stood and watched the results of their efforts. The landslide cut through the fog, swirling it. It gathered in the loose dirt below and grew with every passing moment. A low rumble surrounded them as it gained momentum. He saw guards look up and kick their heels into their horses. Horses plunged at the sound, and their riders attempted to control them. The narrow track between cliff and seashore allowed little room for maneuvering—and none for escape.

He heard Onyx shout, but the words were meaningless. Riders at the beginning of the file urged their mounts forward. Some of them might make it, Giles knew. For others, escape was impossible.

Giles saw Onyx pull his horse around in a vain attempt to escape in the other direction, but it was too late. The leading edge of the landslide hit the bottom of the cliff and cascaded across the track. Onyx's horse reared, then its hind legs were swept from beneath it. It fell heavily onto its side. Onyx lifted one foot from its stirrup.

The earth swept over him. Giles saw one arm raised, the fist clenched, then Onyx disappeared completely, buried under tons of earth.

Giles felt the rope suddenly tighten around his waist. The earth disappeared beneath him, and he swung in empty space along the cliff face. He had been so intent upon the happenings below that he had not felt the ground giving way. He craned his neck and saw Petia and Anji scrambling up the slope.

Keja was already on top, reaching a hand down to assist the others. He called down to Giles, "Don't do anything. I'll pull you up."

After what seemed an eternity, Keja pulled Giles far enough to plant his feet and climb to the top. Willing hands pulled him the last few steps. Keja sat, massaging his hands. "You're a heavy one, aren't you?" he said between gasps. "Not only are you getting old, you're getting fat."

"Did it work, Giles?" Petia asked. "Is Onyx dead?"

"I think so. Nothing would surprise me much with that man, but I saw him buried under the landslide. If he's not dead, then I'll believe his story about being a god."

Larra was a city of remarkable attractions. A castle and a temple dominated the two hills of the city, commerce the middle slopes, and warehouses and dock facilities the level spaces near the ocean. The four companions drew a collective breath as rays of the winter sun reflected from the golden tower of the temple.

The city was clean, the people prosperous and, most of all, several ships had anchored in the harbor. They waited their turn to dock, moorage being at a premium.

Anji touched Giles' arm and pointed. Several of Onyx's guard rode down the street. Their heads were bowed and they slumped in their saddles. They looked neither right nor left. Giles saw that they had nothing to fear from the few battered survivors of Onyx's escort.

Giles felt no sense of triumph at the sight. If anything, the weariness he'd experienced before returned even stronger. Was entry into Paradise worth such death, destruction and hardship? Giles heaved a deep sigh. Soon enough, he'd find out.

And abandon his friends when he did so.

He set his mind to their immediate objectives. A bath, a meal, a bed, a ship. All were easy to find. The *Flying Cloud* sailed to Milbante in two days, and the companions were aboard, the voyage not particularly pleasant. Winter winds and weather and an occasional squall made it a trip during which the companions stayed below a good deal of the time, and more than once fought off seasickness.

But in the god's own time it ended. The ship docked at Dimly New and Giles and the others were mounted once again. Sanustell lay only a few miles down the coast road. The keys, as Giles had to convince Keja once more, rested safely in the vault of the Callant Hanse.

How did Giles tell his small, suspicious friend that he need not fear those of the mercantile house but rather the man who rode beside him?

Chapter Seventeen

"AH, NEW CLOTHES!" KEJA CRIED LIKE A CHILD WITH A NEW toy. He stuck out one arm to admire the crimson sleeve ribbons and the material blousing from the tight velvet cuff.

"You're incredible, Keja," Petia said, watching the style show. "I've never seen such vanity."

"Are you two ready?" Giles asked from across the room. "Anji and I have been ready to go for the last half hour."

Keja turned one last time to see whether his new trousers fit as well as he had thought when he purchased them. They were tight and Petia admired the curve of his bottom in the mirror once again. She would never let on that she thought so, but Keja did have a wonderful body.

Keja picked up his new cloak, heather blue with two broad gray chevrons, and quite dashing. He twirled it to see how the ends layed out, then stood still to admire its drape.

"Come on, Keja," Giles ordered. "The women will all adore you. But they won't have a chance if we don't get out on the street where you can be seen."

Once Giles got them moving toward the Callant

Hanse, he allowed no further delay. On the street he walked determinedly, with Anji trying to match him stride for stride. Petia and Keja walked along behind, but Petia kept the young rogue from stopping to admire the goods in shop windows. When they reached the marketplace, she had a more difficult time. Keja wanted to paw every item laid out in the stalls, his quick glances roving from one table to another. Giles and Anji got farther ahead and Petia pulled Keja by the arm.

At the Callant Hanse they announced themselves and their business. They were ushered into the consultation room. The young master, Simon Callant, entered and greeted them. "You're all looking satisfied," he said. "I take it you've successfully found the final key."

"Giles nodded.

"And now you want the other four?"

"Not yet," Giles said. "We think we'll give the final one into your keeping for a while."

Surprise showed on Callant's face, but he kept his thoughts to himself. He eyed the gaudy Keja Tchurak. "And you would like to see the other four keys." It was more statement than question.

Keja reddened. "Yes."

Callant pulled the bell rope close to hand. When a young man appeared, he ordered the keys brought from the vault. "And meantime, refreshments, Jaeger."

When the servant poured the wine, Simon Callant toasted the end of a successful endeavor, but true to the philosophy of the great merchant house, Callant asked no questions about how they obtained the key. He talked about the state of the economy, the upcoming goose fair and the hanging of a rogue several weeks back.

When the keys arrived, the servant presented them on a red velvet pillow. Giles nudged Anji, who removed the cord from around his neck. Giles pulled a small knife from its scabbard at his belt, and then snicked the string holding the key. He gestured to Anji, who removed the final key and placed it with the four others.

Giles shivered at the beautiful sight: four gold keys,

each with a semiprecious stone in the round flat portion at the end of the shaft—Peridot, ruby, emerald, amethyst—and the final key, which ought to have been gold, a duplicate in steel. The hair on the back of Giles' neck rose at the sight of them.

"May I?" Keja looked at Giles, who nodded. Keja lifted the keys, one by one, and examined them. Then he passed them along to the others. Anji, last in line, replaced them with reverence.

Giles drained the last of his wine and stood. "Thank you, Master Callant. We will be back." He led the way out of the room while the young banker stared after them.

The days wore on slowly, but no one seemed to mind. The companions had money from the jewels and gold they had brought back from their adventure in Shahal. Petia spent her time teaching Anji to read and write. Giles took long, pensive walks along the seawall. Keja managed to keep himself occupied with the young ladies of Sanustell's society.

Giles carefully kept a close watch on ship movements into the harbor. Few ships crossed from Bericlere during the winter. Harsh winds threatened when the first one called, and the captain and crew of the second were an ugly lot, whom he did not trust. The third would have done, but it was sailing for the far east of Bericlere, and Giles decided to pass.

In the midst of waiting for the proper ship, Giles worried over the course he must follow. He knew he had to trick his friends and steal the five keys to the Gate of Paradise. Only one might enter. That inscription haunted him until he lost weight and began to sleep poorly. Petia thought he had an ague; but even self-centered Keja noticed and inquired often.

Giles knew he had to act soon. But how?

Hints of spring came to trees and shrubs when a fourth vessel called, a clean ship with a wholesome-looking crew. Its next port of call was Arginis, near Klepht, where their adventures had begun, although they hadn't known each other at the time. Giles made arrangements with the captain for passage for himself and his three companions. They made a final visit to Callant Hanse and took possession of the five keys.

Simon Callant stared suspiciously at Giles—or did the grizzled old veteran only imagine it? Giles Grimsmate's hand shook as he secured the five keys and bid the mercantile house owner farewell.

The voyage proved calm, in spite of brisk spring winds. The companions walked the deck from bow to stern and back, enjoying the fresh air. On the tenth day the landmass of Bericlere showed on the horizon, and on the eleventh the ship made land and docked at Arginis. The companions said their good-byes to captain and crew and found an inn for the night.

The Sleeping Kraken was as cozy an inn as they had ever stayed in. Mistress Allyne hovered about them as if they were the first guests she had had in years. She fussed over the fireplace, rattling it up into a full flame and adding another log. She insisted that they warm themselves while she mulled wine for them. When they were warm both inside and out, she showed them to their two rooms. Both had fires burning in fireplaces, and the sea chill in the previously unoccupied rooms fled.

Early the next morning, Keja began the accumulation of gear for their trip to Hawk's Prairie—and the Gate.

That evening Keja staggered into the inn with a grinning Anji at his heels. "Damn the boy," Keja announced. "We looked at every horse in town and some outside. 'Giles wouldn't like that one,' he says. 'No, too old, see the teeth. This one's got a nasty temperament. Bowed tendons on this one, look.' He wouldn't let me buy at least one horse so we could ride. No, we had to walk all over town, and then retrace our steps."

Giles laughed as Keja recited the litany. Petia smiled,

because Giles had not laughed in a long time. She worried about him. Since arriving, he had become increasingly withdrawn.

"But we have four good horses, Giles," Anji said proudly. "The best I could find. They are strong and well mannered and will carry us wherever we want to go. Not one of them will go lame, I promise you."

"I believe you, Anji. You have a gift with horses. Now, you're just in time for supper. Mistress Allyne says that she has something special for us this evening."

Still they lingered in Arginis. Giles, usually the restive one, found dozens of reasons not to continue. And each day spent at the inn wore him down even more.

Finally, Petia said, "The weather has turned fine. The trees have blossomed while we've been here, birds are building nests, the spring lambs have been turned out to pasture—and still we sit."

The others did not speak, eyes on Giles. He rose and paced the room. "Well, I'm ready," he said. "No more delays. This may be the greatest adventure of them all." The words caught in his throat. "We leave in the morning." With that he almost ran from the room.

They rode along the coastal road from Arginis to Klepht, the sun shining stronger than it had for days. Evidence of spring was everywhere. To their left the calm ocean waves lapped on a shingle beach. Listening to the riffle of rocks washed back and forth by each wave lulled the riders. They relaxed in their saddles, enjoying the fresh air and the greenery springing forth at every hand.

All, save Giles. Each clop of his horse took him closer to the Gate and the need to betray the others.

"It hardly seems like we're on the last leg," Petia said. "When we started this, I was sure that we'd never make it. But it didn't make any difference. I was running away and nothing better to do."

"I was running, too, in a sense," Giles said. "I didn't think of it that way at the time, but I couldn't stand my own village, its people, and most of all, its memories. I told myself that I was off to see a bit of the world before I got old. But I was really running."

Keja laughed out loud. "You two don't know the first thing about running. I'm not even going to tell you about some of my chases."

"Speaking of running, Giles, would it be all right if we didn't go through Klepht?" Petia sounded concerned. "I had forgotten until now. I killed a couple of men who followed me out of Klepht, and the city guards' memory is long."

"And I was looking forward to the fish stew at The Laughing Cod." Giles pulled a map from his tunic.

"I'll never think of you without seeing you pulling out a map," Petia laughed.

"They come in handy," Giles answered. "We'll turn off and take to the cliff tops."

By evening they were northeast of Klepht, sheltered in a vale. They were seated around a campfire, content with full stomachs, and reminiscing about their earlier adventures. It was a scene that would repeat itself each evening. They relived the scrapes, the times they had been near death, the good people and the bad whom they had met and, most of all, they delighted again in their triumphs.

Petia retired early, snuggling down in her blankets on the opposite side of the fire, with Anji close by. For a while, Giles and Keja talked in a desultory fashion. Giles got up to add wood to the fire and checked to see if Petia slept soundly.

When he sat down again, he turned, a serious expression on his face. "I've got to talk with you, Keja. I've been waiting for the proper time."

Keja's eyebrows lifted. "What about?"

"The Gate. Specifically, the inscription written on the archway above it. Do you remember it?"

"I can't say that I do," Keja replied. "I remember that there were runes, but I couldn't read them."

"I could. They say that only"—Giles swallowed hard

at the lie—"two people can enter the Gate."

Keja's mouth dropped. "You mean . . ." Keja pointed helplessly at Petia and Anji sleeping opposite the fire.

"It appears that way to me," Giles replied. "Can you imagine what it would be like if all four of us got there and then Petia and Anji discovered that they couldn't enter?"

"What are you proposing, Giles? Come on, spit it out."

"It's obvious, Keja. We've got to take the keys and leave Petia and Anji."

Even devious Keja was taken aback at this. "But after all we've been through, we can't do that!"

"I don't intend to leave them penniless, Keja." Giles frowned. "I'm not that mercenary. With all the wealth we'll have when we unlock the Gate of Paradise, we needn't worry about money, or jewels, or gold for ourselves. I intend to leave them my share that we withdrew at the Callant Hanse. They won't suffer. It will be more wealth than Petia has ever dreamed of. She can settle down with Anji, see that he has schooling, own her own dwelling and horses. She'll have enough to last her the rest of her life and give Anji a good start, as well."

Keja stared into the flames, as if dealing with something he never could have imagined, coming to grips with a new idea. He got up, stirred the fire, added sticks, and poured a cup of tea for himself. When he sat down, a puzzled look crossed his face.

Finally he shook his head. "I thought I was the one who was underhanded. When will we go?" he asked.

"There's plenty of time yet, but we should pick a time and then stick with it. The keys are no problem; they're all in a sealskin packet. We'll go quietly in the middle of the night. We'll be well away by the time they wake."

Keja nodded. "Enough time to reach the Gate with days to spare, so we can take what we want and be away before they catch up with us."

Giles knew exactly how many days it would take to reach Hawk's Prairie and suggested when they should leave. Having gotten Keja's agreement, he smoked one last pipe, then stretched out beneath his blankets. For a while, he thought about his betrayal of the Trans woman and her ward. At last he slept, restlessly.

A week later, as he built up the evening fire, Giles signaled Keja that they would leave that night. Keja nodded. Although there had not been any opportunity to talk further about it, both men had made their preparations. They would leave with a minimum of noise.

After supper Giles asked Keja to help him wash their bowls in a nearby stream. "Tonight," he told the small thief, hating himself for it. "I've got the keys. They'll be asleep soon." Keja nodded his agreement.

Halfway between midnight and dawn Giles placed his hand over Keja's mouth, and shook his shoulder. The man roused himself quickly, threw his blanket over one shoulder, his pack over the other, and crept away to the place where the horses were tied.

Before leaving, Giles placed his own treasure in Petia's pack. Now he looked sadly at Petia and Anji and whispered an apology to them. He saw Petia's lips turn upward in a smile, as if she had heard him and acknowledged.

Giles turned away, his heart heavy. He liked Petia and Anji, perhaps even loved them and would miss them terribly. "Damn," he muttered. If there was a way to explain it to her, he would have stayed and done so.

He walked carefully away to the horses. Without a word to Keja, he threw the saddle on his mount, stuffed the bridle into the top of his pack, and loosened the halter rope. He turned and led the way down to the brook, then waded downstream. His face was a storm cloud, and had Keja been able to see, he would have thought twice about accompanying this man.

For a long while Giles waded through the water, seemingly oblivious of its coldness. He hated himself and thought more than once of turning back. But ahead lay the Gate of Paradise and the promise locked behind it. He had pursued that dream for over two years, and he was not to be denied. But he had never betrayed friends, and he knew he must do it once again before passing into Paradise and the obliteration of his bodily aches, pains and increasing old age.

Paradise meant youth to Giles, a removal of pain. That alone was more valuable than any gold.

At last he turned from the stream, dripping, and tied his horse to a bush so that he could properly saddle and bridle it. He lashed his pack to the back of the cantle and mounted, waiting impatiently for Keja. When Keja was mounted, he nodded curtly and urged the horse into a canter.

The cool night air did little to erase Giles' intense anger with himself. He raged internally for the remainder of the night, and when Keja essayed conversation, Giles cut him short.

But something more than his betrayal niggled at the edges of Giles' mind. An hour before dawn, he stopped, head cocked to one side as if listening.

"What is it?" asked Keja, hardly any happier than Giles over their perfidy.

"Something's wrong." Giles' eyes widened. "Se-grinn!" he cried.

"What? What do you mean? He's back in . . ." Keja's voice trailed off. "Why should he stay at Onyx's citadel," the small thief said, "when the Black Lord is dead?"

"He knows where we go and has had a month or more to go directly while we dawdled."

As one they cried, "Petia!"

They spun and galloped back toward the camp they'd vacated. As Giles rode, a sense of impending disaster mounted. Just out of earshot of the camp, he halted their rush. They dismounted. He fingered the sword dangling at his belt but did not draw it.

"Giles!" Keja whispered urgently. "Listen!"

The snuffling of hounds came on the wind. Giles drew his sword; Keja followed his lead. The wind in their face carried wet animal scents. Giles' entire body came alive once again as he prepared for combat.

When one of Segrinn's hell hounds bounded out of shadow, Giles reacted instinctively. The sword tip spitted the animal, but the hound's weight carried Giles to the ground. Keja finished the animal with a powerful overhead cut that severed its spine.

Keja started to gloat. Giles silenced him. A dozen feet away stood a large, black figure. The glint of wan firelight reflected off the dagger blade.

Giles moved with purpose—and a silent tread that hadn't been his for twenty years. The sword spun around, edge at the hidden figure's throat.

Segrinn squalled as the blade bit deeply into his throat. Giles spun him around and Keja kicked the dagger out of the slaver's hand.

"Quiet, or I cut your throat," Giles whispered hotly into the man's ear. Segrinn's struggles subsided.

"You'll not get away with this," Segrinn said in low tones. "You might have taken care of that fool Onyx, but not the son of Lord Ambrose! The cat-Trans will be mine again! I swear it!"

"He's mad, Giles," Keja said. "Listen to him. You'd think he had the sword at your throat."

"Name your price. I want the Trans bitch!"

Keja faded into the dark, returning a few minutes later. "He's alone. No sign of soldiers. And that was the only hound."

"Wealth!" cried Segrinn, beginning to froth at the mouth. "Gold! I want the bitch!"

Giles cut deeper and felt liquid drip down the sword blade and onto his hand. "Silence!" he hissed.

Segrinn ignored him. "Onyx was a fool. He wanted only those ridiculous keys. I want Petia Darya!"

"What of your troops?" asked Giles, still worrying.

"Dead, with Onyx. Even his hawk perished with him! You killed the man who bonded you away from murder charges. Ingrate!"

"Onyx killed the priest," Giles growled. "He left me to take the blame." He had suspected Onyx has been responsible for his release but hadn't known for sure until this moment. But all that lay in the past—the distant past.

"I want her!" Segrinn heaved and tossed Giles over his shoulder. As he swung through the air, Giles jerked hard on his sword. A fountain of blood showered down from Segrinn's severed neck. But the huge man seemed not to notice. Head bobbing at a crazy angle, he lurched toward the camp where Petia still slept peacefully.

Keja moved with lightning speed. His sword cut at Segrinn's legs. Hamstrings slashed, the insane slaver toppled and lay twitching in the mud. Giles and Keja stood, staring at the body.

"He'll never bother her again," Keja said, shock in his voice.

"Get the horses. We'll drag his carcass away. The hound, too." Giles peered through the thicket toward the dying campfire. Petia hadn't stirred.

"You're still going on to Hawk's Prairie? Without Petia and Anji?" Keja seemed even more shocked at this.

Giles made an impatient gesture. He had given Petia one final present. But even killing Segrinn and saving her from his insane lust seemed small recompense for stealing Paradise.

Chapter Eighteen

THE DAY DAWNED WITH CLOUDS IN THE SKY AND AN OCCA-sional shower. Giles rode hunched in the saddle. He was exhausted from the long ride, for he had pushed his horse through the night. Beside him rode Keja Tchurak, a curious expression on his face. Giles interpreted it well—another measure of his growing ability for treachery.

"Giles," Keja said, "there's something I don't understand."

"What?" Giles asked, instantly alert.

"The Gate of Paradise—if we're to believe Onyx —was a form of punishment. He had to recover the five keys before he returned to his pantheon as a god."

"So?"

"Why should the Gate allow *two* through? Wouldn't it be more reasonable that the gods intended only one, Onyx, to return?"

"Maybe Onyx lied."

"I've considered that," Keja said, frowning. "He might have been as obsessed as Segrinn was, in his own way, but I don't believe he lied."

"Look!" Giles cried. "There's the Gate! Out there!"

207

As Keja turned in the saddle, Giles neatly clipped him on the side of the head. The small thief tumbled from the saddle to lay motionless on the ground. Giles hastened to dismount, checking to be certain Keja wasn't seriously injured. With trembling fingers, Giles used Keja's precious ropes to bind the thief securely to a small tree.

Keja's eyelids trembled, then opened. It took several seconds to focus. Then he asked, "Why, Giles?"

"Forgive me, Keja. Please."

"I can hardly believe this is you. Pleading? Begging me?"

"I'm sorry, but what lies on the far side of the Gate is more precious to me than any gold." He hunkered down, his face close to Keja's. "Youth, Keja. Vitality! No more will my arthritic joints pain me in the mornings. You can't know how difficult it's been for me to keep up with you and Petia." His face softened. "And Anji. I see so much in him that I want again for my own."

"Why did you bring me this far?"

Giles smiled without humor. "Divide and conquer. I learned the lesson well during the War. Together with Petia, the pair of you might have stopped me. Now?" Giles shrugged. "She might not even pursue, thinking us knaves."

"And you leave me to die of starvation."

Giles laughed and stood. "Hardly. You're a clever one. Those knots won't survive your efforts longer than a few hours. But by then I'll have reached the Gate."

"Giles?"

"Good-bye, Keja. Please don't think ill of me. You're young and quick and have ample booty."

Giles turned and left before he relented. He had learned during the War that a friend at your back counted for more than even a full belly and warm bed. And in the past twelve hours he had betrayed three friends.

But the reward! The Gate of Paradise!

Giles mounted and rode full out, mud from Hawk's Prairie rising under his horse's hooves.

* * *

Though he had tied Keja well, he knew that young thief would undo his bonds in a short time. The track led down, leveling gently as it neared the bottom. Giles Grimsmate looked down, unable to see the Gate from this vantage, but knowing that it was there. When the gods had set it there, they had done a remarkable job of camouflage. Only those with a key in hand might see it.

Giles glanced at the sky; the sun appeared and he saw spring moisture burning off. He urged his horse forward.

When Giles arrived at the spot he remembered so well, he dismounted, tying his horse to a bush. He pulled a leather pouch from his belt and emptied the five keys into his hand.

The Gate of Paradise appeared out of thin air before him. Walking slowly toward the Gate, he smiled mirthlessly as he read the runic inscription: ONLY ONE MAY ENTER.

The locks were just as he had left them over two years earlier. They showed no wear or evidence of exposure to the elements. Indeed, they looked as if the locksmith had just finished burnishing them.

Methodically, hands trembling, Giles inserted the keys into the five locks. He did not unlock any until he was certain that each key was in its own lock. Then, starting at the top, he turned the keys. Each lock snapped open with a loud crack, as if released from long imprisonment. He pulled the shanks from the staples and released the hasps, hooking the locks into the shanks to hang open. When he had finished with the last one, he tugged at the massive gate and stood back.

It swung open slowly, effortlessly. All his dreams would be realized on the other side.

For a moment Giles stood, holding his breath. Then he edged closer and stared inside. He cried in frustration. There was no wealth visible, no chests overflowing with gold and jewels. A barren chamber stretched before him, walls of unadorned rock. There was no furniture, no tables, chairs, chests, wardrobes. In the distance an object emerged from the floor, but it was too far away to identify.

Hand on sword, Giles took a tentative step into the cool chamber. Quiet, an air of peace, enveloped him. It was as if he had walked into a temple, away from the bustle of life, and found a profound serenity. His anxiety ceased; he knew that he was safe. Assured, he walked to the one visible object.

Closer, Giles saw a stone pedestal which seemed to grow out of the solid stone. When he reached it, he found that it was a crudely carved seat, devoid of marks or inscriptions. He stood, unsure, gazing around the chamber. Suddenly he laughed, a laugh that started deep in his gut and rolled out, echoing from the barren walls around him.

There was no treasure.

Wiping his eyes with the back of his hand, he stumbled backward and sat on the stone seat. He'd wait for Keja, and they could share the humor of their quest. Truly, the gods played mortals for fools. His laughter finally subsided to a mere chuckle, and he pulled a handkerchief from his sleeve and wiped his eyes again.

He took a deep breath and leaned back.

A voice whispered, "Be content."

Giles sat up, alert, wondering if he were hallucinating. Again the voice came, "Be content." It was a voice filled with age, wisdom and great love, and the peace which Giles had felt on first entering the chamber welled up within him.

Giles sat back, savoring the feeling. He began to think about the times of his life when he had been content. There were happy times before the War, his childhood and young manhood. He remembered courting his wife, their marriage and their joy at the births of their sons.

Then the War came, a long, terrible, exhausting struggle. Even then there had been moments of true happiness with good comrades. Men had given of themselves, were always there in times of need, and Giles had enjoyed good times between battles. Giles had counted those men as brothers.

His thoughts turned to the past two years. The quest

for the keys had been as difficult a thing as he had ever done, but every step of the way he was accompanied by two of the closest, staunchest friends he had ever known. Keja, vain, not always the brightest, getting in scrapes and having to be rescued. Giles chuckled at the vision of Keja in the treasure room of Shahal, backed up against the wall by the giant snake. But who had rescued him from the temple in Kasha, carrying him up the stairs? Who had flooded the cave fortress of the Flame Sorceress? A poor thief, a great lover, a man who enjoyed life, a true friend and what more could one ask?

And Petia? He smiled at the image of Petia as mother, for that was what she had become. Another thief, even less skilled than Keja. But she always came through when she was needed, slipping into her cat persona and accomplishing things he and Keja could never do.

They were his two greatest friends: two thieves, one a Trans. And the boy, Anji, also a Trans and a slave when they had met. Giles had opposed bringing the boy along, but Anji had contributed more than his share to the success of their adventures. A bright lad who would grow up to bring some good into the world.

"By the gods, I am content," Giles said, his mood brightening. "Life has not always treated me kindly, but it has treated me fairly." He stretched cramped joints. "There is no treasure here. A legend had promised it, but the legend was false. And whose fault is that? Mine or the legends?" Giles shook his head. He'd been foolish believing in Paradise. But he wasted no time castigating himself for it. Without hope what was there in the world?

Giles slid forward to the front of the stone seat. "Yes," he whispered back. "Yes, by the gods, I am content." He stood, stepped forward and disappeared.

Keja stared at the Gate. He peered from the inscription carved above it to the locks hanging open to the ironwork gate standing ajar. He stepped to the entrance. "Giles!" he called. "Giles, answer me!"

211

Only silence greeted him. He looked furtively behind him. Perhaps Giles had already left and was watching him, laughing himself to death. He saw no one, yet Giles' horse was tethered nearby, and the Gate stood open. He peered into the dark, cool interior and called again.

His voice echoed back from the walls, but no other sound could be heard. Pulling his sword, Keja passed warily through the Gate. The empty chamber surprised him; had Giles already looted so much treasure? He made his way cautiously, alert, just a little fearful.

He walked uneasily the length of the chamber, more perplexed with each step. No treasure. This was not at all what Keja had been led to expect. The room should be a treasure chamber, piled high with gold, silver, jewels, pieces of art. Only emptiness and silence met him, a cold stone chamber inhabited by echoes that mocked.

Keja approached the stone pedestal silently, anticipating Giles hiding on the opposite side, a big grin on his face, laughing at the joke the gods had played on them. He gave the stone seat a wide berth, in spite of expecting to find Giles there. He had been a thief too long to let down his guard.

As he rounded the pedestal, he found the seat empty. An object glinted on the floor in front of the seat. It was a sword, and Keja recognized it as the one Giles had purchased in Sanustell.

He picked it up, looking around the chamber, wondering where Giles could be. The chamber was not so large that he could not see to the far end. No one was in sight, not Giles or anyone else. He examined the sword carefully, then realized how foolish it was to think that it might hold a clue.

Frowning, he sat gingerly on the edge of the stone seat. The words came clearly, repeated three times. "Be content."

As Giles had done before him, Keja leaned back, musing about his past deeds. Life had been a short one, so far, but interesting. Inimitably Keja, his first thoughts went to the women he had loved. There had been so many, each with her own special, precious personality. His affairs had been tense, frenzied, emotional, sometimes suspenseful, occasionally peaceful and loving for a short time. He would not have missed a one.

His childhood he skipped over quickly. It had been unpleasant and the less he thought about it the better. His life as a thief and rogue had been exciting, although not entirely successful. He wondered if there was any other trade he might pursue with more success. Shaking his head wryly, he thought not.

But perhaps he was wrong.

Throwing in with Giles and Petia had been the best thing that had happened to his life, he decided. The last two years had been more exciting than anything he had done previously. They had become deep and true friends, helping each other, living adventures unlike any others in the world, he had no doubt. He was saddened that it was over.

"I can never be content," Keja said aloud. *Giles* had been content. He, too, must have thought over his life and found it good, as good as might be expected in these uneasy times with all their upheaval. Giles had admitted that he was content and . . .

. . . had gone beyond.

"I'm not content," Keja said almost joyously. "How can I be when all of life lies before me? There's still much to do, women to love, the world to be experienced. I'm young, healthy, have plenty of time. I want to see all the world has to offer. No, I'm *not* content."

Keja grinned broadly now, happy that it had been Giles who had passed through the Gate first. Keja wasn't content and didn't intend to be! The world offered too much for a rogue!

He stood, laughing and walked from the stone seat. He lifted Giles' sword and held it vertically in front of his face in salute to his companion of the last two years.

"Good-bye, Giles," he whispered. "Be with the gods. I'm off to find Petia and Anji and see what mischief we can get into. If they're willing, there's lots to see before we settle down. I wish that you would be with us, but you've made your decision. I'll miss you, we'll all miss you. But there are still worlds to conquer."

He saluted again and strode away toward the Gate and the light of day outside. The Gate of Paradise. Keja chuckled and the hollow echoes multiplied until the chamber resounded eerily with the chuckles of a hundred voices. The Gate of Paradise was truly named. Men had searched for it over the centuries, led on by the legend of its treasures.

Five keys, and they had found them all. Keja drew near the Gate and wondered if Giles had left them in the locks. He passed through and turned. The locks still dangled from their staples. And from each of them, the shank of a key protruded. He pulled the keys from the locks and, starting at the top, closed each hasp and carefully pushed the shank of each lock home. The clicks were solid and satisfactory.

He stowed the keys in a soft leather bag, which he placed in the pouch at his belt, closing the leather-and-bone catch securely. The keys out of his hand, the Gate vanished. Keja stiffened, reached into the pouch and touched the keys. The Gate popped back into sight. He tested the locks one last time, then patted the pouch.

Keja didn't know if the Gate to Paradise would ever allow another through. Giles might be the only mortal ever to pass through, but Keja doubted it. The gods might enjoy a joke, but they occasionally dispensed mercy to mortals.

There might be a time when he would want those keys, a time when he might feel content with the life he had led. But not yet. When that time came scores of years from now, Keja believed that the Gate would lead him to Paradise, just as it had Giles Grimsmate.

He stepped back; the Gate had once again vanished.

Keja stared through where the Gate stood and spied the top of the hill where he had left his mount tied next to Giles' horse. Petia sat beside the track. Anji knelt beside her, and Petia's arms circled the boy's shoulders.

Keja tensed until he saw the smile on Petia's face and the joy mirrored in Anji's.

"Mother and child," Keja muttered. And that didn't seem bad at all.

"Great treasures?" Petia called down to him.

Keja raised empty hands to her and laughed. "Take as much as you want," he called back.

He clambered up the hill toward the two Trans. When he reached them, he stood and surveyed the surroundings, the plain below, and the hilly country to north and south. Unsought and unwanted, the image of Lord Onyx flashed through Keja's mind. He had watched the Black Lord and his horse vanish beneath tons of earth, but the image of one raised fist, a black-studded gauntlet surrounding the wrist, shaken in absolute defiance of his death, had invaded Keja's dreams during more than one night's sleep. The Gate of Paradise had been left by the gods. Giles proved that. He had to believe that Onyx had been a god. Once.

But Onyx had died. And Segrinn, too. Keja's buoyant good spirits pushed them from his thoughts.

He collapsed onto the ground beside Petia and Anji. "No treasures," he said. "And no Giles." He described the chamber and what he had found there. "We're no richer than we were when we started," he finished.

Petia laughed. "Yes, we are. Giles left me his share of what we brought back from Bandanarra. You must still have some of yours. Even gaudy clothes such as you're sporting now couldn't have cost *that* much. Anji and I will do well. What about you, dear Keja?"

Keja shrugged, then grinned. "I've had a wonderful adventure, my Pet. I've enjoyed every second of it —well, almost. I'm certainly no worse off than I was when I started, and I do have a few coins left. And you have one gift from Giles beyond compare." Keja told of Segrinn's death, then climbed to his feet and touched Anji's arm. "Take good care of Petia," he said.

Then he turned, collected his horse and swung himself up into the saddle. He saluted the startled Petia and swung his mount back onto the trail heading west.

He topped the rise and gave the horse its head as the track descended down into a vale. Springtime, a nice time of the year, new beginnings. For the first time in ages, a ballad sprung to his lips and he sang the words with gusto. He reached the bottom of the track and let his horse drink from the crystal stream that ran through it.

Unclear words wafted to him from the top of the hill behind. He saw two horses on the skyline. The words came again, clearer.

"Keja. Wait. Wait for us!"

Keja waited.